The Pri...

She heard and scented Varis's approach, quickly straightening up and reaching for her dressing gown, slipping into it while still wet. She cursed the females for introducing her to those forbidden sensations, once tasted, never more to be denied. She cursed herself, a female into her Fourth Season, for not having the knowledge or courage to discover these sensations herself sooner.

And she cursed Varis for interrupting her, even as his presence brought with it opportunity.

He entered, immediately noticing the change in her. 'What has happened?'

'I . . . dined with Kami and Tameri.'

Varis grunted. 'No doubt an enjoyable experience.'

'No doubt.' She walked up to him, sensing his discomfort, determined to overcome it. Her arousal, her need was still strong. 'Varis . . . do you remember when you first took me? As your First?'

His face creased with pleasant recollection. 'Yes. You were beautiful in your inaugural gown.'

She was beside him, her hand on his belly, snaking it around him, her breasts against his arms and chest. 'And so sweet and wet, bent over, receiving your cock that first time, your hands on my hips . . . so masterful . . .'

He smiled with the memory. 'Yes . . .'

'I only wanted to serve you then.' Her hand moved lower. 'I am still sweet, and wet . . .'

The Pride
Edie Bingham

BLACK LACE

Black Lace books contain sexual fantasies.
In real life, always practise safe sex.

First published in 2005 by
Black Lace
Thames Wharf Studios
Rainville Road
London W6 9HA

Design by Smith & Gilmour, London
Printed and bound by Mackays of Chatham PLC

ISBN 0 352 33997 7

1

It could have been all the hassle and grief inflicted on her during the day. Or that idiot at the bar who kept groping her. Or it could have been that she had just snagged her best blouse on that doornail.

Whatever, it was enough, enough for Kami Ösbank to smash her fist against the offending door, cracking the frame, her whole body shaking visibly, and shriek, 'You fucking bastard!'

The whole room went quiet, turning in unison towards the bar, collective breaths held, awaiting an equally explosive response from the target of her fury. However, the owner and barman, a rotund, hatched-faced, moustached man with leathery, copper skin, simply nodded and replied in a whiskey voice of fractured English, 'Ah, yes, apologies. I will pay for a new blouse.'

'Yes, you fucking will! Bastard!' Kami's eyes blazed with hazel fire, and the muscles in her frame were tight beneath her dark tanned skin, her mane of honey-tipped chocolate-brown hair framing a livid face. She spun in place and stormed towards the doors, ignoring the oohs and ahhs of the patrons.

The Oasis was an all-purpose restaurant/bar/disco, and, like most establishments in town catering for the Western tourists, was dressed up in a faux-Hawaiian motif: palm trees, inflatable pineapples and bananas suspended over the tables, and framed pictures of hula girls. These last shimmied as Kami slammed doors shut.

Four men in T-shirts, shorts and flip-flops, de rigueur

fashion for the British male tourist abroad, sat laughing and whistling at the end of the bar, before turning to the barman, who had returned to his duties. One of them, Josh, the youngest of the group and the object of Kami's earlier displeasure, looked as pained and angry as his embarrassment of ginger hair, pressing a bar towel to his mouth where she had struck him. 'Bitch. Shouldn't look like that, if she didn't want it.'

Peter, a broad-shouldered black man with shaven head and bright teeth framed by the stubble of a moustache and beard, grinned. 'Hot little tigress there.'

His friend Ryan, a tall, lithe, rangy man with fair hair, grunted, his Welsh lilt slurred. 'You just gonna let her wreck your place, Abdul?'

The owner sighed, as he heard bottles being broken, crates smashed, in the alleyway outside, before someone started up the music. 'Doors can be fixed more easily than limbs, friend.'

Josh snorted. 'I thought you Arabs kept your women in place?'

The Turkish barman shrugged. 'We have a saying: "Women are storms, don't try to fight them, just keep your head down until they pass".'

He chuckled at this. They didn't. Perhaps it lost something in the translation.

Ryan pointed a finger at him. 'She needs seeing to.' Then he indicated his three mates. 'We know how to deal with birds like her back home.'

The owner restrained a burst of derisive laughter. 'That's no bird that just flew out, my friend –'

Now Ryan's face darkened, as if sensing the barman's doubt. 'I'm not your "friend". You think we're pussies like you?'

'No, no –'

Peter leaned forwards, cradling his empty beer mug. 'She's asking for it.'

Josh, flanking Ryan's other side, copied Peter. '*Begging* for it.'

That made the others laugh. The barman's face tightened. 'Boys, have another round, on the house –'

'What, this pig's piss?' Peter slammed his glass down and stood up, Josh following. They looked to each other, smiles rising on their mouths, unspoken challenges exchanged – then all looked to the fourth member of the quartet: Tony, a hard-looking man with a comma of black hair hanging over his swarthy features. Of the four of them, he was the highest-ranking back in their platoon, and whether on base or on leave here, the others did nothing without him.

Thus, when Tony finished his beer, quietly nodded and rose to join them, they whooped with anticipation at the hunt.

The barman called after them, 'My friends, don't –'

Josh waved at him. 'Go back to your camels, Abdul. We've got it sorted.' As one, the pack departed, knocking a chair or two over, possibly accidentally, probably not.

The owner watched them depart, his hands tightening against the cushioned border of his bar. Worried.

For them.

They stopped outside for a quick piss, seeing evidence of the woman's further outbursts, and joking about it. Then, as if having caught scent of their prey, they half-ran down the street, the shadows in the alley hiding the claw marks on the wooden-framed walls.

Kami was certain she had had worse evenings. Damned if she could think when, though.

She should have seen it coming. Perhaps she even

had, but chose to ignore the warning signs. She would apologise to Sedat tomorrow. But tonight, tonight . . .

She paused at a crossroad in the town and screeched, 'Bastards!'

Then dared someone, anyone, to answer her back.

However, no one did. The winding, sloping streets of Meraklisi beckoned beneath the stark, star-studded indigo canopy of a summer evening, while further away, the rippling reflection of moonlight on the waters caught her eye once or twice. Closer, she caught the sounds of music and laughter, of merriment and motor vehicles, the scents of cooking and alcohol, the fresh, salty breeze from the bay below. It was an assortment of sensory goodies, like a box of multi-flavoured Turkish delights, and normally she revelled in them all.

But not tonight. Tonight, Kami was distracted, unable to focus, to keep her wits about her. If there were no distractions . . .

'Hey! Hey, sweetheart! Wait up for us!'

English. Young. Drunk. Arrogant. Open in their desires – usually a sought-after trait, for her purposes – but with all the coarse clumsiness of the monkeys that were their close cousins. 'Oi, sweetie!'

She turned in place to shout, 'Fuck off!', and in a moment of ungainliness nearly tripped over her own feet. This provoked laughter, and quickly she reached down, removed the offending shoe, and hurled it at her pursuers.

It struck the ginger-haired man in the head, sending his mates into fits of giggles, and the target into cursing.

A part of Kami instinctively measured them up, once closer: the dark-skinned one was powerfully built but clumsy, the ginger-haired one young and predictable, and the fair-haired one loud but cowardly. However, the last, the muscular-looking, dark-haired one, stayed in the rear, silent, watching, evaluating her as she did him. He was the pack leader, acknowledged or otherwise.

He was the one to watch out for, when she made her move.

Her move?

Then she realised she had decided already. And despite the tension, the torrent of emotion and hunger that remained, she felt relieved. It was foolish, so foolish, out here, in the open, but . . .

But *nothing*.

She reached down and removed her other shoe, playfully flinging it at her prey this time. 'Come on, boys! Don't lose your courage now!' Then she was running barefoot down the hill with phenomenal speed, ignoring the harsh concrete beneath her, the men in hot pursuit.

The bottom of the hill fed into one end of a wide, stone-cobbled and tree-lined causeway circling the crescent bay, a band of shallow white-grey sand that lay there while dark waters lapped at it, and fishing and tour boats rocked gently further out. It was late, and the shops which lined the causeway had closed hours ago, but it wasn't yet so late that people had begun filing out of the pubs.

Peter was the first one to find the woman's white blouse, lying abandoned in the street. He brought it to his nose and breathed in deeply, whooping with delight. Ryan was beside him, fighting for it, while Josh staggered into them, wondering what was going on.

It took Tony to walk around them and retrieve the abandoned black skirt and matching knickers. 'Lads – wouldn't you rather have what was in these?'

The three men glanced about quickly, Ryan asking, 'Where the fuck did she go?'

Peter moved onto the pavement, near one tree, staring in the inky blackness shrouding over the waters. 'She must have gone for a swim!'

Ryan giggled, like a child let loose in a toy shop. 'Darling! Where are you?'

The answer came in the leap from the poplar tree nearest to him, landing more softly than any of them could expect. The nude figure was crouched on all fours, feet and hands pressed together, full breasts squeezed into maximum cleavage, her back cambered at an angle that would have been excruciating for anyone else, balancing by the grace of the long swaying tail jutting from the base of her spine. Tiny dark rosette spots ran along her bronzed limbs, the sides of her breasts and her face. The eyes stayed fixed, unwavering, on the four men.

Then the fair-haired one turned.

He made himself the first.

She leaped from her crouching position as if propelled by a steel coil, moving with phenomenal swiftness and grace through the air, twisting and striking his chest with one swipe of her hand. There was a tear of cloth, and he staggered back, hands on his chest, shrieking and falling over his own feet into the street.

The others just continued to stare, as fixed as deer in headlights.

But Kami kept moving, dropped into a twist that would put an acrobat to shame, and sent a powerhouse straight-leg kick into the back of one of the ginger one's own, sending him flailing to one side, striking the pavement hard. She twisted further onto him, slashing open the boy's shirt, then clawing his belly, leaving deep red tracks.

'Fuck!' Somehow, the black one ignored the urge to fly, and moved to grab at her arm. In response she gripped his own with a strength that belied her size, claws sinking into his flesh, twisting until his body contorted, affording her the opportunity to drive her foot into his groin. Breath whooshed from his body, and he doubled over like folded paper.

The ginger one wailed at all this, a wail quickly cut off as she struck him across the face and knocked him out.

Then she saw the leader, turning to scurry into the dark, no doubt relying on it and the soft sand cushioning his footfalls to hide him.

And with anyone not possessing her senses, it might have. As it was, he could not have stood out more to her if he had been on fire and screaming.

He was the one she would take.

Tony ran, stumbled, as if the minuscule waves lapping at his feet were responsible. He lost one flip-flop, and never even noticed it, as he continued to glance behind him. But the darkness surrounded him, metres away, cloaked him. Protected him.

His breath escaped rapid-fire from his body, and his skin felt on fire from the beer and the fear. What the fuck was that thing? He'd not seen anything move that fast before . . .

He hit the wet sand face first, and only his forearms before him kept him from breaking his nose. He swallowed brine and sand, coughing and sputtering as he twisted about, felt the weight of a body on top of him . . .

Hers.

She near-crouched on him, one foot resting on his chest. So close, so close . . .

He jumped as her hand darted out, as if to strike his face – stopping just inches from his nose. She extended her forefinger, as if to display the curved, centimetre-long milky-white claw jutting from a slit at the tip of the finger, barely touching his skin, and smiled, her voice sibilant, triumphant. 'Mine.'

Tony swallowed, paralysed, as the claw trailed down to his lips, his chin, his throat, his chest, and she repeated, 'Mine.'

Kami continued, his eyes following the claw down to his stomach, his abdomen – to the bulge in his shorts. And her smile became a grin. *'Mine.'* Then she bent down, as if to sink her fangs into his neck, but instead licked him with a hot velvet tongue and an inescapable magnetic gaze that made him hold his breath, his cock pulsing and hardening. He became aware of the woman's ample, creamy cleavage, so close, the heady mixture that he could not escape; trickles of cold sweat tickled his back, or was it sea water? His senses focused, grew more vivid; he found himself breathing heavily and, somehow, becoming passive in the proximity of the woman.

Her hands moved over him, tearing playfully at his T-shirt, repeatedly, seemingly at random, though expertly enough not to scratch his skin. Her scent was strong, dizzying.

Then she pointed to his crotch. 'Pull those down.'

'Wha –'

Pain shot through him – his *face*! She'd scratched his face! It felt like she had touched bone, though he knew better. He had flinched, but then froze in place, as he felt the claws at his throat now, the trilling, soft-yet-deadly words on his ears. 'I said pull those *down*.'

She could have removed them herself, or shredded them as she had done his T-shirt. But he somehow realised that his doing it himself was symbolic of his submission to her. And Tony obeyed, careful not to disturb her overmuch as he manoeuvred beneath her, tugging his shorts and briefs down to his knees; he couldn't draw them down any further. A wave of embarrassment shot through him. Embarrassment – and excitement; his cock, long and thick even at rest, was now throbbing fully to life, the shaft at maximum stiffness, pointing in her direction like some divining rod, its head emerging glistening from its hood, as if pushed up by his balls, now resting inside his body.

Kami moved her fingers softly across his stomach, making his guts twitch and twist within, anticipating those claws. However, she had withdrawn them for now, leaving only the ends of her slender fingers to dance over his groin and send waves of pleasure through him. He held his breath as he felt her fingers wrap around his hardened shaft, squeezing lightly as if testing its sturdiness.

He moaned and sank back on the sand, his heart rate quickening, no longer with fear but with an arousal that was just as incapacitating. He could feel her tail swish against his legs, softly brushing his thighs, as if reminding him of her dangerous potential; it unnerved and excited him in equal measure.

Then her gaze caught his. 'Taste me,' she said. And she straddled his head, taking him by the hair and manoeuvring herself to get his face towards her crotch, then swinging her hips forwards.

Her pubic hair was fine, very fine, and straight, like a soft mane framing her open sex. And her musk ... Tony breathed in her scent deeply, finding it so powerful, so attractive, so undeniably feminine, and yet feral. Given her inhuman nature, that should not have seemed so surprising. The desire to have her, taste her, overwhelmed him. He felt like a starving man smelling freshly baked bread; greedily he extended his tongue and pressed forwards, the tip of his tongue stroking the folds and creases of her hot, wet labia, and the damask skin within.

Kami relaxed noticeably as his tongue slid into her dark passage to taste the soft lining of her sex. Sighing with unmasked enjoyment, she flexed her claws lazily against his scalp. He began to lick and suck at her sweet opening, his tongue delving deep into her, producing loud trills and purrs from her as her head fell back. Revelling in his ministrations now, she pushed more fervently onto his face, her hands tangling in his hair as she ground herself against his hungry mouth. He licked and sucked in earnest now, fired by her obvious arousal and a need to please her, his tongue and lips embracing her sex as her juices flowed freely. Finally, she growled loudly and bucked onto his face, as a climax surged through her.

She fell back onto his belly, satisfied – for the moment. The water was lapping around him more now; it drew the sand away from his outline and made him feel like he was sinking into its cold depths. His cock was straining for relief. Then she twisted about, and her face and hands were near his groin, fingers flexing her claws, in, out, in, out. She gently flicked at it, making him start, moan, and making her purr with delight at her absolute control over him. Lust and desire filled her eyes, as did triumph at having been sated by him at her bidding.

'You're good,' she purred. 'You *smell* good.'

'I – I –' was all he could gasp. His mind reeled, afraid, excited, and oh-so-aroused.

Before he could say more, she bent forwards and licked him with a broad, velvet-soft tongue from the base of his shaft up to the very tip, making him gasp loudly and struggle reflexively to get out from under her. Her hand shot out to his balls, claws extended, pricking at his soft wrinkled skin. He froze.

Then she removed her claws from his testicles and turned about again, straddling him, face to face, lowering her hot, wet sex onto his straining manhood.

Kami rode him, rode him quickly and furiously, relentlessly bending backwards, pointing her breasts to the sky, then forwards, until they rested on his chest, the nipples peaked. He stared in utter fascination and rapture as she bounced up and down on his aching flesh, moaning and growling, and scratching him some more. Oddly, he no longer cared, no longer felt the pain, only the overwhelming desire for climax.

She kept riding him.

Tony's body floated, and he felt disembodied from it, looking down at the carnal scene. He finally came, inside her, bliss shooting through him to make him moan and wail, feeling like a sponge being squeezed dry, one too many times.

Eternity passed. She continued to ride him, ignoring his weak protests.

She came.

She mewled, and scratched him again.

Beyond bliss, Tony was only distantly aware of the woman rising from his twitching, come-soaked cock. Her fingers stroked slowly across the sensitised tip, gathering his come and making him gasp again. Lifting her hand to her lips, she flicked out her tongue and licked her fingers one by one. Then she patted his cheek, as one might do to a pet that had performed his tricks to order. 'Now go, forget what you saw. Never come back.'

Then she leaped out of sight. Exhaustion paralysed

him, and he lay there in the sand, shorts and boxers still around his knees.

Kami scurried back for her clothes. The other men had left, but she didn't stick around, dressing as she raced home, her satisfaction quickly waning into displeasure at her actions. Stupid, stupid bitch! Risking her identity, her very life, like that. How big an idiot could she be?

'You're the biggest idiot on the planet.'

Mark Healey stepped back into the shade of the hotel canopy to read the LCD power display on his camera, never looking over at his friend, but noting, 'No, don't hold back, say what's on your mind.'

Greg Eddings licked at the foamy head of his beer, the first that morning. 'OK: you let people walk all over you, let them take what they want. You never know how to just raise a hand and tell people: enough is enough.'

Mark raised a hand in his direction. 'Enough is enough.'

Greg was a gaunt, glib man in his early thirties, with a crooked grin and high forehead capped with crinkly fair hair, who, clad in his baggy yellow T-shirt and matching shorts, seemed to have left his sense of fashion back in Manchester along with his sense of irony. 'Now take Chrissie. Chrissie had you pussy-whipped from day bloody one. You let her call all the shots.'

Mark paused, melancholy memories flashing unbidden before his mind's eye. 'Well, she seemed very good at it.' Mark Healey was the same age as Greg, though his broader goatee-clad face and figure, straighter black hair, and more conservative dark-blue short-sleeved shirt and cool beige trousers made him seem older. He certainly felt older than Greg. Sometimes not in a good way.

Greg turned in his high stool at the poolside bar, pausing to glance over at some bikini-clad women coming to take the last few recliners not yet claimed with towels. Then he was back in his stride. 'She was no good. Her entire family were trash, Mark. You're well out of it, mate, trust me.'

Mark put the camera back into its carrying case. 'You still shagged her sister at that Christmas party.'

Greg smiled without irony or apology at the memory. 'Even trash needs love. But I'm gonna get some class action out here...' He then paused again to say to the passing women, 'Morning, girls, I'm the hotel's official sun-lotion applicator, I'll be right over.'

Mark rolled his eyes, hoped he wouldn't regret asking, but went ahead anyway. 'It's not too late to come along, you know.'

Greg turned back to him, pursed his lips in theatrical deliberation, then replied, 'Thanks, mate, but, as exciting as it would be to get sunstroke climbing over some dusty ruins learning about the Battle of Cunnilingus, I think I'd better stay here and keep the British end up.' He leaned in closer, his voice lower. 'You know, most normal blokes will be staying by the pool getting a tan, a beer, and an eyeful of the topless babes.'

'Say hi to all the normal blokes, then.' Mark rose and put on his cap. 'See you tonight.'

Greg grinned and nodded, waving him off as he started towards the pool. 'Have fun; I know *I* will.'

Mark relaxed visibly as he left him and the hotel behind for the day, squinting under the brim of his cap, marvelling at the blinding brilliance of the sun in a sky of naked blue. The hotel was basic, as most in Turkey were, but this one's principal selling feature was seclusion: it wasn't on the main road, but set back, and cloistered by thick growths of ivy and begonias on the high walls. And yet one turn around the corner, and he was on the main road, dodging youngsters on mopeds and noisy vans, and pitchmen enticing him to purchase bottled water, postcards, phone cards, Turkish delight . . .

He stopped for water, not having a taste for Turkish delight, and not having anyone back home to call or send postcards to.

The tour minibus was parked in the pre-arranged spot, and tourists from other hotels in the immediate area had gathered, people – couples – of different ages and origins, but all older than him. He was aware of his single status, and yet wasn't as bothered about it as he was back home, when he'd gone the rounds, having to explain why Chrissie wasn't out with him that night. It was refreshing.

Two figures stepped off the bus as he approached, two women in the black slacks and baby-blue tops of the reps of the travel agency with whom Mark had booked the holiday. The first one was tall, lanky, her flaxen hair drawn back from her narrow face, thin lips bridging high, sun-pink cheekbones, then seemingly pushing them out as she smiled and began checking names off her clipboard before allowing people onto the bus.

The second was a little shorter, more curvaceous, a classical figure with thick chocolate-brown shoulder-length hair mixed with lighter strands of blonde, framing bronzed cheeks, soft hazel eyes, elfin nose and full russet lips. She stood at the bus doorway, ensuring all boarded safely, smiling with genuine warmth at each in turn. There was something very arresting about her:

the way she held herself, the way she regarded everyone with a casual concentration. It made Mark glad he
was wearing shades as he gave his name.

Her voice was like honey. 'Good morning, Mr Healey.
My name's Kami Ösbank.'

2

Mark climbed on board, taking a seat near the front. Finally, the reps boarded, speaking to each other, before the brunette – Kami? Was that her name again? – smiled as she sat down beside him. The driver closed the door and started up the engine.

The bus rocked as it wound its way through the narrow streets, moving at a mad pace up the hills and onto the larger roads leading out of the city. Throughout, Mark remained acutely aware of her proximity, of the unruly strands of lighter golden hair snaking through the dark brown depths, the way her breasts, full and firm, tremored slightly within her blouse. Then there was that fragrance, something indefinable, yet potent and attractive. Chrissie preferred flowery perfumes . . .

He sighed, closed his eyes, and mentally counted to ten. He'd been determined to keep her out of his head for the duration of this holiday, and in less than two days in Turkey, he'd only thought of her – what, twelve times? You wouldn't think they had broken up just three months before . . .

'Excuse me?'

He opened his eyes and turned his head. 'Huh?'

It was her, staring directly at him now. Her voice was low, lilting, foreign, and yet discernible over the growl of the engine. 'Are you feeling ill? I know our driver's a maniac. If you need any –'

'I'm fine, really. Thanks.' He reached into his case

and drew out his guidebook, his breath quickening as he tried to keep the woman – all women – out of his mind.

Then she rose, faced the rear of the bus, produced a small black microphone and switched it on, easily keeping balance with the bus's rocking. 'Good morning, everybody! Or, as we say here, *Günaydin*! My name's Kami Ösbank, and my co-worker in the rear of the bus is Janeane Wade, and we both wish to welcome you on our journey today to Usal.' She went on into the familiar chatter about keeping hydrated while outside, sun protection, and the scheduled stops on the way.

And Mark found himself watching the brunette, unable to look down again into the contents of his book, until she was sitting down beside him again, smiling. 'Is this your first time in Turkey, Mark?'

He drew breath, simultaneously relishing the sound of her voice and bristling at the instant familiarity that most reps employed. It was a familiarity he usually didn't feel or display in return, and was not prepared to do so now. 'No, I've been before, several times.'

She crossed her legs and settled back into her seat, casually fixing up a couple of rebellious strands of hair. 'Oh? And have you been to Usal before?'

He swallowed, wishing he could move to get his water without breaking the aura of disinterest he was trying to building around him. 'Yes, three years ago.'

She drew closer, reaching across him to the air conditioning controls above. His heart pounded at her closeness, relishing it and rejecting it at the same time. 'Just making us a bit more comfortable, hope you don't mind,' she whispered, almost toppling onto him as the bus turned a bend. 'Whoa – sorry, you seemed a little stifled –'

That was it. He pulled away from her contact, until

the back of his head was resting against the window. His face felt flushed, paper-thin and radiating all the heat from his body. 'Miss Ösbank, I'd really like to read my book now. Is that possible?'

She blinked at him, looking as if he'd slapped her across the face. Then her calm professional smile returned. 'I'm sorry,' she breathed, her cheeks flushing, obviously a little embarrassed. 'Of course.' And she turned and faced the front of the bus again, without another word. At least, not to him.

'The area that would later be called Usal was first settled 3000 years ago by the Phrygians, taking advantage of the local hot springs. Later Hittite, Roman and Christian settlements followed, but these ruins here date from the Seljuk period of the late eleventh century, who made Usal a caravanserai, a way-station for contemporary traders...'

Mark knew the rest, and departed from the group to take pictures. The remains of Usal rose from the uneven shrub-dotted hills surrounding it like defiant weeds, the cracked fortress-like walls and hexagonal turrets plain in façade as if by erosion rather than design, the intricate patterns of Arabic script and tiles of the period reserved for the arched doorways.

And as he walked through the remains of the mosques, the baths and kitchens and sleeping quarters, he imagined what it was like at its zenith, when the Seljuk Turks produced extraordinary achievements in craftsmanship and commerce. It never ceased to amaze him, that feeling of stepping back in time to another age. He felt almost giddy. Or maybe it had been the relief from getting away from the party, and in particular Miss Ösbank.

Then he stopped himself, literally. Bloody women!

Why did he let them get under his damned skin so easily? All he had wanted was some peace and quiet to enjoy this holiday as best he could under the circumstances! Was that too much to ask? Was it his fault that she'd made advances to him?

He sat down on a stone bench and reviewed the digital photos he had taken already, as the tour party appeared, with Miss Ösbank leading the way; he was afraid to look up.

The woman, however, was no longer prepared to leave him alone, at least indirectly, as she brought the party towards him. 'In the summer of 1097, European Crusaders had marched through Anatolia towards Jerusalem, one party stopping here to try to pillage the caravanserai; both Seljuks and Crusaders ended up massacring each other.'

'Actually,' Mark found himself interjecting, 'there *was* an account by the Duke Hugh de Chaumont that both sides had been attacked by monsters who had travelled south from the sea.'

'Yes,' the guide replied, deadpan. 'That sounds much more plausible.' That brought the expected titters from the crowd, and she followed with, 'Now, if the rest of you go with Janeane, she'll take you to the rug-weaving demonstration, while I ask Mr Healey if he's out to steal my job from me.'

They stood facing each other as the other guide led the party away, Mark working up the courage to say, 'I'm not.'

'Not what?'

'Not out for your job; I'm not a smiley-type person.'

'That's a shame. The one time I've seen you smile was rather attractive.'

He made a nervous sound, one he had hoped to sound more casual.

She drew a little closer, glancing about, as if distracted by the tiny black birds nesting in the cluster of growth overhead. 'I knew about Chaumont's account, but as an apocryphal footnote, not exactly general knowledge. You don't really believe it, do you?'

'Why not?' he countered, though his eyes revealed his teasing. 'He *was* in charge of the Crusaders who stopped here.'

'He was also a murdering religious zealot who bedded his sister; such things tend to tarnish his veracity for me.' She grinned, and looked more closely at him. 'Are you a historian, then?'

'A teacher, Classical Studies at Manchester University. But history's been a personal love for me for years.'

'Why?'

He blinked; the last person to ask that question had been Chrissie, and she had asked with that mixture of arrogance and ignorance that only the truly self-righteous could fully employ.

Miss Ösbank, on the other hand, seemed genuinely curious, and for a moment it had thrown him. Then he recovered, pretending to find something new and startling on the wall as he replied. 'I had a very good teacher when I was young; she brought the past to life, made it more than names and dates and battles and treaties. She made me feel a part of it, showed me why things now are the way they are.' Then he looked over at her, somewhat embarrassed. 'Sorry. That probably sounds stupid.'

To his relief, she shook her head, and her face took on a wistful expression. 'Not at all. I had someone similar in my life.' Now they suddenly found themselves close together, and it seemed to be her turn to be embarrassed. Then she detoured with, 'There's a Roman mural in a cave passage near here, part of a library anteroom. It was only discovered last year.'

He brightened, intrigued. 'Really?'

'Yes, but we can't put it on the tour, because of the delicacy of the find.' She waved an arm out invitingly. 'However, I can make an exception for a fellow lover of history . . .'

Time more than the elements had battered the mural, like so much in the ruins. However, it was still distinctive.

The passage was cool, pitch black to preserve the find; Mark and Kami had to use torches while inside. The air was dry, musty. But it was the woman's proximity to Mark now that was sending chills down his spine – and electrifying his cock.

'Remarkable, isn't it?'

Mark assumed she meant the mural, and nodded. And admittedly it was: clear depictions of men, women, couples, groups, all engaged in various explicit sexual acts. 'Ah, I take it this was the adult section of the library?'

'Yes.' She reached out and touched his side, made him shudder. 'Kept apart from the main library to spare sensitivities.'

'I, um, can understand that.'

'Well, I don't.' She drew closer, faced him, pressed against him. As she spoke he could feel her breath on his lips; the hands holding the torches dropped to their sides, taking the light with them, and Mark became acutely aware of how this woman excited all his other senses beside sight. 'Sex is not something that should be hidden. Nor sexual desire.' She was closer to him now; he could almost feel her full breasts against him, but if that happened, she could not fail to feel his growing erection against her thigh. Instinctively he backed away a little as she continued. 'It's a primal urge, like hunger. We don't deny it when we get hungry, do we? We don't get ashamed. We simply . . . eat.'

Mark's head spun, and his mouth dried, and he imagined her hand moving towards his groin . . .

And then he pulled himself back to reality, lifting the torch to light their exit. 'Food, huh? I'm famished for some lunch.'

He felt the woman stiffen beside him, perhaps feeling she'd been insulted, or at least in bewilderment. Finally, she made a shrugging sound and replied, 'As you wish, Mr Healey.'

Mark thought that after this, both of them would avoid each other for the rest of the day. Yet they drew back together, to talk and argue and question each other's knowledge, even as they sat and ate the pre-prepared cold lunch of fruits and breads with the rest of the tour party, beneath the shade of the trees. It was a surprisingly pleasant experience for him; he had a prior impression of tour guides as having soup-dish knowledge of the local area, wide-seeming but shallow, but this woman was erasing that notion. She was entertaining, engaging company.

The day took on a new and unexpected turn on the way back, starting with a conversation between two silver-haired women in the seats behind Mark and Miss Ösbank, examining souvenirs they had purchased. 'She's beautiful, isn't she? So cute –'

Kami turned to see. 'You're not likely to find her curled up in a basket at the foot of your bed, ladies.'

This prompted Mark to glance behind him as well, at the small ebony statue of a female figure, the head feline in its pointed ears and snout, brandishing objects in the arms crossed over her chest, a far more tasteful choice than the multi-breasted Artemises or the über-phallic Priapuses. 'Bastet?'

Kami smiled and nodded, elaborating for the women. 'The Egyptian goddess of cats, a valuable ally in the protection of their granaries. She was also a goddess of perfumes and fertility, and under other names served as a bloodthirsty avenger, slayer of men.'

Under his breath, Mark muttered, 'Perfect job for a woman.'

He immediately regretted it, as it became obvious that Miss Ösbank had heard him. She looked down at him with an amused expression. 'Oh? And how's that?'

He flushed. 'I, ah, was just noting that, of all the feline deities of the Egyptian, Hittite and Kush pantheons, it was always the goddesses that were employed to create havoc. Sekhmet, Astarteth, Mafdet, Ptah, Tawaret, Urt-Hekau –'

'I know the rest.' She sat down again, reaching into the bag at her feet for some bottled water. 'So you think the female of the species is naturally more deadly than the male?'

'That's not the point. Our ancestors created these deities to represent aspects of our psyches as well as aspects of nature. And our ancestors recognised that women have an aggressive, malicious side to them. Or am I wrong?'

'No. Even *I've* been known to lose my temper once or twice.' She made a show of deliberately staring ahead. 'It's amazing, how the sexes can share identical qualities, yet be labelled differently. A man is strong, a woman aggressive, a man cunning, a woman malicious. Just because a woman might not conform to a man's notions of feminine qualities –'

'I don't think that way.'

'I'm glad to hear it. But some men desire the passion of a woman's spirit, but reject her fury, as if you can truly separate the two.' She sensed his reaction to that. 'What do you think about that?'

He considered his reply, and almost told her the truth, feeling like everyone on the bus was listening. Then he settled for, 'Do you want to have dinner tonight?'

Mark heard the words as if they weren't his own. Afterwards, he would relentlessly analyse why he had asked her. Of course, he didn't deny that he had been physically attracted to her from the start, or that he had enjoyed her company on an intellectual level, as he had with few others. And maybe he had asked her to deflect further embarrassment to himself, or perhaps he had to prove something to her. Or himself.

Whatever the reason, she smiled and replied, 'Yes.'

And the butterflies in his stomach hopped onto motorbikes and began riding around.

Mark found Greg still around the hotel pool, now reclining on a lounger under the shade of a wilting tree, wolfing down a greasy burger. He had cast aside his shirt and shorts, and his swimming trunks and skin gave the appearance of his just having hopped out of the water. He beamed Cheshire and swallowed as Mark appeared. 'Oi, mate, about time! Thought you'd got left behind with all the relics!'

'Your concern is touching.' Mark plopped down onto the empty white plastic chair beside Greg and watched the people in the pool: mostly children, splashing about and ignoring their parents' orders to come out and get ready for tea. 'What happened to your two honeys?'

Greg set down his burger and reached for his beer. 'Cheryl and Maura. Or Moira. From Glasgow. They're nurses.' He chuckled, Sid James-style. 'And you know what that means.'

Mark took the beer for a sip. 'You get to play doctor?'

'Well, I *do* have a terrific thermometer.'

'You have all the subtlety of a pair of clown shoes, you know that?'

Greg took his beer back. 'Can't wound me, mate, I've got us set up tonight with Cheryl and Maura/Moira. Cheryl's mine, you can rummage your way through the Glaswegian to work out the other girl's name yourself.'

'Sorry, I'm busy, I've – I've already got a date.' He said it with as much pride as could paper over his anxiety. 'Someone I met on the trip today.'

Greg's jaw dropped, and he sat up to face his friend, his face pale, his voice low. 'Mark, mate, I know breaking up with Chrissie hurt you, but this has gone well past hurt and deep into seriously sick.'

'Pardon?'

'What is it, the walking frames, the ointment smell? I mean, older women are all right, but apart from getting a slap-up breakfast the next morning –'

'It's one of the tour guides, idiot.'

'Oh? What's wrong with her? Blind? Big-nosed? A hunch?'

Mark retrieved the beer, staring ahead as he pictured the woman again, his heartbeat quickening. 'She's ... gorgeous. Beautiful brown hair, delicate hazel eyes, full lips, a figure to die for – and more brains than any dozen of your honeys.'

'So she's totally perfect, then?'

Mark considered the question. 'Well, she *is* a bit forward. Obvious. In your face, so to speak.'

Greg shrugged. 'Ah ... sounds like a complete and utter bitch; I'll take her off your hands, shall I?' Then his grin dropped. 'Oi, what about tonight? You're leaving me to entertain the nurses on my lonesome?'

'Yep.' Mark finished Greg's beer and rose to leave. 'And you never even thanked me.'

The room was starkly furnished, and there was a slightly off-kilter, unfinished feel to it all: the terracotta floor tiles didn't quite reach one of the milk-white walls, the balcony doors didn't shut properly without effort, and the dresser drawers were mismatched. However, he supposed the room served its purpose for the money paid, and the majority of its occupants would be too exhausted or pissed by evening's end to care.

Chrissie wouldn't have cared. When he'd purchased the holiday six months ago, all she could talk about at first was the anticipation of long nights of dancing and drinking. Later, when all she could talk about was ending their relationship, he tried and failed to get a refund, then decided to take the holiday anyway, with the more-than-willing Greg along to take Chrissie's place in every way.

Well, perhaps not in *every* way.

Mark was prepared to spend the week doing things he preferred for a change: sightseeing, relaxing by the pool.

Going on a date with Kami – Miss Ösbank – had been an unexpected bonus.

The butterflies remained, however.

It was just dinner, he reminded himself.

He sat on the edge of the bed and thought of her

again: that mass of hair, soft and fine, flowing around her, those piercing, inviting eyes, those equally inviting lips, that figure, how her breasts moulded themselves inside her shirt . . .

Oh God, he was so hard.

He edged his way backwards until his head rested on the firm linen pillow at the head of the bed, and he kicked off his walking shoes and flexed his toes. Nearby, the glass balcony doors were ajar, and a soft breeze made the wiry curtains flutter; beyond, the hotel bar's techno music failed to obscure the more distant wail of the local mosque for evening prayer.

Mark's cock stiffened inside his clothes.

He could still smell her scent, could feel her presence beside him on the bus, making the hairs on his arm rise.

His focus was on a more prominent rising, though, and he realised how long it had been since he'd last come, by himself or with anyone else. He'd locked the door, certain Greg would not return for a while.

He unzipped his trousers before his cock burst through the fabric, unbuttoned them and raised his buttocks enough to draw his trousers and briefs down to his knees. It continued to swell as he pictured her again, and it rose relentlessly from a wiry thicket of curls, pale and deepening to red at the tip.

He pictured those times when he'd seen her from the rear, relishing the sight of her buttocks and hips in those slacks. She had a woman's figure, one of classical beauty and design, and his hand fastened around his cock as he started a slow pumping action, glancing once at it to see the head glistening excitedly with pre-come. He wanted the delicious sensation to last forever, as he wanted to keep the memory of her closeness fresh in his mind, even if nothing further came of knowing her.

As he brought himself closer to climax, he pushed aside all images and memories of Chrissie, which would certainly tarnish the bliss he was experiencing now. Instead, he imagined Kami, imagined making love to her, looking and touching and tasting her in every way, feeling nothing more than the need to take her, please her, fuck her.

Then the rush, and his balls, heavy and tight, contracted into his body and the first spurt shot from his cock. He came in earnest, violent, long-overdue throbs of sensation firing through him like electricity as he emitted three more rapid-fire jets onto his groin and belly.

He lay back, his sticky fingers still holding his organ, as if to support it for its inevitable wilting. A final random spasm shot through him, like an errant echo, and he wished it had been her hand.

Guilt crept into him now, guilt for making a strange woman the object of his fantasy.

It was only going to be dinner, he reminded himself.

However, it could be more. If he acted more like Greg. Well, why not?

3

'Well?'

Kami kept a swift pace up the road that led to their home, knowing it was the only way to keep the more easily winded Janeane moving. Without slowing, she turned and replied, 'I'm going out tonight.'

'Well, duh. With Professor Stuck-up?'

'He's not ... completely stuck up.'

'I'd hope not, since you spent all day with him, leaving me to do all the work.'

'Aww, did I neglect you?' Kami teased, shaking her hair back to catch the last of the sun's rays before it disappeared over the distant hills.

'*Sicharim Magazina.*'

'It's "*Sicharim Agazina*", unless a threat to kick my magazine instead of my ass is considered intimidating in America. But at least your Turkish is improving.'

Janeane replied with a more understandable gesture as she fished through her jacket for her keys. The road on the top of the hill led to a collection of white-faced residential apartments, some still unfinished. Janeane and Kami's ground-floor flat was in one of the completed units, and while the trek up the hill could be tiring for Janeane, the relative quiet and the view of the town below more than compensated.

The flat interior was what one previous erudite visitor had charitably described as 'eclectically furnished'. In truth, it was an unholy hodgepodge of styles: ornate oak chairs and shocking pink beanbags, Andy Warhol reproductions on the walls, CDs and shoes scattered on the tile floor, table lamps made of glowing fibre-optic wires, and an elegant Persian rug before the TV.

And two daytime occupants: fat tabby grey toms, curled up on either end of the settee.

'Shoo! Shoo!' Janeane slipped out of her jacket and made a half-hearted attempt to swipe at the cats. They leaped off and skidded onto the rug, looking back to hiss in protest before padding over to Kami for protection. Janeane perched herself on one arm of the settee to kick off her shoes. 'You spoil those fat flea-bitten bastards.'

Kami knelt down to scratch behind their ears as they rubbed against her shins. 'I give them a little sugar, and they give me a lot of attention. Like all males.'

'Bite me.' Janeane began unbuttoning her shirt as she departed for the bathroom. 'Come on in and tell me about the professor.'

Kami rose and entered the open kitchen area to feed the boys, before grabbing a peach from the fridge, washing it, and then following the trail of clothes into the bathroom. The tight enclosure of salmon-pink tiles sweated from the steam bleeding from behind the wrinkled yellow plastic shower curtain bordering the tub.

Kami planted herself on the toilet seat, resting her feet on the adjacent edge of the tub and biting into her peach. She regarded the slim, shrouded figure behind the curtain, listened to the drumbeat of water on tile and flesh, and smelled the sweet apple scent of Janeane's favourite shampoo. She swallowed the bite in her mouth and noted, 'You need to put on weight.'

'What?' came the muffled reply.

'You need curves. You don't look healthy.'

Janeane snorted. 'Girl, if I thought it'd avoid my

waist and aim for my tits and ass, I'd scoff down a barrel of chocolate fudge ripple right now.' She paused, and then ventured, 'You piss me off with that damned body of yours. You know...'

Her voice trailed away, but Kami knew, had sensed and scented the physical attraction many times. Janeane enjoyed both women and men, and did not hide it as Kami had seen others do. More than once their mutual need for touch and intimacy had led them to share beds, where they'd talk and kiss and stroke each other for the longest time. Kami certainly relished the attention received, the desire, but she could not let it go further.

'Well, what's he like?'

Kami took another bite as she considered it. 'He smells right.'

'You and men's smells. Anything else?'

'He's clever, but doesn't talk down to me. He has a lovely accent. His eyes notice you.' She smiled with the memory. Then the smile dropped. 'But he's strange. Quiet. He actually seems to listen.'

'A man who listens to women, huh? You sure he wasn't gay?'

'Not unless the hard-on he carried with him for most of the day was because of the ruins.'

'Well, they are impressive erections in their own right.' Janeane chuckled at her own quip, and then asked, 'Sounds like you've lucked out there.'

'What? No. Great company, yes, but not exactly satisfaction guaranteed – a bit too ... lightweight for my taste.'

The water stopped; moments later, Janeane drew the curtain aside and stood there in her naked glory, a curious expression on her face. 'Towel, please.'

Kami handed her a thick blue terry towel from the

wall rail beside her, watching as Janeane dried herself, a brisk routine Kami had witnessed more than once: first she rubbed at the slim calves, then the thighs, across her flat belly, her small, pert breasts, her slender arms, before burying her head into the material to dry her hair.

Kami took in the sight, the scent of her friend, the body language. 'What is it?'

Janeane emerged from the towel and wrapped it around herself, covering herself from breast to thigh. 'Somehow I don't think you'd be interested.' She padded out of the tub and the bathroom, leaving it at that.

Kami finished her peach, dropped the remains in the bin and followed Janeane into her bedroom, curling up on the bed and watching as her friend squatted on a nearby stool beside her dresser mirror to blow-dry her hair. 'Go on, you're dying to have a go.'

Janeane stared back through her reflection, speaking up over the whine of the dryer. 'I've never seen you spend so much time with a "lightweight" as you did today.'

Kami winced, as if only at the dryer's sound. 'That was different. Look, it was so obvious that he wanted to fuck. But he did nothing. No initiative, until the end.'

Janeane switched off the dryer and began brushing her hair. 'Well, maybe he wanted to get to know you better, so he could eventually be more intimate with you.'

Kami shifted to perch on the foot of the bed, a metre away from Janeane. 'That's not how men operate, though. And I wouldn't want them to, either. Too creepy. I think being with women for so long has confused you.'

'I'm no stranger to the ways of the cock.' Janeane set her brush down and turned to Kami. 'Let's try something, then: pretend I'm Mark, and that we're on a date. Stand up.'

'Why? No. It's stupid.'

Janeane rose, removed her towel and slipped into a baggy grey sweatshirt that reached just below her bum. 'Afraid?'

Kami scowled and rose, arms crossed over her chest, challenging her friend. 'No.'

Janeane breathed in, her expression changed, and she drew closer, gazing into Kami's eyes, her voice low, deliberate. 'Kami, have you any idea how fucking lovely you are in the light of the setting sun?'

Kami looked away. 'Crap, this isn't going to work.'

'Then you have nothing to lose.' Janeane drew closer, until they stood almost touching, Janeane's hands reaching up to stroke Kami's hair; Janeane smiled slightly. 'You have no idea how long I've wanted to do this.' Janeane lowered her voice, her fingers moving to Kami's face, stroking it, cupping it. 'How close I've wanted to get to you.'

Kami's breath quickened at the touch, warming her insides and making her head spin. She felt the strength gradually leak from her as Janeane gently but insistently moved her backwards, until she nearly fell as she sat down on the edge of the bed again, Janeane's hands turning Kami's face upwards. 'Look, Jan –'

'Shush. The name is Mark, and I can't help myself, Kami. The thought of touching you, tasting you, is too much to keep back.' Slowly, Janeane bent down and let her lips gently touch Kami's; a moan escaped from her throat as she tasted Kami's sweet lips. Kami started when she felt the hand reach up and grasp the back of her neck. Then Kami moaned back and opened her mouth as she pulled the other woman's closer to her own. She felt her sex pulse as she pressed her tongue towards Janeane's mouth, and a moan sounded within Janeane when she opened her mouth to let it inside.

Then it was Kami's turn to gasp again as Janeane closed her lips around the intruding tongue and pulled her in, softly. Chills began to run up and down her spine. Soon, the two women's tongues were dancing with one another.

Janeane pulled back reluctantly, gazing into Kami's eyes, her lips glistening. 'You're the most amazing woman I've ever met. I want to take you, please you, in ways you've never experienced before.'

Kami gasped. 'Jan –'

'No: Mark.' She smiled again. 'All I want is to please you, give you the pleasure you deserve . . .' Her hands moved to Kami's shoulders, guiding her down until Kami was lying back, and Janeane was almost on top of her. Still gazing down, her blonde hair falling over her head, her eyes wide, intent, her fingers stroked Kami's face. 'You have no idea how much you enslave me.'

'Ja – Jan –'

'Mark . . . my name is Mark. Say my name.'

Janeane's fingers reached Kami's neck, her throat. 'M – Mark.'

'Oh my, so sweet to hear my name on your soft lips,' Janeane replied smoothly, her voice honeyed as she drew closer and began kissing and licking the nape of Kami's neck.

'Oh – oh, that's good.'

'Tell me, darling. Tell me what you need.' Janeane began nibbling along Kami's neck and shoulder, unbuttoning Kami's shirt and drawing it open, revealing full breasts in a frilly white bra. 'Trust me, let me in. I promise I'll take you to those places only a very lucky few have reached. Let me take you, Kami . . .' She darted her tongue along the edge of Kami's ear. 'Give yourself to me.'

'I – I –'

Janeane's hand curled to let the fingertips delicately stroke the sensitive, exposed upper portion of Kami's left breast, until the coral-coloured nipple hardened into a tight, pursed bud of flesh beneath the material of the bra. 'Oh, my sweet Kami, you are so fucking heavenly.'

Kami remained lost, silent, breathing hard under the continued ministration, her arms reaching up to encircle Janeane.

However, Janeane gently pushed them down again. 'Just close your eyes, trust me, I said I'd drive, didn't I?' Janeane chuckled. 'You feel so soft and warm beneath me.'

'Oh, fucking hell –' was all Kami could whisper, her head tipped back, eyes closed, sinking fast.

Janeane's fingers trailed down, down over Kami's fleshy belly, passing over the belt of her trousers, the zip, lightly trailing one finger down over the seam until her hand rested on Kami's pussy mound. 'Sweetheart, will you let me? Please?'

'Yes – yes –'

Janeane pressed down with the palm of her hand. 'Oh, God, Kami, I want you, I want to be inside you. You've made me want you so much today. I can't wait any longer. Will you let me take you all the way, darling?'

'Oh, God . . . yes . . . *yes* . . .'

'You want me inside, taking you? Can I have you, Kami? All of you?'

'Yes! Oh fuck yes!'

They kissed again, hot and moist and wanting.

Then Janeane released her, rose to her feet and returned to her usual self. 'Right, now get out, I've got things to do.'

Kami sat up again, her heart racing, her pussy throbbing. She peered up from under her hair with an equal mixture of confusion, arousal and frustration. 'What the –'

Janeane was flushed, and not from the recent shower. 'Go. Before I forget myself.' She chuckled, distractedly. 'Look at you, your freckles have risen again.'

Kami flushed further, reality crashing in and a measure of embarrassment flooding over her. 'I'm going.' She departed and made her way back to her own room, locking the door as quickly and quietly as she could, the intensity within her body making her feel as if she was ready to burst out of her skin. She pulled at her clothes, making two buttons fly from her blouse as she stripped, as if her clothes were as much on fire as her pussy felt. She saw her arms and, after removing her bra, her breasts, saw the markings now visible on the surface of her skin, a manifestation of her arousal – and her true nature – that was impossible to ignore.

The floor creaked as she kicked off her shoes, fought with her trousers and won, then those hated knickers, flinging all clothes aside to stretch and bask in glorious nudity.

And her tail – ah, that felt *glorious*! It lengthened, engorged with her blood, then rose swaying from the hidden fold at the base of her spine to its full length, happy and free again.

A moment's relief from the clothing, and then the hunger returned to the forefront of her awareness. She dropped to the floor at the side of her dishevelled bed, her aching breasts pressed hard against the mattress, her thighs parted, her hand between them, working madly at her aching clitoris, as her tail twitched and swayed in ecstasy. All that had just happened had been almost too much. And her whole body reminded her that it had been over a week since the incident on the beach; Kami had struggled to keep a low profile since then.

From Janeane's room came the sounds of climax, sounds Kami desperately wanted to echo, and offer back to her friend. She listened, and fed herself. And as she drew closer, the hairs on her limbs rising, thickening, her eyes aching behind her contacts, she thought of Mark, of how he smelled and looked and sounded. She imagined him behind her, inside her, taking her in a way she could never risk in real life, taking, further, further...

Kami hissed through clenched teeth as she came, the sound like steam. She leaned forwards until her head buried itself in the mattress, eyes unfocused, tongue darting out to taste the air, to feel her heart slow again.

After a while, her tail sagged, and she regained control of her limbs, helping herself up onto the bed and pulling the sheets over her. Relief washed over her – relief, and a nagging sense of discontent.

Perhaps Janeane was right. Not about men. As far as Kami was concerned, men were like her toms: capricious, self-centred, urge-driven engines. She accepted that, liked that, because she could take what she wanted from them as they did from her, and then send them away without any hard feelings. Trust was simply out of the question.

Rather, Janeane might have been right about playing coy, if it encouraged Mark.

He *did* smell lovely.

Thoughts of Mark Healey remained with her as she cooled down under the sheets. Her past encounters with men had always been spontaneous, in the moment, without too much thought, especially with her true nature revealed. She'd never had to wait so long for a man.

She hoped it would be worth it.

The sky had deepened to violet upon the withdrawal of the sun, and the air was noticeably cooler. The bright lights of the many clubs and bars in town complemented the darkness and coolness. The sounds of revelry were more artificial than actual, but it was still early in the evening.

Mark stood at the entrance to his hotel, bobbing on each foot anxiously, sticking his hands into his trouser pockets in an attempt to appear casual, but knowing his movements only looked suspect. He wore a light linen jacket and matching trousers, and a dark shirt, a simple but good-looking set.

He needed to swagger. He needed to be as cool and glib and confident as Greg was.

She wasn't going to show up, he convinced himself. She and her mate were having a real good laugh right now at his expense . . .

'Hello.'

He started; Kami had crept up on him from behind. She wore a gorgeous flowing lemony cotton dress, ankle-length, sleeveless, tied at the waist to accentuate a figure that needed little encouragement, the open-neck V-collar dipping to a generous cleavage. She stood there, hands behind her back, one high heel twisting slightly in the dirt, looking up at him on the steps.

'Jesus –'

'No,' she replied sweetly. 'I heard he was shorter and darker. Are you ready?'

Mark swallowed. 'Ready?'

'To eat. I'm famished.'

Mark's stomach growled on cue.

'You too, huh?' she noted, smiling.

Mark breathed out, wishing his body didn't betray him so much in her presence. 'So, where shall we eat?'

'This is Sedat's,' Kami announced, as she took a seat opposite Mark.

Mark was conscious of the stares Kami received from many of the patrons at the bar at the far end, and how she smiled and waved at a few who called out her name, but he put that down to her evident familiarity with the venue. 'Is the food good?'

Kami blinked, as if not having considered the question before. 'Well, there's lots of it, and Sedat likes to keep me happy.'

Feeling an acute pang of jealousy, Mark remembered his agenda, and leaned in towards her. Mustering as much cockiness and swagger as he could, he dived in. 'I don't blame him; someone as foxy as you should be kept happy – and by a guy who knows how.' Mark shuddered inside. Surely this is never going to wash, he mused to himself.

She smiled, though to Mark it seemed false. 'Really?' She rested her chin on her raised hand. 'My, Mr Healey, you *are* the bold one.'

Mark smiled back. 'With a sweet piece of work like you, a guy has to be bold.'

Kami tilted her head, letting her hair fall over one side of her face and allowing her fingers to trail through it absently. 'Who, little old me?' She giggled. In the background, the speakers started playing a soft piano jazz number. 'Oh, this is my favourite song!'

This time it was Mark who was confused. Was she taking the piss? Was she laughing at him behind that sweet little girlie routine? Mark frowned, and then jumped visibly when she abruptly turned and barked, 'Sedat!'

A moustached, portly man in smart clothes appeared, smiling. 'Ahh, sweet Kami, you grace us with your presence tonight.'

Now she smiled sweetly at him. 'How true.' She reached out and pulled him in close, whispering something in Turkish into Sedat's ear. Sedat straightened, regarded Mark, and then tapped his nose knowingly. 'Now be a dear and bring us two big English breakfasts, a plate of chips, and a pitcher of beer,' Kami ordered. Sedat smiled widely, nodded and departed, and Kami winked at Mark. 'I know what Englishmen like for their suppers.'

Mark smiled back. His nervousness reached new levels at the thought that now both Kami and Sedat were enjoying a big joke at his expense. He took a deep breath, beginning to wish he'd just been himself. However, he was in too deep now. He gamely reached for another Gregism. 'Who cares about the meal? I'd rather move straight to the dessert in front of me.'

After a stunned pause, Kami giggled again. 'Please, Mr Healey, you'll sweep me off my feet with such talk!'

Mark blinked again, briefly bemused. She has to be playing with me, he thought, then he forced out another wide grin to paper over the confusions. 'Baby, lie back and enjoy the ride, because I'm the man that can take you places you've never been –'

Suddenly she dropped her napkin and her sweet girlie expression and frowned, giving in to the need to understand what was going on. 'OK, I need to know, why? Why are you talking like that?'

Mark tried hard to keep grinning. Inside his head

was screaming at him to stop with the unctuousness – he'd been rumbled. Nevertheless, the power of Greg compelled him. 'What's, er, wrong with telling a hot, sexy woman how I feel about her?' Mark stuttered, still trying to salvage the few scraps of dignity he mistakenly thought he had left.

'Because everything about you says you're uncomfortable saying all that: your posture, your tone, the look in your eyes, your scent –'

He sat back, stunned, resigned to his failure, and let her words sink in, searching in vain for a witty retort. 'Huh? My scent?'

'Don't change the subject. What you're saying isn't you, and it's confusing.'

'Well, you're damned right it's confusing, but what about *you*? Fluttering your eyelashes and acting all coy! Is that *you*, then?'

Now Kami's cheeks burned with embarrassment at her own masquerade.

Silence dropped between them. After a moment, they settled back in their chairs, regarding each other as if for the first time. Mark finally broke the silence. 'Kami, I'm sorry. I got the impression you'd go for the take-charge kind of man, but I'm crap at it. And I just got out of a bad relationship. And even though parts of me would like it to be otherwise, I'm not the type to just jump into bed with a woman.'

He was blushing now. 'But I *do* like you, and I *do* enjoy your company. So, how about we just be ourselves, and enjoy the evening as friends?' He took a deep breath and looked at her. He was sure he'd blown it now, and sighed, getting up from his chair to leave. Kami reached out and took his hand. He sat down again, his heart racing and his cheeks burning.

Kami didn't seem to know what to say, at least not

at first. But when she did, she sounded intrigued. 'I think I'd like that very much, Mark.'

He smiled. 'Good. Great!' There was an embarrassing quiet again, as they both looked down at their napkins, reeling a little from the earlier charades.

Breaking the awkwardness perfectly, Sedat arrived with their meals, and they spent the rest of the evening eating, talking, laughing, drinking and forgetting their earlier masquerades.

4

It was near midnight before they realised the time, and the couple walked out into a night lit as much by the stars above as by the lights in the neighbouring streets, the sounds of their footsteps loud in the quiet surroundings, the scent of the sea in the air. He looked out. 'It's a lovely little town.'

Kami's eyes followed his gaze. 'Little? It's huge compared to where I came from.'

'And where's that?'

'Just a nameless place in Anatolia. Not much to talk about.' Suddenly she twisted and fell forwards, her dress ripping as she sat heavily on the pavement.

'Kami?' Mark stopped and dropped to one knee. 'Are you OK?'

She grimaced and glared at her feet. 'Fuck, fuck, *fucking bastard*!' She kicked forwards, trying to extricate her feet from the tangle that the lower half of her dress had become, and then winced. 'Fucking shoes, I hate them!' She reached down and ripped the hem of her dress further to give herself greater freedom. 'They're my flatmate's; I'll kill her for letting me take them when she wasn't looking.'

Mark swallowed. 'Here, let me see.' He reached for the foot with the broken heel on the shoe.

'*No!*' she hissed at him through clenched teeth, her hand shooting out to grasp his wrist in an iron grip that made him wince.

Mark looked into eyes that were fierce and bright,

felt the hot breath harsh through flared nostrils, felt his own heart race with alarm, urging him to withdraw.

But then he put aside his own fear, and looked past her rage, to see the other emotions she hid behind it: the embarrassment at her own clumsiness, the fear of being vulnerable like this in front of someone else. It was familiar to him.

And Mark reached out with his other hand, to touch hers gently, his voice soft and tender. 'Kami, I'm your friend, aren't I? I promise I'm not going to hurt you. C'mon, you want to let me help, don't you? As a friend?'

After anxious heartbeats, Kami released her grip on him and leaned back onto her elbows, her hair fallen over her face. She shook it away. 'Sorry.'

'It's OK.' He moved to examine her ankle. 'You've twisted it.'

'Really?' she spat, with sarcastic fervour. She removed the shoes, flinging them both away. But her rage had already melted into an annoyed grouse.

He deftly touched several areas, gauging her reaction. 'Think you can stand?'

'Of course I can.' She started to help herself up, struggling. 'Fuck!'

He rose, and then held out his hand, saying nothing.

Kami stared at it, glared at it – and then accepted it. But she was unable to put her foot down properly. She cursed again, this time in Turkish.

'Right,' Mark decided, bending down to slip his arm around the back of her thighs.

Kami grabbed a handful of his shirt. 'What the hell are you doing?'

He froze. 'Whoa! It's OK, I'm – I'm going to carry you. You can't get back home on your own steam, can you?'

Kami blew out an exasperated breath of air and released him. 'Suppose not.'

He nodded, and lifted her up in his arms, Kami's body sinking so that the backs of her knees rested over one arm, and the hand of the other slipped into her armpit, the fingers almost touching the side of her breast. Her dress, now ripped, exposed her legs to her knees. 'Oh my – could you put your arms around my neck, for a little extra support?'

She nodded, her skin contact with him increasing, her torso twisted so that her breasts pressed against his chest. He felt dizzy, and her hair tickled his face. 'Bloody hell . . .'

'Look, are you OK?' she asked.

'Yes. I was just, ah, well, I'm not used to having a friend in such a . . . vulnerable position,' Mark continued gamely. 'I realise this might be embarrassing for you, so I'll just get on with it, shall I?' He waited for the blood to start flowing properly through his body before setting off, under Kami's directions. He'd kept in reasonable shape, but his arms still ached when they finally reached Kami's building, and he set her down so that she could unlock the door and hobble inside. 'Perhaps I should carry you to bed?'

Kami turned and looked at him quizzically.

'I mean, I didn't mean it like that –'

'I know.'

Mark breathed in, and then looked at the road. 'Well, if you're OK, I should go –'

'Thanks for the lift, Mark.'

He shrugged. 'No problem – what's wrong?'

Kami was frowning, though more to herself than to him. 'I never had a man for a friend, just a friend, before. It never came up, somehow. It'll take some getting used to, I think.' Now she smiled, warmly. 'Don't worry, so far I like the feeling.'

Mark smiled back.

'Come here.'

His breath caught in his throat, but he obliged, drawing closer, as Kami pressed her lips against his, a simple gesture of affection, but one which reached deep inside him as he stepped back.

'Thank you again, Mark,' she said to him, her voice a caress to his ears, a spark to his blood. 'Good night.'

Mark somehow made his way down the hill, the blossoming erection in his trousers refusing to leave despite all attempts at distraction. He mentally kicked himself for not staying, for not casting aside his intention to remain just good friends, and doing what his heart, his groin, wanted.

But he couldn't, not after all the fuss he'd made.

The music was loud around the hotel bar, and suffused the very walls and floors of the building as he made his way upstairs and into his room, the noise even drowning out the sound of his key and the lock. The room was dark, half-lit by the indirect light from outside, through the open balcony doors. At first, he thought Greg was out, with the nurses.

He only realised his latest mistake when he practically walked in on them in one of the beds.

The clothes were scattered over the floor, amidst the flotsam of beer bottles and ashtrays and discarded pillows. The bed creaked, barely audible over the music outside. And Mark stood by the bathroom door, watching as Greg writhed on the bed with two naked women, a full-bodied blonde and a thinner brunette, their limbs snaking and caressing and possessing. The air was thick with sex, even with the fresh air from the open balcony doors. No one had even noticed Mark's entry.

He wanted to leave immediately. Really.

The blonde lay back, her head tilted to one side to avoid the headboard, as Greg knelt up between her legs, supporting her thighs with his hands as he thrust into her, grunting and cursing, his face contorted in sublime effort. The brunette lay beside the blonde, her face hidden by her hair as she licked and caressed the blonde's breasts, before moving to the woman's mouth to plant deep, hot kisses.

'Hey, Moira,' Greg was grunting. 'Gimme some, baby.'

The brunette rose and knelt up, the nipples of her small round breasts pert as she drew closer and clasped Greg's head in her hands, kissing him now with equal fervour.

Mark swallowed, his mouth suddenly incredibly dry, and made his way out on unsteady feet.

The beach was deserted, at least the part Mark had arrived at, past a collection of overturned, beached rowing-boats. The trees that lined the causeway partially shielded the area from the street, but as the town's bars and clubs were on the other side of the bay, Mark may as well have been the only man in town.

The dark water lapped softly against the light sand. It was inviting; Mark's head still spun as he sat down on the cool sand beside a boat and removed his shoes and socks, and then struggled with his shirt and trousers, forcing himself to continue before he chickened out completely. Just a quick dip to cool himself, he assured himself. Or more particularly, to cool the erect shaft inside his shorts that continued to vex him. He nearly banged his head on the boat as he flung off the shorts, and then crouched to gather his clothes and keep them together.

He was naked, in public. And rather erect.

He faced the waters, his breath rapid, his head woozy from the alcohol and constant arousal.

And then he made a dash for the bay, his cock pointing the way.

Kami hobbled inside, ignoring her greeting toms, hearing and smelling Janeane before seeing her friend emerge from her bedroom, clad in a short powder-blue cotton shirt that left her naked from the midriff down. She beamed at her flatmate. 'Kami! Babe! How was your date?'

Drawing closer, Kami could scent the alcohol – and the arousal. 'It was ... different.'

Janeane's mouth opened. 'Oh, honey, you're hurt! Did he do that?'

'I did it – in your shoes.'

'Sweetie!' She rushed over, put an arm around Kami and led her into Kami's bedroom. 'Here, let me take care of you.'

Kami was aware of Janeane's own unsteadiness, of the arm around her, how the hand had made its way towards her breast. 'I'll be fine.'

'No, no – I know what I'm doing,' she slurred. Releasing Kami, Janeane worked at the zip at the back of the dress, allowing Kami to shuck it off and leave herself in just a pair of black silk knickers and matching bra.

Janeane was behind her, her hands on Kami's waist, her breath on Kami's shoulders, murmuring as she swayed, 'My poor darling.'

Kami pulled away and turned to face her. 'You're drunk.'

Janeane nodded at that, swaying, her expression displaying that sense of naked self-awareness that comes with inebriation. 'I just – I –'

Kami sighed, distracted but sympathetic, and took her hand. 'Come to bed.'

And they lay together like spoons, Kami behind her as usual, one arm around her, murmuring softly and comfortingly to her friend.

Janeane quickly drifted off into snoring slumber.

But Kami lay there in the darkness, acutely aware of the time. She was too distracted, too aroused – and too angry with herself for not changing her tactics and inviting Mark in. What the hell was she doing in bed now? She didn't sleep the long, deep sleep of those around her; she should still be on the prowl.

So she crept out of bed, dressed herself in her favourite gypsy lace top tied at the front, hip-hugging chino trousers and comfortable flat sandals, and departed soon after, determined to find relief. Her hobbling had lessened and the swelling was down: good. She sought a man; she reasoned, Mark wouldn't mind, since he wanted them to be just friends, after all. A friend wouldn't begrudge a friend, would they?

She set off, satisfied with her logic. It was near one, and there were a few clubs still open. Some men were hanging around in the streets; perhaps there would be a good-smelling one she could take for some quick pleasure. Some man who knew what he wanted, how to act. Some – some –

Some tedious hunk of flesh.

She stopped and breathed out, wondering what was wrong with her. She could get another man, any other man. He could fulfil her.

But he wouldn't be Mark.

And every fibre of her being told her that sex with him would be infinitely more satisfying. And not just sex. Everything.

Then she caught a familiar scent downwind, and

followed it. Could it be him? Had he not gone back to the hotel? Maybe he'd gone to find some woman? Damn him, wasn't she good enough?

She followed the scent down to a deserted stretch of the beach. It was indeed Mark, and she was relieved to find him alone. She crept behind some overturned boats and watched. He was undressing, revealing a broad-barrelled chest, tan lines at the upper arms and neck, and sporting a diamond clump of hair at the centre of his chest.

Kami licked her lips when he bent to remove his footwear, then his trousers, finally struggling and removing his briefs. He seemed somewhat unsteady. She kept still, suffused with curiosity and arousal at the sight of his cock: a good size, but not too big, even fully erect as it was now, the head flaring and darker than the clump of hairs at the base, crowning his balls. She watched him take a deep breath, then race towards the water. And Kami raced for his clothes.

Shit, shit, *shit*!

Mark's body shuddered as he entered the water, managing to go only as far as his knees before finally turning back. Bloody hell! What idiot's idea was it to go for a moonlight swim? Madness!

On the other hand, his erection had disappeared. So he returned to his clothes, hating the feel of the sand now clinging to his wet feet.

His clothes – they were gone!

His stomach sank.

'Lose something?'

Mark spun in place; Kami stood there, having crept up on him again. 'Kami? What the hell?' His hands dived to cover his groin.

Kami leaned against a boat, arms folded casually

across her chest. 'I'm all for freedom, but the locals are a bit more prudish.'

Mark could feel himself turn seven shades of red in the darkness, and he glanced around him, certain someone would spot him. 'Kami, stop fooling around and give me my clothes back!'

'Hmm . . .' She drew closer, dropping her arms as her eyes deliberately ran over him. She grinned. 'Sorry, but I'm not used to having a friend in such a vulnerable position. But I realise this might be embarrassing for you –'

Mark's words returned to haunt him, and his face burned. 'Kami, I'm begging you –'

'Oh, Mark, you look cold.' She was closer now; he caught her scent. Then she reached out and embraced him, pressing his naked body close to hers, forcing his hands away from his groin. Her touch moved up and down his back, and her hair tickled his face. 'You poor dear, you're shivering.'

Mark buried his face in her mass of hair, and he caught her scent fully, felt her lovely warm breasts through her shirt, the heat from her sex against his own. 'O-Oh?'

'Well, parts of you seem to be.' She pulled back and gazed down, to see his cock pulsing quickly back to life, opening her eyes wide with mock amazement. 'Oh my, Mr Healey,' she purred, returning to her earlier sweet girlie character for a moment, just to tease.

Mark's head was spinning, as much from his own predicament as from his acute re-arousal. 'OK, Kami, I'm sorry. The whole "friends" thing was –'

'Shhh . . .' She brought a tender fingertip to his lips, silencing him, then let the finger descend along his chest. 'I'm the one who's sorry.'

His whole body was trembling now. 'Y – you?'

'Why, yes.' Her hand moved to his groin, through his pubic hair. 'I fear my presence has contributed in some small way to this growing ... discomfort ... you seem to be feeling right now. I should make it up to you.'

She dropped to her knees.

Mark's breath caught in his throat. 'Kami, bloody hell –'

She was at eye level to his cock now, but looked up at him. 'Mark, we're friends. What kind of a friend would I be if I left you in this state after getting you like this in the first place?'

His face was a picture of the conflict within him. 'But – I don't –'

'And what kind of a friend would *you* be if you left a friend feeling guilty? I'm simply helping a friend in need. Nothing more. Right?'

Mark looked ready to grasp any straw of justification. And he did, nodding weakly. 'Well – oh boy – if you feel you should ...'

Slowly Kami lowered her mouth and smelled him, breathing hot breath on his sensitive skin. He smelled quite wonderful to her, and she was very particular about men's scent. She ran her tongue over her soft lips then licked his cock slowly, from tip to root, before hungrily taking another slow lick, as if he were an ice cream, sliding her tongue around his head. Pursing her lips, she gently reached around his shaft and pulled his cock head to her mouth, rubbing the glistening tip on her full lips before opening them and taking the head into her warm waiting mouth.

Kami moaned softly with delight and the tiny vibrations sent shivers through Mark, who was now having great trouble standing. With soft sucking motions, Kami moved from the tip of his hot, hard stem downwards towards his balls, while somewhere above her, Mark whimpered in agonised anticipation. Kami laid the whole length of her tongue under the head of his cock, and licked, leaving it clean and shiny, and desperate for release.

'Oh God, Kami!' he gasped.

'Shh . . .' Kami pressed her face into his sweaty pubic hair, sliding her lips lower, over rough curls and the soft, smooth, hot skin of his inner thigh, before taking one of his balls into her mouth and twirling it delicately with her tongue. His scrotum tightened instantly.

She felt his hands grab her shoulders, and she put her arms around his thighs to steady him, her breasts pressed against his legs.

'Oh – oh, Kami –'

'Mmm, you're yummy, friend.' She cupped her hand around his balls, bringing them out from between his legs, gently manipulating them while teasing his stiff penis with flicks of her tongue, darting in, licking him in hot stabs. She reached around and clamped her hands on his buttocks, her claws not quite pricking his skin. He moaned loudly as his legs almost buckled.

Then she was back on him, slowly sliding her lips over the tip, taking it deeper and deeper into her mouth. Her tongue swirled, stroking and caressing the wet-hot fiery skin of his shaft. Kami pressed down, ringing the shaft, and slid her mouth back and forth, increasing her speed, hearing him moan faster, faster, her hot wet tongue lathering saliva on the bulging contours.

Mark then exploded in her mouth. As he came, Kami clamped his crotch to her face, swallowing, drinking him dry, until his clenched, sweaty buttocks relaxed, his hands fell from her shoulders, and he swayed, barely able to stand on his feet.

'Son of a –' he murmured, pulling back and falling to his knees, still firm but spent.

Kami fell back onto her haunches, licking her lips and relishing his taste. Then she departed, returning with his clothes. 'Come on, let's get you dressed before someone comes along.' Kami lay back on the soft sand bank as Mark shrugged on his trousers, then collapsed on the beach beside her, using his jacket as a makeshift blanket for them both. He lay with her head on his chest, Kami purring contentedly beside him.

5

The sky was blushing with the dawn when they'd awakened. Slowly, reluctantly, they'd risen and, with unspoken accord, made their way back towards Kami's flat.

They were outside that door again, the cool air flowing about them, a replay of just a few hours before. They'd said nothing since the beach: nothing seemed to come to either of them. Both worried about messing up again, yet both were aware of their own eagerness for this to become more than just friendship now.

Then both tried to speak at once. 'Mark –'

'Kami –'

Kami shivered, thinking it'd be easier to just go inside, when Mark pulled her gently to him.

His scent was intoxicating, but that was nothing compared to the feel of his arms. She fought to hold onto her fears as they ebbed away, replaced almost immediately by a low, throbbing desire for him, for his legs and arms to encircle her, and for her to draw him into her warm depths. He bent to kiss her, cupping her neck and bringing her soft mouth to his.

She felt his boldness grow as he ground against her. He kissed her passionately, as if devouring it. Kami felt dizzy, her heart and mind racing with these new delicious ministrations. How the hell was he doing that? Kami could feel a warm glow between her thighs, nudging at her consciousness, telling her to definitely stay put. Mark's mouth was still on hers, holding her captive. Then he pulled away, leaving Kami surging after his kiss.

His hands reached out, two sets of fingers interlocking, separating, arranging themselves in a new pattern, thumbs stroking the other's palm. All she could do was stare at his hands holding hers, her mouth open, her voice – and, it seemed, her will – totally absent. An electric huskiness crept into his voice as he firmly pulled her back to him with a calm determination which made her shiver.

'Can we go inside, Kami? Please?' His voice was deeper now, reverberating in her ears.

Suddenly her mouth was dry, and she was lost to it, to the low pulse between her thighs. A deep insistent need was dominating her thoughts. A need that was very familiar. A need for him. To take him. To have him. Her head was spinning.

'Kami?'

His voice pulled her from her thoughts back into his arms, and she nodded weakly as he unlocked the door. 'Oh God, Kami,' he whispered into her ear, flicking the lobe with his tongue. The slightest touch took her breath away. He embraced her again, his lips meeting hers as before, this time seeming to feel the fire awakening in her as she hungrily took him deep into her mouth. His kiss was hypnotic, and she sank into his embrace as if surrendering to him.

Finally he pulled back, steadying her as she swooned noticeably. Strengthened and resolute, Mark swept her up off her feet and carried her towards the sofa, setting her down gently and leaning back on his haunches as if to regard his prize.

Against all her instincts, Kami just lay back. This was intoxicating. Her entire being was hungry to be taken by this man, pleased by him, satisfied by him. Kami wondered if any of the turmoil she was feeling now was visible. If it was, Mark didn't react to it. He looked back at her unblinkingly, holding her captive even by his gaze. Without taking his eyes from hers he leaned forwards a little, whispering softly as if to calm her fears, whispering nothing in particular. Whispering her name.

She felt his hand at her cheek, then it moved down over her soft neck and traced her throat with his fingertips. She arched her back as his fingers danced over her cleavage, feeling her nipples harden in anticipation. Staring intently at the path his fingers traced, Mark seemed lost on a journey of discovery. Slowly he unlaced her top, parting it until he could see all of her sweet lace bra and her breasts, which were now practically climbing out of the cups in their eagerness to be touched again. Kami felt his warm breath on them, sending shards of pleasure through her and increasing her desire still further.

She tried to speak, to tell him how much she wanted him to touch her breasts, but all she could muster was a low moan of desperation. She need not have worried. It was as though Mark sensed her every thought. His hands moved inside her flimsy bra, brushing the hard nipples and cupping her breasts gently. He bent forwards as he drew one breast from her top and licked tentatively across the upper part, closing his eyes in ecstasy as if tasting her very soul.

Then his mouth was upon her again, licking and sucking at her breast, making her breathless with excitement. Whilst one hand was caressing and gently pinching her left breast, Mark's mouth nibbled at the right one. The sensations building in Kami were like none she had ever experienced.

His tongue flicked over her taut, sensitive nipples

again, sending another wave of pleasure coursing through her. Kami could feel her soaking sex pulsing insistently, and the warmth of her arousal infused her loins. She felt Mark squeezing and kneading her breasts more fervently now as his own passions rose. He sucked greedily on her flesh, biting firmly as he took her sweet, pert nipples into his hot mouth.

Mark's hand moved down between her legs and he delved firmly between her puffy lips. It was electrifying. Kami suddenly froze as she realised she was going to climax, and she let out a surprised cry as it burst from her in waves of heat and pleasure. She moaned with sheer delight and a measure of disbelief that he had made her come with such a short brush at her sex.

Breathlessly she slumped on the sofa, whilst Mark stroked her tender bosom and whispered soothingly to her. 'Kami, that was so beautiful,' he murmured. 'You're unbelievable.'

Her head swam. She was soaking and feeling deliciously drugged. As if he sensed her arousal, Kami was suddenly aware of Mark's fingers in her trousers again, undoing the zip and sliding it down slowly. She moaned with desire for him.

'Oh, Mark, please –' she purred, her hips thrusting rhythmically, urging him downwards towards her hot centre. She lifted her hips slightly to allow him to slide her trousers and knickers down to her knees. Mark stroked her soft mound, toying with the fluffy fur of her pussy and watching as she trembled. He stared down at her, drinking in the sight of her with her breasts bared, her top unlaced and pushed back, and her pants pushed down to her knees.

Mark leaned forwards, closer to her sex, breathing deeply before taking a long leisurely lick at her swollen sex, already coated with her juices. He clasped her hips and plunged his tongue deep into her, making her moan with delight. Kami was swimming in ecstasy, her hips thrusting against his mouth, lost in desire for him. She could feel his hot tongue licking and sucking on her swollen lips, and her pussy twitched and tingled as she climbed a familiar path.

'Mark, I'm gonna – oh God – oh please – oh *my* –' Kami purred loudly as she built to another climax, finally grabbing his hair and thrusting herself into his face as she came. She thrashed on the sofa as the waves of pleasure hit her repeatedly, then finally let go of Mark, her arms falling limply to her side, her breathing laboured.

Mark was fumbling with his own clothes now, struggling to free his visible erection from his trousers. 'Oh God, Kami, I have to have you. I have to have you, now –' Finally climbing free of his trousers, Mark straddled her prone body and lifted her legs up to move between them. Kami gathered her strength and reached out for his hard cock, guiding him between her legs. Mark grasped her ankles and lifted them up, placing them on his broad shoulders as she pulled his hard shaft into her.

Kami moaned loudly and gripped the sofa as Mark thrust deep into her. She was overwhelmed with the sweet sensations rushing through her sex as he took her, his thrusts deep and rhythmic, and he smiled down at her as he drove into her. 'Oh good God, Kami ... my sweet Kami –' The sound of his voice was so sensual. His constant whispers were like a low, breathy symphony, and she couldn't help but dance. After what seemed like an eternity, Mark's whispers faded, giving way to rumbling moans of arousal. His eyes closed as she felt his rhythm change to a more urgent gallop.

Kami purred and growled and bucked wildly as Mark thrust into her, sweat pouring from him as he fucked her. 'I want you, Kami – I have to – have you –'

Finally, he cried out as his cock spasmed. Kami growled loudly back at him. 'Take me, Mark, you have me – I'm yours – I'm –' Kami purred with delight as she felt him come inside her, his hot fluids coating her soft walls, now spasming as she climaxed too. Together they growled and purred as their passions ebbed away, Kami gasping for air as Mark slumped onto her chest, exhausted. He reached up as they lay locked together, stroking her face. 'Bloody hell, Kami,' he whispered in her ear as the last waves of pleasure coursed through her. 'Oh, my beautiful Kami –'

Kami stroked his heaving chest gently as he used his last breath to tell her over and over what a beautiful woman she was. Then he drifted off with his arms still locked around her. Lying there, nuzzling into his warm shoulder as he slept, Kami felt completely and utterly satisfied. She listened to the gentle rhythm of his breathing as her head rose and fell on his chest, lulling her, rocking her towards sleep. A warmth enveloped her, soothing every muscle, every tendon. She slipped quietly away to slumber, purring contentedly . . .

And was rudely awakened by Mark tearing himself violently from beneath her still sleeping form. 'What the hell? Kami – what the hell *are* you? Oh, Christ –'

Kami shook herself free of her slumber, gathering her consciousness quickly as she gathered the rug up to cover her naked body. As she watched Mark recoil from her, the realisation hit. Her tail swished behind her briefly and then disappeared as she hastily covered herself. Mark was mumbling, walking backwards and shaking visibly, glancing away only to pick up his clothes and cover the front of himself with them. 'You've a – I fucking saw *something*, Kami –'

'Mark, stop –'

'Jesus, I *felt* it, moving on me. It was fucking real, Kami. Oh my God. What the hell are you?'

'Mark, wait –' She tried to will her tail to deflate, to return to her body. She drew closer to him.

He backed off, stumbling.

'Mark!' she snapped, far more frighteningly than she would have preferred, but desperate not to have him panic and leave.

But it only made things worse. He was gone. The door slammed loudly, sharply, accentuating the silence after it. Kami stood alone in the room, her tail swishing gently behind her.

Mark burst into the room. 'Get up; we're getting out of here.'

Morning light streamed into the room, but the trio remained sound asleep, Greg sharing his bed with the brunette, the blonde in Mark's. All stirred with varying degrees of recovery, Greg first with the offering, 'Wuz – what?'

Mark barely acknowledged him, dropping to his suitcase, flipping it open and moving to the dresser drawer. 'Come on, we have to get out of here.'

'Is the place on fire?' Greg mumbled.

'No.'

'Then fuck off.' Greg's head hit the pillow again.

Mark showed little care in packing, stopping only to shake Greg. 'Get up! I said we have to get out of here!'

Greg rose again onto one elbow, eyes blinking. 'What's going on, mate?'

Mark stopped, tried to catch his breath, and could

scarcely put into words what had just happened, as if recounting it would make it happen again. 'I was – I was in bed with Kami –'

'Oh, good on you, my lad –'

'Shut up! I saw her change!' Mark faced Greg again now. 'She – she turned into this creature, this cat thing –'

Greg sat up now and sniffed the air. 'You're pissed.'

'I'm not!' Struck by a thought, Mark moved to close and lock the balcony doors. 'It really happened!'

At that, the brunette beside Greg sat up, eyes still shut, the sheet dropping to reveal her breasts before she covered herself again; lipstick was smeared from her mouth across her left cheek. 'What the fuck –'

Greg patted her on the shoulder. 'Forget it, Maura –'

'It's Moira, dickhead, I've told you a thousand fucking times!'

'We've got to leave!' Mark insisted, darting to the bathroom for his toiletries, then returning and dropping them haphazardly into his open suitcase.

'But we've only been here two frigging days!'

'She could come after us!'

'Is he high?' Moira asked warily, dropping and curling up, pulling the sheet away from Greg.

'No, just some bad booze.' Greg stepped out of bed and slipped into his briefs. 'Mate, calm down, you're scaring the honeys, and you're not doing too well with me, either.'

Mark stopped and ran a hand over his forehead, surprised at the amount of sweat he was producing. 'We should call the police.'

'And tell them what? That some woman you fucked tonight turned into a giant cat? They'd laugh at you – or worse, have you locked up.'

Mark considered this, feeling himself grow pale, and calmed down a little. 'Maybe you're right.'

'There's no maybe about it.' Greg smiled at him. 'Now, you need to take your mind off what you think you saw.' He indicated the blonde in bed. 'Cheryl's a hottie with her mouth.'

The woman snored in reply.

'When she's awake.'

Mark breathed in, considering everything that had happened. And it had been real, too real. Only Greg was right: Mark couldn't tell anyone and convince them – not even his best friend.

Nevertheless, that didn't mean he had to stick around and wait for Kami to show up looking for him. 'Greg, I have to go. I can't stay here.'

Greg nodded after a moment. 'Fine. But you better work out what you're really running away from.'

Mark did. He went to the hotel's television lounge and phoned the travel agency reps to lie about a family emergency back home requiring an immediate departure.

He slept fitfully on a low, battered couch, his suitcase by his side, his sleep disturbed less by the infrequent interruptions from staff and guests than by his own thoughts. And his own doubts.

Did he really see what he thought he saw?

His head pounded at the very notion of it. But what he'd seen was real, so real: the tail, the eyes, the pleading in Kami's voice for him not to leave, to wait while she explained.

Yet maybe it was just a joke on her part, a trick of the light, something drink-induced?

On the other hand, was it his need for her to be real,

to be something he wanted in his life, that was warping his perception, making him ignore the evidence of his eyes?

'Mr Healey?' It was the young girl from the desk. 'Call for you.'

He assumed it was the agency again. He was wrong. 'Mark?'

His heart raced. 'I don't want to talk, Kami.'

'You have to. Please listen, come back, I'll explain everything –'

A part of him wanted that, but the vocal half retorted with, 'No! I'm going home today. Don't call me again.'

'Mark –'

He hung up before he surrendered to the anguish so clear in her voice.

Janeane started at the sounds of destruction in the next room. Eyes bleary, half-closed and unwilling to open further, she stumbled out of bed in her half-nude, dishevelled state into the living room.

She woke rapidly at the sight of Kami in her dressing gown, screaming and kicking the heavy settee across the room as if it weighed nothing, before turning and punching the wall behind her, smashing the plaster like tissue and leaving oval indentations. 'Kami, no –'

She drew closer, but Kami backed away, her face a hideous mask of rage and terror, inducing an instinctive fear in Janeane. She stopped and held out her arms, forcing herself to appear as non-threatening as possible. Kami had had wobblers before, but she'd never seen her this bad until now. 'Kami ... Kami ...'

She remained still, and spoke softly, gently. Later, she couldn't recall exactly what she had said, nor did it matter. Eventually, Kami fell to her knees, Janeane joining her, holding her, keeping her safe as the woman broke down.

Through the sobbing, Kami explained what happened. 'I – I scared him – my temper – he wouldn't listen – he's leaving –'

Janeane frowned. 'Leaving?'

She was about to enquire further about what Kami could have done to make the man want to cut his holiday short, until Kami added, 'He – he can't leave – I have to – have to tell him –'

Janeane nodded. 'You'll tell him ... whatever it is you have to tell him. We'll see to that.'

They served the breakfast buffet at the usual time, though he didn't eat until the agency contacted him, to let him know they'd found a last-minute seat on a flight at noon, but only if he left now.

A taxi had been ordered already, to take him to the airport in Altinkum; Mark felt a sense of relief for the first time when they drove out of town.

Relief. And regret.

He still couldn't get Kami out of his mind: her beauty, her allure, their shared chemistry, and especially how well they'd made the hottest, sweetest love.

He drifted off, head tapping slightly against the taxi-door window with each pothole.

Mark heard the voice before he realised the taxi had stopped. 'Out, get out here.'

Drowsy, inattentive, Mark stepped out of the taxi and shut the door, coughing at the cloud of dust inexplicably surrounding him, then jumping as the taxi suddenly drove off with a roar, leaving him calling after it, and coughing some more. 'Hey! My bag –'

He glanced about as the dust settled, awareness quickly returning with his adrenaline; awareness and bafflement. The taxi had abandoned him at a deserted roadside petrol station, some rust-spattered, boarded-up, graffiti-branded square building with the remains of several pumps looking like grave markers. He glanced around, but saw nothing else in the area, no other buildings, no other people, no road signs, nothing beyond but a vista of rugged hills freckled with olive-green shrubbery under a stark blue sky.

Anxiety rose again within him, and he drew up to the building, hoping to find some clue to his where-abouts, perhaps even a phone inside . . .

'Mark.'

Kami appeared from around the nearest corner.

Mark stepped back, his pulse doubled, feeling exposed, vulnerable out here, alone. 'You – you arranged this.'

She wore a simple but elegant wraparound purple print cotton sundress, knee-length, sleeveless, tied at her right hip, with flat shoes, a round straw hat, and wide sunglasses. She folded her hands unthreateningly before her as she stepped closer, slowly, carefully, her pace betraying only a slight limp. 'I do work for your travel agency; I thought it'd be better to get you out here –'

He nodded, still retreating, his mouth dry. 'No wit-nesses, right? So now you –'

'Now I can what? Kill you? Eat you? Gnaw on your bones?' She shook her head. 'No, Mark. That's the last thing I'd do to you. I brought you here so I can explain who and what I really am.'

Mark was glancing at the road, praying for some traffic to appear from either end, someone he could flag down for help, anyone. 'No thanks, really, maybe some other time –'

Kami stopped moving towards him. 'Mark, last night I put my trust in you, something I've never done with any man before. Now I'm asking you to do the same for me.' She glanced behind her. 'There's a lovely place just down the hill, peaceful and secluded; I hope you'll follow me there. Otherwise, just walk down the road along the curve, and you'll be back in town in an hour or two; the driver was instructed to take your bag to our agency office, and you can get a later flight.'

He watched her depart, unable to take his eyes off her rear end, straining to see where he'd seen the tail last night.

Her presence again had brought it all back – the shock, the fear.

And the desire.

He followed her.

6

Kami's description of the glade where he'd found her had been apt: a natural grotto of soft green-gold grass, white and slate marble boulders around which ancient gnarled trees had grown, their full branches overhanging to provide canopies of shade from the light and heat. Birds and insects twittered and buzzed around them, oblivious to their presence, and there was a scent of olive wood in the air.

Kami was reclining against a boulder, one knee raised and the foot flat on the grass, her hands folded around the shin, watching him come closer then stop a metre away. She had cast aside her hat, and her sable-fine brown-black hair spread around and behind her head like an aura.

Mark took in the sight of her; she looked so remarkably beautiful, like she'd stepped out of some classic water-colour. 'Kami, I have to know – what I saw last night –'

'Was real.' She removed her shades; golden eyes gazed unflinchingly up at him, the irises more oval than round. 'My eyes, in their normal state.'

'My God.' He swallowed. 'And the rest?'

'Yes. All real.' She glanced away. 'But do you know what you saw? What you *really* saw?'

'Are you trying to say I imagined it?'

'No, Mark.' She looked up at him again, the light from above narrowing her irises further. 'What I'm saying is that what you saw this morning was something that had never happened with anyone else, before you. Because I'd never felt so close to anyone enough to let my defences drop like that, before you. I never trusted anyone so much, before you. You need to know that, believe that, before we can go on.'

Mark breathed in, his hands absently rubbing his forearms, his heart aching. 'Kami, are you a ... werewolf or something?'

She shook her head. 'I'm no legend, no magical creature. I don't transform, I just hide the truth. I'm not ... fully human, but I'm not supernatural. I'm flesh and blood, mortal, like you.'

'So what *are* you? An alien? A mutant? Something genetically engineered?'

'Does it really matter?' Kami walked over to a carpet of rough olive-green grass and sat down upon it, twisting her legs under her, peering up at him wordlessly. After a moment, he joined her, and for a while, it was as if they'd taken time out to listen to the sounds of life around them.

Finally, she said in a rushed breathless voice, 'My full, real name is Kami-Merysitkheti. As for my people, we have no name for ourselves, as we've never needed one; we knew who we were, and wanted few others to know. Some humans have called us the Pride, because of the statues of lions that sit at the gates to our home; it is a name that has stayed with us.'

'Us? There's more like you?'

Kami reached out and smoothed down her dress. 'Not very many. Once we lived in the open, with humans; that changed, and we took steps to withdraw from human affairs, to remove all traces that we were more than myth. It took centuries, but with tenacity – and the human propensity for war and destruction – we've managed it. And we've remained separate, concealed and safe ever since.'

Mark leaned back, trying to take it all in, the notion of a hidden race, like something out of an Edgar Rice Burroughs novel, but existing in the 21st century. Was it possible? It didn't seem at all likely. And yet living proof now sat before him; very, very attractive proof, too. 'And nothing remained of your people that I would know of?'

'Nothing much, except wherever we've lived. In Central America, you'll still find pictographs of the Olmec's Jaguar gods. In Africa, we were the Lamaklihs, the Leopard Men who devoured the unworthy. The Karadjeri of Western Australia revered us as the Ngariman, and the Chinese knew us as the People of the Yellow Tiger. And closer to home, we were the inspiration for the Egyptian worship of cats –'

'Bastet.' He blinked. '*You* were the monsters of de Chaumont's account? You destroyed Usal?'

'My ancestors did. After generations among the Tucano and the Mayans, we had returned to this part of the world, seeking a new home, and found ourselves caught between the Crusaders and the Seljuks. We did not seek conflict with humans. But they did. To their cost.' At his expression, she continued. 'We had to, Mark, our existence had been threatened; seeing how your own race has treated each other over millennia, are our actions that surprising? And historians like me have done what we could over time to erase any clues.' She smiled, embarrassed – but relieved too, as if this opening up to him released a heavy burden from her.

'And where are your people now?'

The smile evaporated. 'Don't ask me that, Mark. You can't know how difficult it is. How terrified you've made me.'

Mark's eyes widened. 'I – terrified *you*?'

Kami nodded weakly, glancing away. 'Here, in this

place, among your people, I am under constant threat; a threat I feel for myself as much for my race. And not just a physical threat. But I opened to you, Mark, like no other. Gave myself over to you, like no other, Pride or man.' She stared nakedly at him again. 'Do you know what a power you have over me?'

Her confession, her admission, moved him. 'I – I've never made much of an impact on anyone before.'

'You have now. I'm stronger, faster than you; I can perceive things you can hardly be aware of. But still you leave me feeling so helpless, at your mercy. Afraid: afraid of you staying. Afraid of you leaving. I – I –'

He reached out, his own fears gone, chased away by Kami's, and the very reasons for his being afraid nowhere to be found. He took her hand, found it trembling, took her other, and cupped them both in his own, as she continued. 'Mark, please don't dwell on my differences, because I can't believe they mean anything. I laugh and cry. I hunger and tire. I have loves and hates. I do stupid things.' Kami's voice faltered as Mark's hand stroked the fine, almost invisible hairs on her forearm, along the grain. 'When – when you ran off this morning, the look on your face – I was – I was devastated – I –'

Mark shifted, drawing closer until he felt her breath on his face. He gazed into her eyes, his hands moving up to her hair, her face. He couldn't deny his feelings any more.

He didn't want to deny them, either.

She'd broken her silence.

And now it was his turn. 'Kami, I do stupid things too. When I said last night I'm careful about who I get close to now, I meant for my sake. Because when I fall in love, it's fast, and it's deep, and it's all-consuming. And that's what I'm feeling for you, Kami. I tried to convince myself that what I was feeling was wrong, that it was too quick. But I couldn't. Then I saw you last night, and it scared me. But now I'm more afraid of losing you. And I –'

He lost the rest of what he had to say, as he fell into those golden eyes, wide, glazed, heavy with expectant tears. And their lips sought and found each other, parting to let their tongues meet and caress in a fresh, frantic longing, a longing matched by the couple's limbs as they fell into each other's arms, dropping fully to the ground, clinging to each other for dear life. Mark's cock reacted strongly to the heat it felt from Kami's sex, so close, separated from it only by a few meagre layers of clothing, unmindful of the emotions at play. He felt her tears drop onto his face.

Sometime later, they pulled back, without fully releasing each other, to catch their breath. Mark lay back, Kami half over him, her hair draping down to block out the light from above. He reached up and lightly stroked her cheek, from her hairline down to her jaw, feeling the downy, invisible hair. He watched Kami's eyes close, then open, and saw her lips moisten and swell, ever so slightly.

Then he noticed freckle-like markings appear along her bronzed skin, tiny spots that resembled the tracks of some living thing making its way along her flesh, leading down past her ear to her shoulder. So unusual; she settled, her head on his chest, her breath catching in her throat every so often, her body trembling in echoes of her earlier catharsis.

He watched, fascinated, his hand dropping to her shoulder, stroking, finding and raising tiny, almost imperceptible hairs along the tanned skin – and more of the markings, drawing down but moving away from her breast to the soft skin at her sides. At this, Kami sighed and moved slightly, allowing the loop of her dress to slip a little more from her shoulder, and letting her full, warm breasts lie against him, her hand on his chest, fingers flexing tiny jabs through his shirt. He lifted his head, and gently kissed wherever he touched.

'Oh . . .' She tilted her head back, rolling onto her back as Mark rose up onto one elbow and leaned over her, stroking and kissing along her upper arm, drawing the markings to the surface. He breathed in, taking her scent in, fascinated by it as he was by the rest of her. He looked up at her face, watched the eyes close, watched the skin at the base of her throat flutter. He wanted to see more.

His fingertips moved across to the outer curve of her breast.

Her eyes opened.

Mark tried to read her expression, finally swallowing and asking, 'May I?'

Slivers of doubt and apprehension seemed to prick her before she nodded.

Slowly, carefully, he drew down the top of her dress, exposing the upper portion of her breast to the outline of her aureoles; he watched, spellbound, as his strokes summoned the markings along Kami's curves, then along the inside of her arm.

Mark leaned in and planted a tight trail of pecks along her marks; he felt her nipple tighten through her dress against his cheek; Kami's arm encircled him round his back, gripping the loose skin between his shoulder blades through his shirt, her breath quickening. 'That's – that's –'

Somehow, the material had pulled away from Kami's breast completely. And somehow, his mouth found its way towards her nipple, the tip of his tongue darting from between his lips to flick at the flesh, until his lips fixed themselves around the bud, sucking slowly, rhythmically, feeling Kami squirm – and sharp nails flexing into the flesh on his back. His eyes opened, and saw the tiny hairs on her skin rise and stiffen.

He started when Kami's head suddenly lolled back, and the prickling on his back intensified. He pulled away and gasped, as did Kami, who breathed, 'S-sorry – claws – don't stop –'

He had no time to ponder this new feature, nor much desire to; he still had a thousand questions for her, and wanted to take a lifetime to ask them. One hand moved to encircle the breast he was kissing and sucking, while the other moved up to stroke her cheek and hairline. Kami reached up and clasped his forearm, to help guide him as his extended, parted fingers brushed through her thick hair, reaching her scalp, again and again; he felt as much as heard the trilling she produced, and his cock twitched in response. His kisses moved down to the underside of her breast, to flesh moist with sweat and heat, the tip of his middle finger barely touching Kami's nipple.

'M – Mark – God –'

He drew back to look up at her, cradling the back of her head as he kissed her once more, both of them embracing, sharing heat and moisture, their legs entwining. Mark was more conscious now of how strong she was, compared with any other woman he'd known – and most men, too. All that strength just under the surface, the proverbial velvet glove around the iron fist, something else she'd been holding back, yet another facet she'd had to keep hidden from everyone around her.

He wanted to see more; his hand moved to the tie at her hip. Kami's body stiffened, and her nails – claws –

were out again. Mark moved to the side of her head, whispering, 'Should I stop?'

At first, there was just her breathing, and her fear, the latter solidified with her words. 'Don't – don't ask me anything now.'

His hand continued, unravelling the knot, loosening her dress; her breathing increased slightly, as if he'd tightened it instead. She bit her lip, gasped. 'I'm – I'm dizzy – sit up –'

He did; she followed, clinging to him, staring into his eyes, letting him see her jumble of emotions. Then she pulled him in again, kissing her, mumbling into his mouth, as he loosened the knot further, drawing one end of her dress away from her. His hand moved to stroke her belly, her side, her back, finding more of the silky fur along her spine, stroking down, down, stopping near the base of her tail. She moaned into his mouth, clinging to him as much from fear as from desire, and Mark continued to stroke her. He was aware that her breast and part of her belly was bare and pressed against him, very warm, and very soft . . .

She was moving in her embrace of him, letting more of her dress fall away. Then Kami rose, allowing Mark to see her naked from the waist up, her dress now a sarong, her hair flowing behind her, the sun draping her, a vision.

And then she straddled Mark, her thighs parted, the heat from her sex like a furnace against his, her breasts in his face for him to kiss and lick, her arms around his neck, while he slipped his arms under hers and continued to stroke her back. Her nipples tightened against his tongue, and her hands moved up into his hair, gripping him as she growled, 'God go lower –'

He took the cue, his hands sliding down to her

buttocks, cupping the full, fleshy cheeks, aware of but not focusing on the tail he felt swishing about. She moved her crotch against his, gyrating it wantonly; Mark's cock cried for relief, and as her musk rose, reaching his nostrils, his hunger doubled.

His hands moved down, reaching the curves under her buttocks, then between the cheeks, finding a thicker tuft of fur leading to her rear entrance.

And then Kami froze, stiffening and shuddering with orgasm, clasping her hands onto Mark's head. He felt the energy radiate from her, and clung to her, rode it with her, desperately wishing he was inside her now.

Then she pulled back, to reach down and struggle with the remains of her dress, watching her own hands, her hair falling down over her breasts. 'Mark, I need you inside –'

He needed it too, needed to feel Kami's body on him, around him, enveloping and embracing him. He undid his trousers, lifting himself up to slide them down, but couldn't get them past his thighs.

Kami wouldn't let him, reaching down to grasp his cock, to claim it for her own, stroking the length, daubing the pre-come at the slit with her thumb and painting the velvety head fully with it, until Mark fell back onto his elbows, his mouth dry, his head spinning. 'No – no more –'

'Yes,' Kami purred, urgent and sweet and jubilant, lifting up her dress and draping it over his lap as she lowered herself onto his shaft, her hot, sweet pocket sliding down over him. She reached out and pulled him up straight to embrace her. 'Yes, more.'

They kissed again as they rocked together, Mark's cock sliding deep inside her, then back, until only the head remained, before sliding deep into her again. They clung to each other as if for dear life, their union a declaration, their fucking a defiance of their fears.

Kami pulled at the front of Mark's shirt, and he heard the buttons fly, seeing them bounce off her, uncaring of anything but his need to press his naked flesh against hers, to let their scents and fluids mingle. His hands moved up her back to her shoulder blades, echoing Kami's own motions, his lips on her neck, nipping and sucking. He was filled with a need to claim this incredible woman for himself, even as he was driven to please her, and keep pleasing her, and be worthy of her.

Kami came again, a sharp, sustained pulse, this time around his cock, drawing him along as he gripped her and lost control, rapidly, fervently thrusting up into her, spurting deep inside her and lengthening, strengthening her own climax. She withdrew her claws, clinging to him for dear life.

They continued to hang onto each other, immobile, even after Mark began to wilt. Afterwaves of Kami's orgasm conspired to push him out of her.

But when Mark began to shift his whole body, Kami's claws were back at his neck, her teeth on his earlobe as she hissed, 'Don't move.' But then she added, 'Please.'

'OK.' His voice sounded strange, as if he hadn't heard it in days. 'Don't feel like moving much anyway.'

She was trilling again. 'We don't have to move; I can get you hard again, back inside me.'

He blinked. 'What? Are you kidding? No way.'

She laughed quietly, knowing better.

Greg's jaw dropped when he saw his friend step into the hotel bar, catch his eye, stride over to his table and slump into an adjacent chair; Mark was hobbling with his bag beside him, his shirt torn, his chest scratched. 'Mate, what happened, did the plane crash?'

'Changed my mind.' Mark snatched the burger sitting on the plate before Greg and began devouring it voraciously, reaching for his beer.

'Oh, go right ahead, I'm not bothered.' Greg signalled to the girl behind the bar for a repeat order. 'The girls were asking about you, thought maybe we could –' Then he stopped and stared, and finally grinned. 'Oi, I know this, this is sex famishment! You've been shagging!'

His mouth full, Mark gave him a thumbs-up sign.

'You dirty dog!' Greg chuckled, slapping him on the shoulder. 'So, no cat woman, then?'

Mark swallowed quickly, shaking his head. 'Course not, you tool.' His mind was racing ahead, past the shower, change of clothes and nap he'd planned on, before seeing Kami again this evening.

Not that he'd expected to get much of the last, what with his mind running in top gear. He was head over heels with a woman quite literally unlike any he had ever known, and who felt the same way about him!

Who could sleep with *that* in their brain?

7

Kami was lost in a bliss of her own as she made her way up the hill, the sun bearing down through her hat and widening her already-huge grin.

So distracted was she, in fact, that she didn't notice the large black sedan parked outside her building until she was almost upon it.

Inside, she threw off her hat and strode into the living room, beaming. 'Hello again!'

Janeane was there, having finally dressed after helping plan Kami's conspiracy. 'And about time too, young lady! Your aunt and uncle will think I have no control over you.'

'Few can control our Kami.' The woman who sat in the recliner, Kami's toms in attendance at her feet, shared the same skin colour as Kami, but was older, and taller by half a head, with carmine roots in her hair. She rose to her feet, straightening out her blue pinstripe business jacket and pencil skirt before holding out her arms to embrace Kami warmly. Kami's heart raced as she took in the familiar scent, while the woman stepped back and cupped Kami's face in her long, slender hands. 'Look at you.'

Behind her, Janeane rose to her feet. 'Right, I'll let you have some quiet time together, while I go for a paper.'

Kami glanced at her. 'Thanks. By the way: it worked.'

Janeane beamed. 'You owe me dinner.' She looked at the woman, and Kami could see that behind the courtesy, Janeane was strongly attracted to the visitor. 'A pleasure to see you again, Mrs Fehr. Please pass my regards to your husband.'

'I shall, my dear.' The woman broke contact with Kami to plant a kiss on Janeane's cheek. 'Thank you again for your hospitality.'

Janeane left with a blush, a broad grin and a skip in her step; Kami waited until she had departed before noting, 'You'll have her talking all night now. And where's "Uncle"?'

'Behind you.'

Kami started, seeing the man step into the room from the direction of the bathroom. 'The locks on those windows are inadequate; I'll arrange for improvements right away.' He strode to the curtained sliding glass door that led out to the patio area.

Kami frowned to herself, having smelled him in the flat but missed his appearance. 'That's not necessary, Major.'

He glanced back at her. 'With all due respect, Mistress Kami, I would be remiss in my duties if I did not do all in my power to protect the children.' Ardeth Fehr was a tall, vigorous-looking man in his mid-forties, his short raven hair peppered with iron grey at the sides, a cleft lower lip hidden behind a thick but trimmed beard and moustache. He wore a dark, sober suit, spoke in a cultured, educated manner, and moved with the silent resolve of a predator, making Kami imagine at times he was more Pride than man.

The woman looked at him. 'And you serve us commendably.'

'You honour me, Mistress Seska.' He offered a slight bow. 'And now, I shall allow you time together, though it pains me to remind you of the meeting in Izmir –'

'I know, Ardeth.'

On his departure, Seska slipped back into her native tongue, a language never recorded, and barely unchanged in ten millennia. 'It has been too long, Student.'

'Yes.' They embraced again, basking in the warmth of each other's familiarity. Finally, Kami whispered the dreaded question. 'Has something happened?'

'No. As far as the First is concerned, we're still looking for you.'

'Ardeth seemed concerned about the locks.'

Seska smiled. 'Ardeth is who he is. And I am here because I dearly miss the company of not only kin, but a kindred spirit.'

Kami embraced her mentor and friend, scenting the older female's desire, potent and heady. But even as they kissed, and she felt some small desire, Kami, to her surprise, felt nothing more. It was strange, like eating food that had inexplicably lost its flavour. Seska had done more than rescue her, she had awakened her to new sensual delights: she recalled the long hours they had spent reclining naked together, kissing and stroking and licking each other to unparalleled heights of bliss. And this visit should have offered her a return to those pleasures.

Now, however, things had changed.

And Seska was perceptive enough to notice, pulling back. 'What's wrong?'

Kami shook her head. 'Nothing.' She tried, really tried to get into the mood.

But Seska stopped her, her eyes narrowing. 'You can't hide the truth from me, little one. Tell me about this man I smell on you.'

Kami tried not to react, failed, then shrugged, pulling away. 'He's just a man.'

'Liar. His scent is thick on you, thick enough for him to know who and what you are. Is he the first you've taken?'

Kami knew what she meant, and knew she couldn't hide the truth. 'I didn't *take* him.' At Seska's reaction, she added, with some pride, 'I didn't have to.'

Seska tensed. 'Foolish child. No man or woman not made yours can be trusted.'

Kami bristled at the response, thick with condescension. 'This one can, Respected.' Kami made her tone as resolute as she could while still maintaining deference. 'He's kind, and gentle –'

'Have you learned nothing from me? From history? Some humans have their charms, and their uses, but they are certainly not to be trusted.'

Kami scowled. 'And what would Ardeth say about that?'

'He believes it, of course, as do all the Swords.'

Kami stared blankly, feeling the pleasures of today bleed from her as if from a mortal wound. 'Well, *I* don't. And I won't have anything to do with anyone who thinks like that.'

Seska's expression soured with unabashed disgust. 'You hold your tail up high for someone who makes a habit of shirking responsibility, firstly in the Pridelands, then leaving me in Ankara to pursue this idle existence. And now you risk our security, trusting in a man you hardly know –'

Kami's head spun. She could hardly believe how quickly, how easily the mood had changed between them. 'Leave Mark out of this. This is really about us.'

Seska suddenly paused, reined in her emotions, and straightened herself up, as if nothing had passed between them. 'Not at all, little one. But Ardeth was correct, I *do* have an appointment, so I must cut this short. Bastet watch over you.' And with that, she strode, all too quickly, to the front door and departed.

Confusion and anger boiled within Kami, both at Seska's reaction and her own. She snarled, lifted up an ugly pink ceramic table lamp with an equally hideous orange tissue-paper shade, and flung it in Seska's direction, shouting, '*Fuck off*!'

Just then the door was opening, Janeane saying, 'Kam –' She shut the door in time for the lamp to shatter against it in a blossom of shards. Behind the door, the American shouted, 'Jesus!'

Kami brought her hand to her mouth. 'Sorry.'

'You should be.' Janeane walked gingerly around the pieces, dropping her newspaper. 'I'm still gonna kick your ass –' Then she saw Kami's expression. 'What happened? Seska and her husband ignored me as they got in their car and –'

Kami's claws flexed into her palms. 'We . . . argued.'

Janeane pursed her lips. 'Come here.' She drew closer, took Kami's hand and led her back around to the front of the settee. Janeane sat down, reclining and opening her legs to let Kami curl up between them, then leaning back onto her until her head rested on Janeane's breast. Janeane wrapped her arms around her friend and stroked her. 'You wanna talk about it, or should we just go straight to calling her a bitch?'

Kami closed her eyes, choosing her next words carefully. 'Jan, do you think I'm right to trust Mark? Someone I hardly know?'

Janeane shrugged. 'I don't know the guy. But how long are you supposed to know someone anyway? There's people I've known all my life that I wouldn't trust to tell me the sky was blue.' She bent down to kiss the top of Kami's head. 'Others I barely know, but trust with my life.'

Kami reached up and clung to her arm. 'What do I do?'

'Trust your instincts. They don't usually let you down.'

The building looked different in the light of day, or at least the dying light of early evening. Mark felt slightly out of breath after climbing the hill, wrestling with all the things he was carrying. He paused outside the flat's door and recalled the night before, standing there with Kami, crossing the line past being just good friends, and learning – becoming – something more. He smiled broadly to himself, and then stopped, feeling foolish just standing there like an idiot.

The blonde tour guide with Kami that first day, Miss Wade, greeted him at the door, clad in shorts and a T-shirt. She smiled politely at him. 'Hello, sport.'

Mark smiled back. 'Hello. Uh, is Kami in?'

'In the shower.' After a moment, she stepped aside, allowing him access.

He glanced about, remembering the settee well – but not the broken furniture or the holes in the walls. 'Everything all right?'

'That depends.' She closed the door and faced him, looking concerned. 'Listen, pal, what do you know about her?'

Mark blinked; did Janeane know of Kami's true nature? It seemed obvious, if they had been living together, but could Mark take that chance, and inadvertently reveal Kami to someone else, after all the promises he had made today to keep her secret safe? Damn, he should have asked who else was in on it! He swallowed and replied, 'I think I know a lot about her. And I want to know a lot more.' It was the bare truth.

That seemed to give Janeane pause, as if she'd

expected a different, perhaps more facetious answer. However, she was evidently resolved to say her piece, and pointed to the wall and damaged furniture. 'She did that this morning, because of something that had happened between you two. I don't know what it was, and I don't want to know, but she's been through a lot lately, and if you ever make her feel that way again, you'll have to deal with me. Understood?'

Mark was simultaneously relieved that he had kept Kami's secret, appalled that he had brought the woman he loved – *loved!* – to such a state, even inadvertently, and pleased that she had such a loyal friend. He nodded. 'Understood.' He indicated the plastic bags in his hands. 'Would you care to join us?'

Now Janeane smiled back, apparently satisfied with his response. 'Thanks, but Kami's very territorial about what's hers.' She winked, then added, 'She said get the food set out on the patio. She'll be out shortly.'

'OK.' Mark entered the kitchen area, carefully stepping around the two cats, who stopped eating long enough to raise their hackles and hiss at him.

It wasn't long before Kami stepped out onto the patio, taking advantage of the brilliant salmon pink of the dusk sky to show off the jet-black bustier she'd chosen, the side zip drawn up just enough to reveal the tops of her stockings. 'Hello again.'

He had set up a small table outside with plates of cold meats, breads, cheeses, salmon, fruits and glasses of wine. He turned from the view of Meraklisi, the lights coming to life below with the advent of night, and breathed out in sincere appreciation. 'Kami ... you look beautiful.'

'Thank you, Mark.' They drew closer and kissed, Mark tasting the lipstick and being careful not to mess it.

Then they held each other for what seemed like ages, and not long enough, before she pulled back, lifting up one leg. 'And heels again. But I'll try to be careful this time.'

'Don't worry, I'll hang onto you.' He pulled back himself, this time to reach for something sitting on the nearest chair: a CD player. 'I bought this today.' He switched on the music. 'Let's dance.'

Kami blanched. 'Dance music is too loud and piercing for my people's hearing –' Then she paused as she heard the first number, nothing shrill and loud at all. 'You can dance to that?'

Mark took her in his arms, held her and swayed slowly with her. 'Find out.'

After a moment, Kami seemed to trust him again, and went with his rhythm, holding his gaze. 'This is good.'

He smiled with undisguised satisfaction. 'I'm glad. In fact, I'm glad for a great many things.'

At some stage, the song ended, and changed to a more familiar, gentle dance between piano and percussion. Kami beamed. 'My favourite song again! And I don't even know the name of it. Sedat lost the CD cover –'

'*Sophisticated Lady.*'

'Huh?'

'*Sophisticated Lady.* I recognised it.' He smiled at her. 'I'm a jazz fan. John Coltrane, Miles Davis, Thelonius Monk –'

Kami beamed back, and he saw the feelings within her welling up, threatening to burst out. 'I'm never letting you go. Do you know that?'

Four hundred miles northwards, in the capital Ankara, a government bureaucrat named Raheel Bibi was not smiling or dancing. He was too busy flying across his living room, striking the wall and landing in a battered heap on the floor. He was young, and had always prided himself on his developed physique. None of which meant anything now.

The figures that had set upon him were taller than him, with saturnine faces, hazelnut-brown hair ponytailed back, their eyes hidden behind sunglasses, and they looked uncomfortable clad in their all-black outfits. Ten minutes before, they had arrived at his door with a third figure, a female dressed head to toe in traditional black Muslim gear, covering all but her eyes. Raheel had thought it was his Mistress Seska, paying an unexpected but very welcome visit; their speech, their body language, had marked them as Pride, as the Priestess of the Swords and her pack.

But he'd been wrong.

The female continued to speak, her voice honey-sweet and commanding. 'This is so foolish. You will tell us where Kami is. Eventually. And then you will transport us to her.'

They'd come, knowing his connection to the Swords, knowing he had forged human identities for their people in the past. They'd questioned him. And though Raheel saw them as his superiors, and had sworn to obey and protect them, Seska had also sworn him to secrecy about his work. 'I – I can't, Mistress –'

The female dropped to one knee before him, reached out, grasped a handful of dark hair and made him face her. 'Yes you can. And once my males have convinced you some more, you will.'

And she was right.

8

Kami stirred first again, marvelling at how deeply her man slept in her arms. Their scents mingled in the room, the aromas of the evening's sex and food. Rose-pink morning light streamed in between the thin wooden blinds on her window. But she kept her eyes closed, content to listen to Mark breathing, a fly buzzing in the far corner of the room, her toms puttering about near the kitchen, and outside, bird-song and the capricious winds playing with litter and leaves.

Her man? She beamed to herself; she had a *man*.

She was resting her head in the hollow of Mark's arm, her lips brushing against the edge of his pectoral muscle. She opened one eye enough to stare at his nipple, and playfully breathed at it until it puckered for her. She loved how his body reacted to her slightest action, even as his mind slept.

A sheet covered their lower halves, a habit on Kami's part in case she'd ever forgotten to lock her door and Janeane walked in. She shifted slightly, and glanced down to see their outlines in the blue cotton sheet. It was strange, having a man here all night. Strange? It was unprecedented; she was used to sending them home after she and they had had their fun, both to protect herself and because, frankly, sex was the only interest she had in them.

Now ... now she never wanted him to leave.

Mark made some slight sounds, talking to himself;

Kami heard the name Chrissie, that bitch woman he'd told her about, and his face took on a disturbed look. Then her eyes drifted to the slight outline in the sheets, between his legs.

Smiling, she gently eased herself away from him, their skin sticking together from sweat and sleep, as she slipped down towards his groin, drawing the sheet away and keeping her hair off him, without waking him. His cock was soft and pink, curved in its flaccid state until the russet head, collared by a dark-tipped foreskin, rested against one ball, almost hidden beneath black curly hair. His musk was strong, and filled her nostrils, and his penis looked so peaceful there, sleeping like its master.

But not for long ... she raised herself over his groin, letting her hair fall down and frame him as she extended her tongue and licked the head, reminding it of who was its mistress. There was a twitch, a pulse, one that came again as she carried on licking him, running the tip of her tongue around the head, again and again, gently nudging beneath the foreskin to taste the grooved rim. And Kami felt the shaft pulse in response, though Mark himself didn't stir.

Bolstered by the reaction, Kami softly engulfed the thickening shaft in her hot mouth, relishing the taste of it once more, swallowing until she felt his pubic hair brushing against her nose and mouth. Her mouth moved slowly up until only the head remained, then down again, her tongue running along the rugged underside. With each pulse of blood into the organ, it grew harder, and she wondered idly if she could make him rock hard without waking him. It would be an interesting experiment.

On the other hand, an awake Mark Healey was so much more preferable. She made a humming sound around his cock, until she heard and felt the rest of him awaken. 'Mmm? Wu –'

Kami withdrew and licked her lips, looking up at his groggy expression. 'Good morning.'

'Hey, what are you up to?'

She turned until she rested the upper half of her body on his thighs, and stared down at his erection, one hand lazily stroking and playing with it. 'Punishing you.'

'Me?' He smiled dreamily. 'For what?'

'Infidelity.' She pursed her lips. 'You were dreaming of another woman.'

'What? Oh yes, *her*.' He grimaced. 'Believe me, the dream was as unpleasant as the reality. It was the day she decided our relationship was going nowhere, and kicked me out of the flat. She'd had all my things packed and outside the door, then had her huge doorman brother beat me up when I tried to get back in and see her.'

Kami took on a dark expression. 'I'll kill anyone who hurts you.'

He blinked when she saw how serious she was. 'Let's forget about her, she's nothing compared to you.'

Kami took this in, then nodded. 'That's true.'

He grinned, then his eyes travelled down the rest of her body.

Kami caught him staring, and playfully stroked his shaft for attention. 'What are you looking at?'

'A very, very attractive woman.' He raised himself up onto his elbows, then winced with discomfort, glancing down at the dark scratches on his chest and belly, some fresher than others, all standing out more pink than his tanned skin. 'Ouch.'

She frowned, genuinely concerned. 'Have I really hurt you? I forget how fragile humans can be –'

He twisted suddenly; not so suddenly that he could surprise her, but still breaking the mock tension. Then she was giggling, and he was on his side, half on top of her, invading her mouth with his tongue, wrapping one leg around hers as if he had a chance of pinning her down, pressing his erection into her thigh. His hand moved up and caressed one of her breasts, evidently enjoying the fullness of it, its heat and soft downy covering. Their tongues danced together, and Kami melted and squirmed under his attentions, wrapping her arms around him.

When their mouths parted, Kami gasped and asked, still teasingly, 'So, not that fragile, then?'

'Let's find out.' Pressing his erection harder against her, Mark shifted his hand along her belly, dipping once into her navel before continuing its descent, cupping her mound, feeling the heat, the wetness of individual strands of her bush, and the puffy flesh against his palm.

Kami's eyes widened in response, and she pressed her fingertips into his back. But Mark shook his head. 'Oh no, not again.' With his other hand he reached up and removed hers, pinning her wrists over her head.

Now she smirked. 'The Assyrian king Sennacherib tried doing this to one of my ancestors he'd caught on the edge of the Black Sea two thousand years ago. He thought he'd had her pinned, but then sheee-ooohhhh –'

Her subsequent words were lost when Mark entered her with his middle finger, gently but insistently penetrating her to the hilt, the walls of her sex tightening around him. Mark drew closer to her ear and licked it before continuing. 'Tell me, Kami, did that king tell your ancestor what I'm going to tell you now? That I think you are the most amazing woman I've ever known? That I find you so fucking attractive? That you get me so hard with the way you look, the way you sound and smell and taste? That I want to make you come more than anything else in the world? That I want to make you come again and again?'

Kami's body writhed in pleasure, her limbs spasming, and a reply she tried to make was lost.

'Oh God, Kami,' he continued, pausing to nip her ear and elicit a soft yelp from her. 'I want to feel this wonderful pussy of yours come at my touch.' As his finger continued to thrust into her, his thumb swivelled up to tease and rub against her clitoris. He watched her lovingly, starting when her arms easily freed themselves from his token grasp only to swiftly reach up further and clasp the twisted brass railings of her headboard, holding on for dear life, her eyes shut and her teeth clenched in acute concentration.

'You're the most beautiful woman I've ever seen. The most amazing. The sexiest. I don't ever want to leave you, Kami. I don't ever want to leave you.'

'I – I –' Words became yelps, yelps became cries, rising, galvanising like her body, suffused with sensation for what seemed like hours. But as she began losing control, Kami considered his words, and how she could realise her deepest desire – and take him. A few scratches, a bite, that's all. It would be easy, so easy now – and he would forgive her afterwards, would forgive her anything, in fact.

But she didn't act upon it, and then her thoughts were lost with the opportunity, as she collapsed on the bed, her pussy having squeezed out Mark's finger, allowing him to lie back again and regard the rivulets of spots that had risen again along her body.

He lay with her, holding and kissing her. But her

mind remained active, contemplating her lost opportunity, and the reasons for her actions – or rather lack of them.

It would have been easy to make Mark hers, the way Seska would have preferred, to make him stay, to ensure his devotion and discretion; males, both Pride and human, were not known for their fidelity, but Pride males could not be put under control the way human males could.

In the end, she realised that she wanted him near her despite such tricks, not because of them.

It was a good feeling.

The city of Danya sat alone in the midst of fertile Anatolian steppes, bordering the mountains and standing on a major crossroads and railway line. Its oldest remaining features lay at its heart, with a huge citadel, mosques and medresseh dating back to the days of the Seljuk Empire. Between these and the modern complexes maintaining new irrigation projects, there was a crowded crescent of flat-roofed buildings and houses, and for one day each week the markets, the largest bazaar in the region, dominated most of its narrow, winding streets.

The tour bus, one of many from the coastal resort towns, pulled up into the huge tree-framed parking lot, and moments later Kami and Janeane, clad in their blue tour-guide uniforms, led an assorted collection of tourists, and Mark, out into the heat. Mark hung back, unwilling to distract them or interfere with their work, and listened to Kami give the usual speech about the dos and dont's here, as well as the rendezvous time to return to Meraklisi.

Then Kami came up and hugged him, smiling. 'I

have to lead the party around while Janeane checks in with the office. I'd ask you to come with me, but you're too much of a distraction.'

'I understand. Think I'll have a look around by myself.'

'OK. But be careful. If you want to buy something expensive, find me to help haggle.' Her gaze narrowed with amusement. 'I can be very persuasive.'

'Don't I know it?' They kissed.

Mark found himself wandering alone, seeking something special to get for Kami. Multicoloured canvases canopied the streets set aside for the marketers, shading the sellers and buyers from the oppressive sun. The scents of fruits, vegetables, meats, sweets and spices filled the air, as did the sounds of music and calls for passers-by not to miss out on the best offers today. Locals as well as tourists filled the streets, and Mark found himself a leaf in a stream, dodging and swirling about them, enjoying the life around him.

He felt alive, too. Each second seemed imbued with a vitality he'd never felt before. Love? Lust? Something unique to his relationship with Kami? He still had so many questions about her and her people, but she naturally remained cagey. If she wasn't the only one around, maybe –

A human-sized meteor struck him from behind.

'You'll find it a dizzying treat,' Kami was concluding to the group. 'But remember that it mainly caters for the needs of the local people, and you won't find too many items out of the ordinary, so if you're looking for things like jewels or gold, wait until you get to the Calleria Shopping Centre. Oh, and if you want to get Janeane or me something, we both like strawberry-flavoured Turkish delight.'

The consequent chuckles were lost on her as she turned, catching a scent in the air, something familiar – but it was hard to pin down, with all the people and other odours around her. Perhaps it was Mark.

She turned back to the crowd. 'So go enjoy – and remember: haggle!'

'Oh, did I miss the haggle speech?' It was Janeane, smirking and setting a hand on Kami's shoulder. 'Hey, you might have a surprise today.'

Kami frowned to herself, still distracted at what she thought she had picked up in the air. 'Oh? What sort?'

'Family.'

Kami glared at her now. 'What?'

'Yeah, apparently a cousin of yours called the office this morning, looking for you. They told him you'd be in Danya today.'

'Oh. Thanks.' Kami's heart raced, but she tried to remain calm. 'Better go find him, then.'

'A cousin, huh?' Janeane grinned. 'Well, if he's anything like your aunt, maybe I should come along and meet him –'

'First my aunt, now my cousin; you're insatiable, you are.' She slapped Janeane on the bum and departed.

'Look who's talking!'

Kami stopped listening. She was concentrating, moving past stalls, barely keeping from bumping into people, eyes darting everywhere, all senses focused. Her mouth had gone dry, and she dearly wished she wasn't in constricting clothes, so she could move more freely. She glanced back, and Janeane and the guests were lost in the anonymous crowds. People, too many people around her, waves of stimuli confusing her, a miasma of sensation. And it had been too long, far too long since she had had to rely on her senses, living among humans.

Then the wind shifted towards her.

And she raced in the opposite direction.

It was in a typical block overlooking the market, one flat behind the ground-floor shop front, divided from the shop by a set of beads in the doorway. The rooms were small, and crowded with furniture, pictures of family and the great reformer Atatürk fighting for space on the walls with tiny shelves holding candles and more personal mementoes. A small portable TV sat in the corner, playing a local football match listened to by a pair of old men who chose to sit in the cooler open doorway to the back alley, drinking tea and playing backgammon while the younger members of their family ran the business up front.

No one expected the sight of Mark being dragged like a carpet past the old men and flung unceremoniously inside. He landed on a low settee, banging his elbow on an adjacent coffee table. Before he could recover, or even react, the hands were on him again, lifting him up to his feet and pitching him against a wall, knocking down shelves. His head rung, and he fought to catch his breath. 'What the hell –'

From the corner of his eye, he saw one of the hands, now a fist, swing towards him with unnerving speed. He slipped and slid to the floor, glancing up to see the fist punch a hole in the wall, sending plaster dust and pieces blossoming onto him.

Mark looked up at the owner of the fist: tall, lean, fit, long sable hair swept back and ponytailed, nose blunt, chin narrow and almost pointed. The face was a stoic mask – framed with Pride markings – and his dark clothes were thick in defiance of the heat, especially the long leather coat. He stood over Mark, legs and arms out as if he was ready to pounce on his prey, and he spoke to him in Turkish.

One of the old men from outside entered and confirmed this for him, speaking angrily in the same language. The stranger barked back, never taking his eyes off Mark. From the corner of his eye Mark saw the old man hurriedly shuffle past, heading towards the shop front.

Then the stranger moved, again with astonishing speed, reaching down and easily lifting Mark up to his feet again, demanding something again, and prompting Mark to respond with a breathless, 'Don't understand –'

The stranger frowned, then grunted. 'American? I speak American.' His speech was guttural, just about functional.

'I'm English, not American, you knob –'

The stranger lifted him up and hurled him into another wall, sending more shelves and pictures falling and flying. Then he stood over him again. 'You all look alike to me, ape. I want Kami.'

'Kami? Who's that?' Even as he replied, Mark knew it was a pathetic, transparent denial.

And so did the stranger, to judge from how he lifted him up and threw him against the last wall, the one leading into the flat's kitchen, sending him tumbling against a rickety table and chairs, scattering them in the cramped confines of the room. Then the stranger followed him inside. 'Her scent is thick on you. You *know* her.' Something moved within the folds of his long coat, behind his legs; Mark saw it was a tail, dark and thick and prehensile, like Kami's.

Then, from the other room, a younger Turkish man in a dirty apron appeared, shouting at the strangers who had invaded his home. The Pride male ignored him, until the Turk was almost upon him – then he spun and swung out, seemingly slapping the Turk across the face. Except that the Pride male had extended his claws. The Turk clutched his face and cried out, staggering away as his attacker picked up a nearby microwave oven and pitched it after him like a cricket ball, narrowly missing the Turk and smashing another, more sizeable hole in the plaster of the wall.

Then he turned back to Mark, his hand still open, claws extended, the spots on the borders of his face strong, suffused with blood. 'I'm still waiting.'

Kami ran, stumbled, kicked off her high heels and flung them under a stall before continuing, hitching up her skirt to give her legs more freedom, ignoring the stares of those around her. All that mattered was her escape, and finding Mark. Would these fucking people just get out of her way? Move!

Her pursuer was still behind her, faster, less impeded than she was by either skirt or courtesy towards humans. She rounded a corner, entering an open door-way into a storage area, with metal shelves packed with large silver food tins, and stacks of cardboard boxes both unmarked and with corporate logos. She was moving towards the door on the other side of the room when her pursuer tackled her, sending them both into one stack of boxes.

Even as she fell, Kami kicked and clawed at her attacker, and even tried sinking her teeth into him, but he was stronger, more determined, pinning her down. He was also instantly recognisable to her. 'Djaben! Let me go! Now, damn it!' The words in Pridespeak came easily to her lips again.

The male called Djaben stepped back, out of her range but still able to subdue her again if she tried to escape. He was only slightly taller than her, but broader in face and frame, his hair a sepia shade, flowing freely behind him; he wore a simple black T-shirt, jeans and trainers, keeping his tail concealed, but his glasses had been knocked away in the struggle with Kami, revealing dark irises bordered in gold. He finally spoke, only slightly out of breath. 'I cannot, Kami. You know this. You must return with us.'

She caught her breath, shifting up to a crouching position but stopping when Djaben reacted to this. 'I don't want to go back, please! There's a man –'

The reluctance on the Pride male's face, his stance, his voice, was obvious. 'Kami, I have my orders; don't make this more difficult –'

'This is wrong! I want to be free, I –' Then she paused, saw his reluctance, and more; the struggle, the closeness to a female like Kami, had aroused, distracted him as well; his markings had risen, as had his bulge.

Good. She raised her skirt to her waist, revealing her stocking-clad legs and white knickers beneath. 'You want me, Djaben. You always have. But I rejected you. I won't reject you now.'

His eyes followed to her crotch, his lips parting, his breath quickening. 'I cannot – you are Chosen –'

'You want this.' Kami slipped her hand beneath her clothes to cup her mound, then let her finger slip across her lips, parting them. Despite herself, she gasped at her own touch, at her heat and wetness and musk, and held her clothes away from her sex long enough to let her scent drift out and catch Djaben. 'It's waiting for you. You made it hungry. It wants you to fill it. And you're just letting it sit here, untouched –'

Anger, frustrated anger, fuelled his response. 'I cannot! You are marked for the First!'

Kami narrowed her gaze at him. 'I know. But we can

do other things. Things I know you have never received from our females.' She rose to her knees, crawling to him. He backed away for a moment, wary of her intentions, but unwilling to move away any further. She drew closer until her face was at his bulge, prominent but not indicative of a full erection. Yet. Her hands reached up to tentatively run along his sides, before moving to his belt and zip and undoing them. She drew out his cock, long and thick and dark, with a flaring head glistening with moisture.

Then she drew in his odour, musky and salty, parted her lips, and took him in entirely. Djaben gasped with instinctive fear – but the sounds almost immediately shattered into groans of approval above her as she ran her tongue along the rim relishing his delicious taste. Her nipples now reacted almost painfully, and she grew wetter and hotter, until her inner thighs were damp.

Kami continued to work her mouth up and down his length, aroused by his taste and feel. With a sucking motion, she manipulated the loose skin insulating his cock, drawing it up to the swollen head and then relieving the pressure, before repeating the cycle. Djaben made more sounds above her, swaying in place.

She readied herself for the moment.

9

The male lifted Mark up to his feet again. 'Tell me where Kami is, or I'll cut you to pieces.'

Mark had no idea whatsoever what was going on, but he knew enough to defy this bastard. 'Go to hell –'

He slammed Mark against the wall repeatedly, then across the kitchen table. Mark tumbled to the floor. Hurt and stunned, he heard rather than saw the male smash the table against the cooker, as if tired of its dominating presence in the kitchen, sending pieces flying. 'Idiot. I can easily break your limbs, remove your eyes, and you will *still* talk.'

However, as he drew closer, Mark raised a weak hand, unable to take any more. 'Wha – please – will tell you –' His voice was barely above a whisper, choked with pain.

'I'm waiting.'

Mark tried to raise himself to a sitting position and failed, then tried rising to his elbows, but failed again. He coughed. 'Help – can't –'

The male impatiently reached down and grasped Mark by the shirt, then hauled him up.

And Mark suddenly grabbed the male back and screamed in his ear.

The stranger cried out and staggered back, clutching his ear, briefly stunned but still trying to grapple with Mark. In response, Mark reached under the Pride male's coat, found his tail, and pulled and twisted with all his might. He yelped and fell to all fours, losing his balance and freeing Mark to reach out, lift up a iron skittle hanging from a hook under some kitchen cabinets and strike him across the back of the head. Then he escaped into the back alley, getting his bearings and ignoring his hundred points of pain. Kami, he had to find Kami...

'Ape!'

Mark wished he'd hung onto the skittle. He stopped and turned to see the extremely angry-looking Pride male staggering towards him, teeth bared. 'You're –'

Then he stopped and tilted his head, as if hearing something no one else could. He grimaced, spoke to Mark in some unfamiliar language, the tone unmistakably profane, and quickly departed in the opposite direction.

Mark shook his head, not knowing why his attacker had run off, though he was confident that it was not because Mark had intimidated him. He held his left forearm as he departed too, unwilling to stick around for the inevitable police intervention.

Where was Kami?

Kami fought with her own growing arousal, focused on Djaben's, as she tasted the thin, salty fluid of his pre-come. Growing closer, closer, his balls rising towards his body, needing release so desperately...

Kami provided it, sucking him in a steady, rapid motion, as he shuddered, shook, called out in Pride-speak, and came. Kami swallowed, clutching his thighs, taking it all in, forcing down her own instinctive arousal at the act.

Then she withdrew and pushed him away, propelling herself to the open doorway, ready to leap off the steps and find Mark...

A figure, fully clad in black but for the eyes, filled the

doorway, one hand shooting out with frightening speed to smack Kami across the face and knock her down with a spin. 'You have troubled us enough, child.' She glanced at the prostrate Djaben, taking in his wilting erection. 'What did you do to her?'

Djaben gritted his teeth and simply shook his head, looking deeply chagrined and thwarted as he hurriedly hid his cock, unable to look at either female. 'Respected, she – she –'

'If you took her –'

'He didn't, Mia,' Kami said simply, wanting to escape but reluctant to see the hapless male needlessly killed.

Mia scowled and neared Kami, sniffing around her, frowning further as she sniffed her face. 'What did you do to *him*?'

All three started as another familiar figure entered from the open doorway. 'Mia, you found her.' Then he saw the scene before him. 'What has happened? Did he –'

'Never mind, Zeel. Where have you been?'

'I found a man, thick with her scent.' Zeel's gaunt face curled with a sneer. 'I was busy ... questioning him.'

Kami directed a furious glare at him. 'If you harmed him –'

'Save your threats,' Mia informed her coldly. 'Your obligation is to obey. Rise; we return now to the Pridelands.'

'Fuck you.' Kami smiled, a grin of satisfaction matched by her voice. 'You'll find it impossible to drag me away from under the eyes of the humans, without drawing attention.'

Mia almost smiled back, choosing instead to reach into the folds of her robes. 'This should last long enough for us to carry you home.' She withdrew a small golden cylinder, now fitted onto one finger like a thimble. With her other hand she carefully removed the blunt cap on it, revealing a much sharper tip beneath. 'Tameri assures me it is safe.'

Kami recognised the device, smelled the coating on the needle, and recoiled as much as she could, with Djaben and Zeel holding her. 'Keep that away from me!'

But the First Female just quickly reached out with it and scratched Kami's shoulder. Then she smiled.

And Kami's eyes rolled into the back of her head.

Mark hobbled back through the markets, his eyes darting about, fighting back the aches and pains, the fear and the deepening shock. 'Kami? Kami!' He had to find her, had to warn her . . .

'Mark?'

Janeane. Her eyes saucered at the sight of him. 'What the hell happened to you?'

'Have you seen Kami? She's in danger.'

'Danger? What's wrong?'

Suddenly Mark realised how trapped he was, how little of the truth he could tell Janeane or anyone else. But he had to say something. 'It was . . . members of Kami's family. They came looking for her.'

'Yes, they phoned the agency, wanted to know where she was.' She looked him over again. 'They did that to you?'

'One of them did.' And he didn't want to think about what they might do to her.

They searched the town for the following three hours, until Mark had gone well past panic and back again, and reluctantly Janeane rounded up the party for the bus ride back to Meraklisi.

Mark sat on the steps of the bus, eyes still darting

about, as if Kami might obey some cinematic rule and appear at the last moment, and he'd take her into his arms – and not lose sight or touch of her again.

Ever.

But she didn't appear.

'Mark.' Janeane perched on the steps above him, pressing the side of her knee against his shoulder; the concern on her face as strong as his. 'We have to go. If she can, she'll call us, or the office. But if you want to report it to the police here –'

'No.'

'No, what?'

He sighed, pale despite the heat and exhaustion and anxiety. He could say nothing that would make the authorities take him seriously, could he? Of course, he could always remain discreet about that aspect of Kami – but given the Pride's apparent success at concealment, any efforts by the authorities to protect her would be fruitless. Worse, he might jeopardise all of Kami's people. But wouldn't that risk be worth it to help her?

My God, she was gone, and they'd only really had such a short time together ... 'We can't go to the police. For one thing, they'll probably just dismiss it as a domestic matter.'

'They're a lot more progressive than that in Turkey –' Her voice dropped. 'Are they involved with the Kurds?'

Mark glanced at her; the Kurdish separatist movement in the Eastern provinces near Iraq remained a thorn in the Turkish government's side. No one really talked about them. And this could work to Mark's advantage. He lowered his voice as well. 'Janeane, all I can say is that we really, really can't go to the authorities to help her. If you don't want to get involved any further –'

'Shut up; I thought I'd already made myself clear.'

He looked away. 'Bloody hell, I don't know where to start.'

'Maybe her aunt could help?'

Mark glanced up. 'Her . . . aunt?'

Janeane nodded. 'Seska Fehr. She's in Ankara.'

Mark rose and faced her now, hope rising within him, his mind racing ahead. Ankara was just a few hours' drive away. 'And you have her number? Her address?'

'Back at the flat.' When she saw the expression on his face, saw him glancing about as if ready to take off for the capital on foot, she reached out and took his hand. 'We'll return to Meraklisi, get cleaned and changed, get whatever money or items you might need, and we'll go together.'

'We? You don't have –'

He stopped when she squeezed his hand. 'Shut up, I know the country better than you. And she is my friend. Now get on board.'

Mark nodded and followed her, still anxious but at least not feeling lost any more, not with the light Janeane had just given him.

Greg was nowhere around the pool and bar, or in the room: good, that made it easier. He made his way to the bathroom and stripped off, wincing repeatedly at both the painful movement of his body and the sight of the ugly purple and maroon bruises patching his chest and back and shoulders. Downing some painkillers, he filled the sink and splashed cold water on his face, gritting his teeth as if under assault again, but enduring it, letting it invigorate him.

He changed into a dark-blue short-sleeve shirt and sandy trousers, and retrieved the rest of his cash, traveller's cheques and passport, stuffing them into his backpack. Then he prepared a note, explaining to Greg that he was going away for a few days for something special with Kami and would get a later flight back, and asking him to take Mark's suitcase back as second luggage.

He hoped Greg would understand, and not worry about him. But ultimately, to Mark, nothing mattered now but finding Kami.

He met Janeane halfway to Kami's and her flat; she had changed as well, into a light but dressy blouse and slacks, with a backpack slung over one shoulder. 'I've let the cats out, and phoned Mrs Fehr's gallery; she's away in Istanbul, but is expected back later this afternoon.'

'You didn't leave a message?'

'Like what? "Hi, we think Kami's been kidnapped, see you later?" Come on, we'll get the next *dolmus*.'

'The bus? Won't a train be faster?'

'Yes, but they're less frequent; we'd lose more time waiting for the next one than if we just took this.' She offered a slight smile of confidence. 'We'll get there as quickly as possible, trust me.'

For the Turkish people, Ankara was a proud monument to the visions of Atatürk. He had transformed it from Angora, a sleepy Anatolian town of a few thousand known primarily for its namesake wool, into the capital of the modern, secular Turkish Republic, a city of three million with wide European-style boulevards, university buildings and placid parks.

Mark woke up to find the *dolmus* driving through the *gecekondu* slums bordering the hills on the edge of the city, a reminder that Ankara, whatever its wealthy and diplomatic neighbourhoods were like, remained located in the provincial heart of the country.

The bus station was in the heart of the New Town development, and Mark felt lost, but Janeane had a pocket map, and seemed to know where they should go.

The directions led them to a high street of expensive-looking boutiques in a pedestrian precinct, most of them beginning to shut for the evening. A tall, reno-vated building of elaborately carved stone and high, narrow windows, topped with overhanging greenery, dominated one corner.

The interior was an open-plan area of polished wooden floors and well-lit displays of paintings and sculptures both old and modern and, as they could see from the brochure, equipped with price tags that in inflated Turkish currency looked like astronomical units. A haughty girl had informed them that no, this was not a public gallery for tourists, and that yes, they were about to close. A moment's explanation and a telephone call later, she was escorting them to an old-fashioned lift that carried them up to Seska Fehr's office.

The third-floor office was air-conditioned, furnished by dark mahogany desks, chairs and display cases flaunting items of pottery, jewellery, and even weap-ons, some of which Mark believed from a cursory glance to be millennia old.

Seska Fehr stood beside her desk, clad in a charcoal jacket and skirt with a dark-blue low-cut silk blouse. She was a striking woman, and Mark had to swallow. He saw so much of Kami in this older woman, in the eyes and the hair and the tiny tracks of freckles on her skin, and most of all in the way she held herself, presenting an unmistakable, unignorable sensuality, coupled with a commanding presence. She eyed them briskly as her assistant departed and closed the door on them, obviously suspecting the reason for the unexpected visit, but maintaining a cordial air. 'Please, take some seats. Who is your friend, Ms Wade?'

'My name's Mark Healey,' he answered for himself, settling into the plush padded chair beside Janeane. 'I've been ... close to Kami recently.'

Seska breathed in deeply, her eyes flickering almost imperceptibly, and Mark realised from his experiences with Kami that the woman was taking in his scent, and whatever accompanying scents he might be carrying, cementing his hopes that she was more than she seemed. 'What's happened to her?'

'We were in Danya this morning, doing a tour of the markets with a group,' Janeane began, looking somewhat distracted as she stared at Seska. 'I'd checked in with our office, and found that some members of Kami's – and yours, I suppose – family had called in that morning, asking for her whereabouts. When I told her this, she took off to find them.'

'When I was alone,' Mark continued, 'a man, who wanted to know where Kami was, attacked me. He was a member of your ... family.'

'Oh?' Seska fixed a gaze on him that spoke more than she revealed with words. 'And you consider yourself an expert in identifying members of my family?'

He felt moved and almost intimidated by her gaze, but he was determined to hold his own. 'Kami's taught me a lot. The resemblance was –' he touched his jaw '– striking.'

'So, neither of you saw Kami with the others? You didn't see what happened to her?'

'No,' Janeane admitted. 'But we've been calling the flat and our office ever since it happened, and she's not contacted either.'

'And what have you told the police?'

'Nothing.'

'Yet,' Mark added, growing wary of the woman's attitude. 'I didn't think it was appropriate. At least, at the time.'

'I assure you, Mr Healey, it still isn't.' She moved to her drinks cabinet, opened the small doors and slid out an extended base to pour sepia-coloured liquid from a crystal decanter into a tiny glass. 'This corroborates a report I received today about an associate, who was made to reveal Kami's location and transport his assailants to Danya.' Without preamble she downed her drink in one, offering nothing to either guest, before turning to them again. 'Thank you for informing me personally. You may leave now.'

Silence hung in the air between the three of them, before Mark broke it with, 'Is that it?'

Seska set the glass down again. 'If you need your expenses reimbursed –'

'What we need is to find Kami, and get her back!'

'That . . . won't be possible.'

'But why not?' Janeane asked. 'They would have taken her back to your village, wouldn't they?'

'One does not just walk in and out of my village. It was difficult enough helping Kami escape the first time.'

'Escape? Who's holding her? Why?'

'None of these questions concern you, Ms Wade.'

'What? She's my friend, my flatmate, I've known her –'

'I've known Kami all her life, young woman.' Seska cut through archly, turning away to face the window, as if hearing the call of the *imam* to evening prayer as the sky began blushing dusk.

'Then you'll know how wrong all this is!' Mark countered.

'Believe me, Mr Healey, if I could help her again, and not jeopardise my current standing –'

'Your standing?' He rose to his feet. 'Is that all you're worried about?'

She faced him now. 'I have responsibilities, obligations, which you could scarcely understand. Do not seek to judge me.'

'I don't care about your responsibilities –'

Janeane rose and stepped in, one hand on Mark's arm, silencing him, before looking at Seska. 'Mrs Fehr, I realise this is difficult for you, but can you please explain *why* Kami was taken? I understand if you can't go into detail, but we're just concerned for her.'

Seska bit back an initial reply, then seemed to soften her features a little. 'Yes, of course.' Her hands moved together, as if gathering and shaping her words. 'It's what might be called an arranged marriage. Kami was selected to bear the children of our . . . chief.'

Mark felt his blood run cold. Janeane looked away, then back again. 'They can't do that to her. It's the twenty-first century!'

Mark's expression hardened. 'That doesn't mean a damn to them, does it, Mrs Fehr?'

Seska matched his expression with one of her own. 'Don't presume to lecture me, Mr Healey; far worse occurs to women throughout the world. I can assure you that Kami will not be harmed.'

'Tell that to the bruiser who threw me around! She needs our help!'

Seska regarded him then took a step forwards, her gaze magnetic, as if putting all her powers of persuasion to bear on him. 'I am aware of the effect Kami can have on a man. But be realistic: you've known her for less than a week. Return to your country, your life, and these feelings will fade.'

Her scent, so like Kami's ... it made him want to listen to her, to do what she suggested. It *did* make sense, a part of him admitted. And yet, that same scent awoke a resolve within him. He shook his head. 'No. I know too much. About her. About *you*. Too much to stop now.'

Seska's face muscles tightened. 'That's a very dangerous thing to tell me, Mr Healey.' But then she sighed. 'You're not going to give up, are you?'

'Would *you*?'

In reply, Seska thumbed her desk intercom. 'Ilona, have Major Fehr call me.' She rose, looking at each of them in turn, her expression determined. 'Would you follow me?'

Mark nodded, as did Janeane, and they followed the woman out of her office and into the lift, Seska producing a key that fitted into a lock in the lift controls.

The lift descended.

Janeane spoke up again. 'How did he know?'

Mark and Seska looked at her. 'Pardon?'

Janeane focused on Mark. 'That man who attacked you? How did he know that you knew Kami, if she wasn't around?'

Seska smiled. 'Mr Healey will have ample time to explain that to you.'

But Mark was distracted by the floor numbers on the brass plate overhead disappearing past the ground floor. 'Where are we going?'

Seska didn't answer.

The gates opened into a featureless corridor bathed in pallid fluorescent light – and two of the tallest, broadest figures Mark had ever seen: two metres in height, identical in their broad, sharp features, clad in simple black kilts with ancient Egyptian-style arm-bands, torcs and gold baldrics crossing their frames from shoulder to hip.

And, to judge from the honey eyes and tails swishing behind them, undeniably Pride.

More swiftly than the humans could have expected, they reached through the opening doors of the lift and pulled them out, to fling them against either wall. Mark tried to make a move for the tail of the one who held him, to duplicate what he'd done in Danya, but this one easily kept him at arm's length.

'Jesus –' Janeane choked out, her eyes wide and face wan.

Seska spoke to the males in a language Mark recognised as Pridespeak, then added in English, 'As I said, Mr Healey – a *very* dangerous thing to say.'

10

'She's cold.'

'That will pass.'

'That drug almost killed her!'

'A mere simulation. You forget yourself, Gatekeeper.'

'I forget nothing . . . Respected.'

It was the need to silence the all-too-loud voices as much as hunger and thirst that had stirred Kami, had made her fight the effects of the narcotic and rise to her elbows.

The bed was firm, woven, familiar in touch and scent, as was the stone room surrounding it: wooden and hand-woven furniture and rugs; a hearth cut into the rock, upon which a small iron pot with a pleasing scent bubbled over a fire; a cask of water in one corner beside some wooden chests. Narrow slits in the walls allowed light in during the day, or, as now, just the cool whistle of the wind. In the background, her captors stood, talking, watching, near a battered-looking rug.

In the foreground, a female appeared: shorter than the males, her hair darker shades of walnut and sable, her nose blunt, her eyes focused with the narrow scrutiny of one of her calling – Tameri, a Healer. 'She's awake. She'll be fine.' She rose and departed, Kami noting the cold, hostile glare she threw at Djaben, a former close mate.

Then someone finally addressed her. 'I knew you couldn't bear to be parted from me for long.'

'Kahotep!' Ignoring the throbbing in her head, Kami

sat up and embraced the older male, welcoming his closeness and scent once again. 'I've missed you!'

'As I, you.' He drew back onto his haunches and smiled. He looked little different from when she'd last seen him, months before: the same ash-grey mane swept back, the same flattened nose, the same white scar down his wrinkled right cheek to his jaw, a souvenir from his own time as a Pride agent in the human world, decades past, the same mischievous grin. And the same emerald-green kilt and short-sleeved tunic, of course; fashion was not as mercurial among their people as it was with humans. 'I have broth ready.'

He moved to the fire, as her abductors drew closer. Mia had changed into the long sleeveless purple dress with wide shoulder straps and the elaborately-crafted gold choker and tiara appropriate for her station, while Zeel and Djaben had returned to their warrior's blue kilts and tunics. Zeel balked. 'You're feeding her?'

'She was drugged for over half a day, and carried in a filthy rug by freight train and horseback. She has been through much.' Kahotep poured broth into a wooden bowl and placed it on a tray with bread and a mug of water. 'Your voice alone is wearing enough on the strongest of us.' He turned his back on him to return to the bedside.

Zeel bristled at the insult, shook off Djaben's silent entreaty to let it lie, and took a step forwards. 'I still find it difficult to understand how our stalwart Gate-keeper could allow Kami to escape.'

Kahotep grunted. 'I daresay, Zeel, you still find it difficult to understand why you shouldn't piss in your own well.'

The younger male stepped forwards. 'Don't push me –'

Kahotep spun in place, teeth and claws bared, eyes alight. 'No, don't push *me*!'

'Enough!' Mia snapped. 'Zeel, the First has already found Kahotep innocent of any collusion or negligence; you dishonour him by such remarks.'

She paused, the unspoken command hanging in the air. Zeel drew in a sharp, apparently distasteful breath, then hissed, 'I . . . apologise, Gatekeeper.'

As contrition went, it was pathetic. But Mia nodded, apparently not expecting anything more. 'Let her finish her meal; she'll need her strength.'

Kami returned to her food, eating hurriedly despite her reluctance to leave Kahotep and the relative sanctuary of his place at the mouth of the Pridelands. Kami had been anxious about his fate when Seska had helped her escape, though he had played no active part in it.

When she had sated her hunger and thirst, she rose, as Mia announced unnecessarily, 'Now, remove that offensive human clothing.'

Kahotep helped Kami to her feet. She turned her back on them and followed him over to the wooden cask in one corner of the room, then undressed, handing each item of clothing over to the Gatekeeper, never looking back. It was still humiliating, though not out of modesty – such concepts were meaningless among the Pride – but because this act, ostensibly to remove traces of the world of man, even their scents, symbolised her casting off of the life she had made away from her people.

Kahotep, for his part, said nothing, but merely accepted her shoes and stockings, her clothes and underwear, placing them in a storage chest with other clothes Pride members might use to infiltrate the outside. Then Kami was naked.

Kahotep's voice was a whisper as he smelled her shirt. 'A male?'

'A man.'

He nodded. 'I will keep it safe.'

She fought back tears, turning to the cask to use a cloth and Pride-made soap to wash and rinse her body, losing Mark's scent from her with each passing heartbeat. She felt that loss more keenly than anything else.

Kahotep took away the confiscated items, allowing Kami to dry herself off briskly. She had to put Mark out of her mind, at least for now – to dwell on him would be to sink into despair.

Kahotep returned to her with clothing more appropriate to her new station: a silk pine-green dress that left her back, arms and shoulders bared, the material bound by gold clasps at her right hip. It opened in traditional tripartite design to bare her legs up to her pelvis, and from behind, to allow her tail freedom – and to provide access for a male. It was beautiful, and something she knew Mark would have loved, too. Had she worn it for him, it would have been an expression of her identity and the strength of the love she had for herself. Here, however, it mocked her former freedom.

Kahotep drew her out of her bleak thoughts, dressing her and combing back her hair with his long fingers. Then he embraced her, his voice a whisper that suffused her with love and support. 'Bastet watch over you, little one.'

'It is well past time,' Mia interjected.

Kami drew back and walked towards the others, Mia silent but looking almost grateful, as if she had been afraid that Kami would have put up a stronger fight. Djaben said nothing.

But Zeel? He couldn't resist one parting shot. 'Don't

cry for your ape, Kami, I'm sure he'll find female company again soon enough.'

Kami's scowl was thick with contempt, as was her reply. 'Sooner than you, Zeel; any female desperate enough for your length inside her will have already succumbed to self-loathing, and thrown herself off the nearest cliff.'

Kahotep's laughter escorted the quartet out of his chambers and down the spiral staircase, centuries-old and stained along the curved, cracked walls by countless torches set and extinguished over time. The four were silent now.

The corridor that awaited them twisted, narrowed, then suddenly turned and widened out, until they found themselves in the Court of the Firsts.

It was not as grand as some human equivalent, but it suited the surroundings and its inhabitants: tooled out of the volcanic tuft into a hexagonal shape, it boasted air chimneys and vents, a hearth offering heat, and other vents positioned to provide reflected sunlight from without. Within sat voluminous pillows, furs and low tables, all surrounded by banners and tapestries lining the walls, depicting many periods and events in the life of the race that had created them. It was a room of stark elegance, a display of wealth in history rather than treasure.

And in the figure who awaited them. He stood, facing the fire, hands folded behind him. He never moved, but just listened, taking in their scents and waiting until the four stood in the centre of the room, three of them descending to the expected submissive posture, on all fours, heads bowed. 'Zeel, Djaben, you have our gratitude for your service. You may leave now.'

The males rose and obeyed.

Varis-Menmaat turned in place to regard the two

females, Mia still on all fours, Kami defiantly standing. One of his large hands moved away from the soft silk material of his red-rich robes, and stretched out. 'Mia, your return pleases us immensely. As does the success of your mission. Attend.'

The First Female rose and stood beside him, glaring at Kami's disobedience as Varis continued, his eyes sweeping over Kami. 'And Kami, I give thanks for your safe homecoming.'

To Kami, there had always been something larger than life about Varis, something beyond the powerful frame, the mane of brown hair turning to iron grey, the worldly lines in the bearded face, the deep, rich voice that caught one's attention without rising beyond a conversational level. She fought a lifetime's worth of conditioning of subservience towards the First Male, and raised her chin. 'Don't thank me; I didn't return willingly.'

Varis appeared slightly amused by her reaction, like a parent dealing with a defiant child. 'Then I shall offer all the thanks to Mia. She carried out an odious charge with honour.'

'Honour?' Kami shot a glare at the older female, feeling no deference whatsoever. 'Her lapdog Zeel assaulted a man to find me!'

'Your point being?'

Mia sidestepped closer to him. 'Her point being that this particular man was her pet.'

Kami resisted the urge to attack her. Somehow. 'He's no pet! He's my lover!'

'*Was* your lover,' Varis corrected simply, his reaction to the idea of Kami's intimacy with a human clear on his face. 'You will never see him again. Better to focus now on the duty you must perform for your people.'

Kami took the anger she felt and used it to force back

the bleakness and anguish that his words threatened to blanket her with completely. 'For you, you mean.'

'Of course.' He dropped Mia's hand and slowly orbited Kami. 'As the Behest states, what serves the First Male, serves the Pride.'

Kami turned in place to keep her eyes on him. 'It doesn't serve *me*! I was happy where I was! Damn the Behest!'

'Silence!' Varis barked, eyes narrowing and teeth bared. He moved a little more quickly around Kami now. 'Do you know what your selfish actions have accomplished?' He stopped and calmed down visibly, though his words remained taut with anger. 'We are nine months into Season, but the females have now stopped visiting the Lair to perform their duties, and the males are growing more aggressive. Dissent blossoms, and it is only a matter of time before we sink into anarchy and dissolution. When you fled, my authority was weakened.'

Kami breathed in, her memories flooding back. Three months ago, when Mia had proven unable to conceive an heir for Varis, his claim at Firstship was threatened. He proved unwilling to renounce her and choose another First Female, so she invoked a little-used edict within the Behest, and Mia claimed a Second for him – whether Kami agreed or not. And despite herself, hearing that the females had now abandoned trying to conceive made guilt gnaw at her. 'Why didn't you choose another?'

'You know why: you are of one of the proper lines. And you are of excellent stock, young, intelligent and fit.' He paused to stroke her tail. 'You will set a fine example to the other females. You will help restore order to our people.' He grunted. 'And of course you will have the honour of receiving my attentions.'

Kami stiffened at his touch, and the resolve she had felt begin to crack with guilt was now galvanised back to full strength. 'Keep your honour and your attentions. I reject them. And you.'

The Firsts froze for a heartbeat, unable or unwilling to believe her response. Then Varis snarled, 'Assume your position!'

'Go chase your tail.'

He attacked, lunging forwards to swing his open hand at her. But Kami had been ready for it, ducking and backing away, claws extended, dropping down instinctively into a stance that would take advantage of her lighter, more lithe frame, watching and letting him make all the moves. She smiled and cooed mockingly. 'What's the matter, "Respected"? Getting too old for dealing with a little female?'

With a growl he took the bait and charged at her. Kami sidestepped easily.

Too easily, it turned out. She'd neglected Mia, who had broken her stance by the fire to tackle Kami. The two females tumbled to the floor, Kami below Mia, losing her breath even as she lashed out, breaking skin as Mia broke hers and moved swiftly for a female nearly twice Kami's age . . .

Until Varis reached out, grasped Mia and flung her away, before pinning Kami's arms behind her and pressing her face down onto the cold floor. Kami kicked back at him, cursing him in every language she knew, even making up a few words. Then she froze, when Varis suddenly clamped his mouth, his teeth, onto her neck, growling through them.

Kami became acutely aware of so much: her dress, torn and tattered, her breasts pressed bare against the stone floor, Varis's sharp teeth and scent on her, the hardness she felt pressing into her.

And of the futility of further resistance.

She relaxed her body, making a soft mewling sound, a sound she never thought she'd make again, letting Varis discern her surrender. His stance shifted, his grip on her neck lessening, but only a little, as if still prepared for trickery.

A wise move, she realised after the fact, when she felt muscles relax she never realised were tensed, her survival instinct unwilling to accept defeat.

He released her neck and snarled to Mia, 'Get them.'

A dishevelled and bruised Mia nodded and obeyed, returning from behind one of the wall banners with a set of heavy-looking black iron chains, fringed in several places by thick rings of several sizes.

Varis manipulated his hold on Kami to allow Mia to secure the cold, heavy iron clamps around Kami's ankles, then her wrists. Finally, her head was lifted up and drawn back, and for a moment Mia stared into Kami's eyes, as if the older female were about to go for her throat. And she did – but with another iron ring. A collar. Kami swallowed, atavistic fear rising like bile within her.

Varis finally rose from her, and Kami tugged at the chains, feeling them clink, the metal heavy on her, mocking any efforts to break free of them. She turned on her side to get away from the cold floor; her dress had been torn in the fight, revealing her left breast and most of her right, but it didn't matter. The chains binding her wrists, ankles and neck all converged onto a central ring before her, like the spokes of a wheel, the length of the chains offering enough movement to walk and crawl and sit, but not enough to run or fight back well.

Varis and Mia stood above her, their own clothes torn, the marks on their skin thick with excitement from the rush of blood during the fight; the stiffness under Varis' robes further defined his state. Mia had regained the bearing and attitude expected of the First Female, but Varis still struggled, as became obvious when he finally spoke. 'It is – regrettable – that your continued defiance forced us to take this action.'

Kami spat. 'Just get on with it.' Until she remembered that, of course, the act would not take place here.

Mia helped her to her feet, then retrieved another chain and attached one end to Kami's collar, holding the other end and guiding Kami out like a pet, and Varis following, as tradition demanded. Along the way, Pride members they encountered stopped and stared.

And followed.

The Lair was the largest enclosure within the Pridelands, a barren fissure in the mountain, cracked open ages ago by some earthquake, striated with dozens of large, flat step-like surfaces that rose up to the crescent-shaped opening to the sky. Thirty generations of careful horticulture and landscaping by the Pride had transformed the Lair into a lush grotto, overgrown with hardy plant life fed by the heat from the springs, and clinging to the rocks and each other, twisting and curling into fists and fringes of green. The water from the springs bubbled out in rivulets towards a central pool. Torches and campfires were scattered throughout, their light never reaching the top of the Lair, where bats and birds nestled.

This was the place where the Pride members came when moods took them. Moods to talk, to eat, to share company, to groom, to fight and to mate. Kami had done all these here, of course, before her flight.

But she never thought she'd be here again, doing anything.

The ground was carpeted with soft grasses and wet earth, easing the aches and pains of Kami's feet after so much time wearing human footwear. Mia held onto the lead, glancing at those who watched them, either to challenge or to invite. Then she tugged the chains towards a large grey boulder half-buried in the earth, scored with generations of claw marks from others who had perched there. Mia pulled Kami face down over the rock, roughly and visibly demonstrating her authority and power over the younger female. Kami felt the cold rock against her front, and the cool air and hot eyes on her rear, as her tail slipped out from between the folds.

She glanced behind her and saw Varis stripping off his torn robes to reveal a bare chest sporting years of scars, and a tripartite kilt of blood-red silk, tented forwards. He glanced about, as if waiting for sufficient witnesses to this act of the restoration of authority. Because that was what this was about. Not love, as she would have received from Mark. Not pleasure, as she would have received from some other humans, or other Pride members. It was not even about producing a child.

It was about power, and possession.

He cast aside the front fold of his kilt, revealing the thick shaft of his cock, dark pink and wet-tipped and pointing towards her. Behind her, more of the Pride arrived, unnaturally silent and rapt; under normal circumstances, it would not have drawn such attention, any more than a human couple talking at an open-air café table. But then it had apparently been months since anyone had mated here.

Despite herself, the scent of Varis's cock triggered a reaction in Kami, the pounding anxiety and excitement of her captive state already making her heart race, the veins in her throat pulse and her sex spasm as she breathed faster.

She pictured Mark, imagined it was him behind her and not this male, imagined she was back in her bedroom, or maybe on the beach again. Her tail twitched at the memory of the human's scent, his touch, and his gentle, hungry smile. Varis positioned himself between her parted legs and knelt down slightly; both hands gripped her hips, stopping to pull away the remains of her dress. Then he gripped her again, the head of his cock sliding up and down the groove of skin between her cheeks, his claws flexing into her skin, as if she might somehow still stop him. When she made no move, he murmured to her, 'Have you finally acknowledged your place, then?'

Kami turned back to glare up at him from behind strands of dark hair, her eyes wide with fury and defiance. 'Fuck you!' She struggled against him, but it only served to open herself up and let him drive his shaft into her. Kami faced front again, ignoring Mia, who was still standing before her, still holding onto Kami's chain. Kami forced her body to relax, not wanting to stiffen at the undesired penetration.

And Varis began thrusting, pushing his hips hard against her buttocks, forcing himself deep into her, hard and fast thrusts that displayed his deep pleasure and satisfaction, his urgent sexual need seeking release, a frantic fucking action. She was aroused, but only a little; this male wasn't a patch on Mark.

So she drew thoughts and memories of Mark into the forefront of her mind, and made noises as Varis pumped harder and faster, until their bodies slapped together rapidly and rhythmically, and his claws deepened their hold on her hips. Around them, the collective mood of the Pride observers was as heavy as their scents, their expectation and excitement almost palpable.

She had quite the audience now to see her sub-mission, her debasement.

So she used it, tilting her head back, closing her eyes and calling out, 'Mark! Oh, Mark, my sweet, wonderful man! Do it! Drive it into me, Mark! Drive it into me, my wonderful *human* lover!'

A bit obvious, she realised, but she knew her audi-ence, knew that subtlety would not be the right approach. And she knew she'd timed it correctly – too late for Mia to react in any way, too late for Varis to do anything more than what he'd wanted to do all along, as he climaxed, with a strangled snarl, filling Kami's sex with hot, thick bursts of come. The action, and the memory of Mark with its consequent feelings, pushed Kami over the edge too.

But still she whispered Mark's name, even as Varis quickly wilted within her and withdrew, and Mia released her hold on the chain. Kami slumped to the cool earth, catching her breath and gathering her strength until she saw Mia walk around to join Varis, to dress him. With a snarl Kami rattled the manacles at them. 'You've had your fun, now get these fucking things off me! Or do you intend to keep me bound forever?'

The notion spread grumbles throughout the spec-tators, even from those Kami knew supported the actions against her; chains were for criminals, for the insane or uncontrollable. But the Firsts were politically astute enough to recognise this; in a deliberately com-manding tone, Varis replied, 'Of course not. You may have been bound to keep you from hurting yourself again, but they are no longer necessary.' Slipping his robe over his head, he looked over at a young female crouching nearby. 'Ankhesen! Help our Second remove her protective chains, and take her to her chambers.'

Ankhesen, a petite young female just into her Initiate phase, with a snub nose and wide golden eyes, rose and straightened her thigh-high sleeveless emerald tunic, then reluctantly dodged around some larger spectators. She glanced about nervously, tail twitching, as if afraid one of the males present would try to claim her, and squatted beside Kami, hands clumsily shaking with the locking mechanisms.

Kami tried to catch her eye, and studied the salad of feelings she saw: fear, admiration, arousal, confusion. All feelings Kami shared, but with Kami they were shackled to a driving bolt of anger. She grasped the removed chains in one hand, rose to her feet and flung them in the direction of the departing Firsts. 'Try to put these on me again, and I'll kill you!'

The chains spun through the air like bolas, landing noisily a metre behind her target. Varis and Mia stopped and turned, and Varis replied simply, 'Try to keep denying your responsibilities, and you'll kill us all.'

And left it at that.

The water was hot, pumped up from the springs and drawn into the sunken pit by mechanisms that were simple, even primitive by human standards, but had remained reliable after generations.

The water lifted up the scented stick of Pride soap and began the slow process of melting its skin into a thin white film.

Varis stood by the pit, allowing Mia to undress him set his damaged attire aside for repair. She knelt to remove the bands of gold and fur from around his shins. 'You did well.'

He grunted. 'I mated; as vain as I am, I don't expect praise for that.'

She smiled back, rising and standing before him to undo the belt of his kilt. 'You know what I mean. Authority must be re-established.'

'You left of your own accord to retrieve Kami when she fled; that is a strange way of demonstrating the importance of authority.' When he was naked, he stepped down into the pit. It was only knee-deep when he stood up, so he bent down to lift a cloth that floated like a raft on the water, and squeezed the contents over himself.

She undressed and followed him into the water. 'She was needed. I know I cannot conceive. You seemed ... reluctant to act, despite the threat of Zeel's line.'

He didn't comment on that, but looked her over. 'It has been difficult for you.'

'Nonsense,' she lied, taking the cloth from him and reaching for the remains of the soap, then lathering and soaking his broad chest, her tone deliberately detached. 'Kami will bear your heir. Order will be restored. And then we will proceed against Seska.'

'No.' He raised his arms, letting her wash his sides, and then turned to offer his back and shoulders. 'She is to be left alone.'

'She almost certainly helped Kami escape. I know she is your sister, Varis, but –'

'But nothing.'

Mia dropped the subject and dabbed at the wounds Kami had inflicted on him, watching the water run in rivulets down the landscape of muscles on her consort's back, racing down towards the curves and grooves of his buttocks. Then she knelt in the water to wash his legs. 'Kami must be watched. She is strong, as was her mother. But she gathered many bad habits among the humans.' At this level, she could smell his sex, and smell Kami's scent on him; when he turned to face her, she was inches away from his shaft, short and thick and resting in its nest of the dark, crinkly hair steepling his scrotum.

She remembered what Kami had done to Djaben. 'Many bad habits.' She washed the front of his thighs, moving up to his balls, his shaft, taking the most care now, feeling the blood pulse within the column of flesh that used to fill her up – until it proved necessary to choose another to bear his heir. She bit back the satisfaction she felt at washing Kami's scent off him. 'We did well to rescue her.'

'Yes.' Varis sounded distant, pensive now.

And then she almost asked him to return with her to the Lair. To forget saving his seed for the Second, to return and eat and laugh and groom each other. To have him take her once more, fill her up, scratch her thighs and slap her buttocks and coat her insides with his come, then lie there wrapped in each other's heat and scent, never mind her barrenness.

But this was her gambit. And she knew her place within it.

11

'So where does it go?'

'What do you mean?'

'I mean they looked two foot long and an inch thick! Something like that has to show even through the baggiest clothing, and I've seen Kami in the skimpiest!'

Mark smiled and examined another poster. 'There are no bones in their tails, just muscle and cartilage wound in a sort of spiral pattern; with practice they can retract them, like an accordion tube, behind a fold hidden at the base of their spines.'

Janeane frowned, and kept pacing, as if she hadn't been around the cell many times already. But it remained unchanged: furs and pillows for a makeshift bed, a chamberpot, table and chairs – and most curious of all, posters covering the walls, pictures and lists of words in Turkish and phonetic equivalents. After some investigation, Mark guessed they were glossaries of Pride words, translated, as well as diagrams of what seemed to be foodstuffs, gestures, ceremonies. 'Oh. As simple as that,' she said finally.

'Simple, but not easy. It's worse for the Pride because their tails help with balance and co-ordination, and engorge with blood when they're excited. Same with their eyes and markings.'

'And the claws?'

'Just under the fingernails, behind folds of skin at the tips.' She'd asked about those twice already, but he didn't mind repeating himself, finding it a relief to talk to someone else about what he'd learned in the past week about the Pride. 'Same with the toes.'

'But everything else about her was –'

'Human.' Mark's smile turned bittersweet from his longing. 'Very human. She didn't lick her paws or chase mice or anything like that. Any other questions?'

After a moment, she replied, 'Yes.' Her hands fidgeted needlessly with her sleeves. 'I knew her longer than you.' She chuckled grimly. 'Or thought I did. But she chose to reveal her biggest secret to – to –'

'To someone she'd only just met?' Mark prompted, understanding but not really knowing at first how to respond, empathising but not believing it right to apologise. 'I saw her true nature by accident; she had to say something to me.'

'She could have come to me before.'

'Yes, she could have. But given how Seska Fehr reacted to our knowledge of her kind, maybe Kami was protecting you?'

'Maybe,' Janeane finally conceded, grumbling. 'There's more. I . . . wanted Kami. Big time.'

'Oh.'

'Yes, "Oh". Look, what I'm trying to say is that I feel stupid for not having noticed just how different she was, OK? Like I really *am* a dizzy blonde. I mean, I was sitting there between her legs once on the bed, when she wore these tight little pants –'

'I get it.' Mark blushed. 'Well, it's not like you knew to look for something, did you?'

Janeane made a sound of assent, not convinced but not willing to press the matter further either. 'Well, if you can get the image of me between Kami's legs out of your head –'

'Never crossed my mind,' he lied.

'– then maybe you can tell me what's going on, where we are.'

He nodded. 'I think this was some underground fallout shelter from the Cold War, something the Fehrs are now using for their own purposes. Can't be difficult to arrange, if her husband is in the Army.'

'That answers the where, but not the what.'

He returned to the posters. 'They seem to be running a school – learning about the Pride: history, language, customs and so on.'

'Uh huh.'

He nodded to one set. 'These pictures seem to be describing the history of Bastet, and the ceremonies and festivals that used to take place.'

'Wonderful.'

'Yes, and illuminating. Most of the information we have on them describes huge bacchanals, like Mardis Gras. But there was so much more lost. Or hidden from man.'

'Mark –'

'There are some indications that the worship goes back even beyond the First Dynasty. I wonder if –'

'I wonder if you're gonna shut up and take some action!' she snapped, kicking at a chair. 'They're gonna kill us!'

He paused at the outburst, and drew closer. 'Jan, I'm sorry I got you into this. I should have told you what I knew.'

'Like I'd have believed you.'

'But if I'd known she was going to react like this –'

Janeane stared ahead, the moment of fear and anger seemingly vanished. 'Did Kami ever tell you how she and I met? She'd impressed the agency with her knowledge of history, so they hired her on the spot, and they asked me to show her around. She seemed so shy, such a country girl, not just new to the area, but new to the world.' She smiled at that. 'I'd coaxed her into going out clubbing. Well, we'd separated for a moment, I went looking for her, and some guys grabbed me, pulled me into an alley ...' Her face paled. 'And then this ferocious woman suddenly appeared from nowhere, knocking men down like they were made of paper. Just to protect me, someone she hardly knew.' Her eyes met his again. 'Nobody tells me to forget my friends and walk away. *Nobody.*'

Just then the door opened, and one of the hulking males entered, beckoning to Mark. 'You. Come.'

Mark didn't move. The male started towards him, as Janeane elbowed him. 'Get going, find out what's happening.'

The male reached out, grabbed Mark and dragged him out. 'Well, since my arm's going anyway ...'

The male strong-armed him along winding corridors, past sets of heavy iron doors, some open to reveal storage and sleeping rooms. Then they entered a larger area, filled with furs and pillows, with banners on the walls, and brass braziers within which burned incense and oil fires. There were also carved stone pillars topped with marble and obsidian images of Bastet, in both her fully feline and half-human appearances, spaced equally about in a wide circle which nearly encompassed the room.

But Mark's attention almost immediately focused on the occupants of the room: twenty or more men, almost all near-naked, standing in a circle; peering closer, he noticed that they possessed Pride-like markings on their skin, but were definitely not Pride. They faced inwards, watching and chanting as Seska, clad in a short toga-like ruby-red outfit, sat astride a naked man on the floor. She writhed and undulated in the heady throes of intercourse, her tail thrashing about behind her, her body occasionally dipping forwards as if her hair sought to embrace the man's head, and her hands moved over his chest and arms.

Mark swallowed and shifted in place, his cock twitching, and forced himself to look away, away from the raw act of sex in the centre of the room, seeing the other men there, men with red claw marks on them, like Mark's own. Then he saw the other male, wearing something more ceremonial than he had before. And it all came to him: ceremony . . .

This whole facility was a temple, evidently for a cult worshipping Bastet. And he was witness to a ceremony.

Within the circle, Seska's thrashing grew more intense, as did the man's thrusts upwards into her, until she was demanding something in Turkish, something which the man was fervently agreeing to.

Then the chanting stopped, the tableau froze, and Mark found himself holding his breath, watching as Seska slowly rose off the man, who was helped back to his feet and carried to some adjacent pillows. Seska turned and slipped a beautiful red silk cloak fringed with gold over her shoulders and clasped it around her neck, then stepped onto a raised dais, her hands clutching the hem of her cloak as if ready to drape herself. Her insouciance was arresting, as if she hadn't just been having sex with someone. 'Who else knows you're here?' she asked Mark.

Mark swallowed, realising he couldn't bluff or lie about it. 'No one. Believe me.'

'I do, Mr Healey.' She stepped down from the dais and drew closer to him. 'And in fact I appreciate your honesty, if not your imprudence in making threats as you did earlier.'

Mark became acutely aware of the Pride male tensing behind him, ready to stop anything he might try against her. 'Let Janeane go, I'm responsible for us being here –'

'Spare us the gallantry, Mr Healey, it has no place here. Here, your beliefs and expectations mean nothing. Here, we make no concessions to gender, race, age or wealth. Here, as it was seventy centuries ago, all humans are equal in stature – below the Pride.'

'But she's not –'

His subsequent words were lost, as the female's hand shot out and fastened itself around his throat like a vice, the claws pressing on his windpipe, threateningly; he felt his eyes bulge and his face turn purple, and listened to the words she spat at him through clenched teeth.

'Every breath you take from this moment onwards will be a gift from me. Cherish them.' She held onto Mark's throat for a moment longer, as if determined to demonstrate her authority, then released him. Mark almost collapsed, but the Pride male caught him, and kept him up.

Mark returned a glare to Seska, and let his hostility flow unchecked. 'There's no reason to harm her, she doesn't threaten your people's security. Neither do I.'

'I am in a better position than you to judge what constitutes a threat to the Pride, Mr Healey. It is one of the reasons I founded the current incarnation of the Swords of Bastet.'

'Swords? What, assassins?'

'Worshippers.' She stepped away to walk around the perimeter of the circle, her hand moving over the statues, her eyes never meeting the acolytes standing beyond the circle, their own eyes averted. 'Ours is a heritage of persecution by humans: Romans, Mongolians, Crusaders, Conquistadors, Nazis, churches. But though we remain hidden, on occasion some of us venture out into the human world, and bring into being the Swords, secret societies attracting the elite: politics, military, business, industry.'

'And through the likes of them, you gain powerful allies.'

'Yes. The Swords existed in the times of the Seljuks, the Ottomans, into the twentieth century; this current incarnation is five years old.' She smiled. 'Kami never got around to telling you about any of this, did she?'

The mention of Kami somehow sounded so wrong coming from Seska just now. 'Kami told me many things, but never anything that would jeopardise your people. I respected that.'

'How charming,' she mocked, but her eyes now as she returned to him seemed to regard him in a new light. 'Intelligence, discretion, tenacity, strength … I'm beginning to see what she saw in you. Would you like the opportunity to walk out of here alive, Mr Healey?'

Now he regarded her, playing in his mind all the possibilities behind the question. 'That – depends. How?'

'By joining us.'

'*What?*'

'By allowing me to induct you into the Swords. It is the only means I know to allow you to live, and guarantee continued discretion.'

'By … worshipping you?'

'My people. I am merely their priestess.'

He glanced around. 'What about Janeane?'

'She is not your concern any more.'

'Yes, she is.'

Seska sighed. 'If it makes you feel any better, Mr Healey, she is safe now. It is tradition not to spill blood during these ceremonies.'

'Ceremonies?'

'Stop feigning ignorance. You understand the power that secret societies can possess, the necessity for ceremony and tradition, among your own kind.' She walked around the room, glancing at the surrounding men. 'Each man here will live or die at my command. As will you.'

Mark watched, his voice lost. These men's faces showed the truth; they were devoted, besotted, enchanted. How? How did she keep these men under her thrall? Was it merely for the privilege of having sex with someone as different as a Pride member? He knew how bizarre and wonderful he felt when he thought of Kami, but that was different – that was love. Mark's face hardened. Was this what he had to do?

Seska smiled triumphantly. 'Well? Do you agree?'

In truth, like her, he knew his answer from the start. But still he hesitated. Secular by nature, the thought of faking devotion to the Pride, especially to Seska, in order to find Kami didn't bother him in the least, being little different from going to church as a child to please his mother. 'What do I have to do?'

'Well, for a start, take off your clothes.' She laughed quietly at his reaction. 'Why so surprised? Were you not observing just now? If it helps, keep in mind that I have seen many men naked, and I don't judge.' But still she watched intently, deliberately.

Incense seemed to climb into his lungs as his fingers fumbled over the buttons of his shirt, cast it to his side for want of anywhere else to set it, then lifted up each foot in turn to remove his shoes and socks, ignoring the men drawing in closer. Seska reached up and unclasped her cloak, then drew it back and allowed Fehr to collect it. He removed his trousers and sent them to join the rest of his clothes, trying to build up an expression of defiance. 'No matter what happens, my feelings for Kami –'

'Spare me the assuage of your conscience.' She wasn't staring now, but was moving and stretching her body, allowing him and the others to see the fit curves of her breasts and hips, the swirl of her tail, the way the silk outfit seemed to flow like water on her. 'This is business, for both of us. Continue undressing.'

Fighting back his modesty, knowing hesitation would only make it worse, Mark complied, kicking aside his boxers and forcing his hands to his sides, trying and failing to appear as nonchalant as possible under the circumstances. It didn't work; his cock twitched before him, regardless.

Seska seemed to possess no reticence, the cut of her outfit allowing peeks at her dark nipples, or the darker bush steepling her long thighs, as she drew closer to him. Her tail twitched in that manner Mark recognised from Kami as signalling her arousal. This close, he smelled her musk, also reminiscent of Kami's; he chose to focus on that association, which made his cock react further.

Men appeared beside him, and began touching his arms and shoulders with something cold and wet. He looked to either side, to see dabs of paint or dye added to his skin: faux Pride markings.

When she was only inches before him she spoke again, her tone suggesting a well-known litany. 'At the dawn of time, Amun-Ra made the world, and from his essence gave birth to the gods and goddesses. And they brought their mortal children to life and set them upon the world to live together.

'But man was not content to share the world. Alone among the children of the gods and goddesses, he killed for sport, or greed, or lust.

'And he did just that, and in bloody war after bloody war he drove to the land of the dead the other children

– of Buto and Hathor, of Osiris and Neith and Anubis –
to make himself master of the world. The other gods
and goddesses had abandoned their children.

'But not Bastet. Her children were the most beautiful,
the most perfect, and she loathed to see them fall to the
hand of man. So she gave her children a gift.'

Before her, Mark tried to focus, to recall his knowledge of Egyptian myth, to understand how it differed
from what Seska was saying, and, more importantly,
why. He thought of Bastet: goddess of cats, of perfumes,
her name deriving from the bas perfume jars ... she ...
they ...

And Seska was still circling him, her scent strong and
impossible to ignore. 'Bastet gave her children the
power to entrance men, distract them, and enslave
them. So when men came to kill, they found themselves
helpless slaves of their own desires. As you do now.'
She faced him again. 'Don't you, Mr Healey?'

The question snapped him back to a semblance of
coherence. 'I – I – uh, no –'

She made a soft murmuring sound of laughter that
caressed him. 'No?' She extended her right hand to his
groin and lightly brushed her fingertips along the
underside of his scrotum, before trailing the sensation
along the base of his member.

Mark closed his eyes and tried to fill his thoughts
with unerotic themes, attempting to distract himself as
she gently stroked and fondled his penis. The futility of
this strategy became immediately evident when Seska
drew even closer, trilling and stroking his face and hair
with her other hand. And once her musk further
invaded his nostrils, already somehow heightened by
the incense burning around him, his resistance was
entirely broken down, his cock rapidly stiffening in her
grip. Having won the battle to get his organ to respond

to her touch, Seska began to sculpt it, to stimulate it to grow in the shape and direction she desired, until it jutted straight out.

'Is that the best you can do, Mr Healey?' she murmured in his ear, her other hand clasping him by the shoulder, pinching him slightly near his collar-bone. Shaking and tongue-tied, he tried to muster a reply, but instead she continued, 'Get on your knees.'

He swayed, trying to reach out and steady himself on her arm, but she twisted her grip on him and gently but firmly forced him down, until his eyes were level with her groin. Her musk here was stronger, her bush almost visible through the silk.

With one hand Seska took hold of Mark's hair, and with the other she drew aside the front of her gown, revealing her sex, the trimmed, fine hair.

'Breathe deeply, Mark Healey, and understand why Bastet was the goddess of perfumes . . .' And she pressed his face into her sex.

He obeyed, and his head spun as he drank in her scent at the source, feeling the heat of her on his face, his nose pressing against the hard bud of her clitoris. Seska moved slightly, parting her legs, almost as if she would straddle his face. Mark's breathing quickened, his cock stiffening further. He'd felt aroused like this before, with Kami, but never to such a degree, and he couldn't figure out why. With the helplessness came mortification, at betraying Kami in this way, at doing something so intimate in front of complete strangers. But he found his chagrin locked away, present but unfelt, as if in a glass box.

Seska raised her right leg and set it upon Mark's left shoulder, leaning in and cambering Mark slightly backwards, so that his mouth and nose gained a more complete access to her sex.

'Now taste me, Mark Healey. Drink from the well of your new mistress.'

And he did, bonding his mouth and lips to her tempting hot centre, his tongue greedily probing her damp, needy furnace as he endeavoured to match the rhythm of her pulsing groin, feeling her strong, hot thighs around his head, unable to form coherent thoughts, lost to the deed.

Seska then withdrew, standing before him triumphantly, her voice suddenly sharp, demanding. 'Get on your back.'

He did, the furs beneath him making his now-sensitised skin tingle, his penis pointing upwards, pre-come glistening on the head.

Nearby, someone began beating a skin drum, and Seska drew closer, to stand over his groin, then slowly squatted down, leaning forwards easily until her hair hung like Spanish moss over his face, and he felt the heat from her pussy on him again, just centimetres away from his aching cock.

Her gaze captured his, and her voice seemed like a whisper, though he knew it was loud enough for the others in the room to hear it. 'From this night onwards, you will belong to Bastet, through me, her chosen agent. You will obey my every command, not out of fear, but adoration, for you will find no lover, no drug, and no god or experience as fulfilling, as satisfying as that which you will feel with me. And you will find yourself counting the days, the hours, until the next rise of the full moon, until the next meeting, when I reward all my acolytes for their devotion.'

And now Seska leaned in still further, taking him by the wrists and pinning them down over his head, her sex still tantalisingly close, her tail flicking across his thighs. She exerted total mastery over his body, and flicked her tongue across his lips, making him shudder and squirm in her grasp, as she asked again, 'Who do you serve?'

Almost angrily now, Mark glared at her and snarled, 'You! You!'

Seska smiled beatifically down at him. 'Of course you do.'

And swallowed his cock in her sex.

Mark gasped and moaned shamelessly as the hot, sweet, wet flesh wrapped itself around his member, taking him into her body until her weight was fully upon him, pinning him onto the ground.

Somewhere nearby, an engine of voices, growling deeply, the acolytes tightening the circle around them, joined the drumbeat.

'And now,' Seska informed him, 'let us complete your baptism.' She squeezed her thighs around his captive legs, bucking her hips on top of him, fucking him at a slow yet relentless pace timed with the drumbeat, a deliberate rhythm designed to maximise her domination and his submission. Mark's hips tried to thrust up, to increase the pace, but Seska's steely legs held him at her mercy.

And then she began pouncing on his neck with her mouth, nipping and biting him here and there: behind the ear, at the shoulder, over one pectoral muscle, the pain quickly eclipsed by other sensations, her growls like venom, coursing into his bloodstream.

The tempo increased as she battered him with her hips, pulling him inside her with unbridled sexual abandon, whipping herself and Mark towards orgasm. She clawed at him and cried out, as white-hot bliss shot through him.

Bliss – and then pain, a pain that made him twist and pass out . . .

12

Kami's chambers were deep within the mountain, but vents still bridged to the outside and caressed the air within in whispers that fluttered the surrounding canopies, offering the illusion of the nomadic tent life that had once been typical for the Pride. Within were scattered pillows, furs, quilts, and chests and shelves filled with the scrolls and artefacts that were the instruments of her trade.

With furs blanketing her from neck to tail, Kami stretched out and wondered what time it was, knowing human time meant nothing here. There were events, meals, seasons, there were all hungers to be sated when they could be, but there was little use for calendars and clocks, except when studying history. And very few did that.

She opened her eyes and lifted her head to look at her unwanted companion: the handmaiden, Ankhesen. 'Why are you here?'

The younger female kept low, indicating an adjacent tray of bread, fruits and honey. 'You must be hungry.'

She was, and sat up and helped herself, nodding to Ankhesen. 'Have some.' When the female just shook her head, staring unabashedly, Kami asked, 'Why don't you take a photo? It'll last longer.'

The female blinked back. 'What's a photo?'

Kami forced herself not to scowl. She'd never realised just how sequestered from humans and human affairs her people were, until she escaped. Even then she'd found herself woefully unprepared for many aspects of outside life. Her encounter with Janeane, and their subsequent bonding, had helped her immeasurably.

Kami ate, dressed and left the handmaiden behind, hissing when she attempted to follow. Kami emerged into the Cross, one of the larger communal areas, an intersection leading to a dozen different tunnels or chambers. It was quiet, even for the Pridelands; varied sleeping patterns and the generally languid, solitary nature of Pride members alone could not account for the stillness.

Males and females, never together, appeared at the Cross, on their way to somewhere else. Kami knew them all, of course – her community could hardly match the human ones she'd known for numbers – but they reacted to her like a stranger.

The males, especially. The hostility some directed towards her was brazen enough to give her pause. But not enough to intimidate her.

She had to confront it.

The Forum was a large, tiered enclosure around a bowled dip in the floor, with rafters of sunlight from ceiling vents, reflected and directed by sets of polished brass disks in strategic places.

When Kami entered the male environment, all eyes were on the struggle occurring on one of the lower tiers: two naked males, grunting and grappling, clawing and biting, encouraged by the spectators.

Kami stood at one of the entrances, watched and soon realised it was no play fight, no training session or exercise. And it wasn't quick either, to judge from the many scratches and cuts covering both combatants, or the heavy scents of sweat and fury in the air.

A moment's scrutiny allowed her to identify the

fighters: Teth, one of the glass-makers, and Ekos, one of the older males who tended the livestock on the surface. Teth was relatively gentle, a good trait for his occupation, and one that had made him memorable to Kami those times when they had mated. Now she saw none of that gentleness in the figure before her, nor in Ekos, who used to make her laugh when she was a child.

Ekos took a swipe at Teth, sending him reeling to the ground, then was upon him, at his throat . . .

'*No!*'

Scores of eyes turned as one on Kami, who then asked, 'Why are you fighting?'

'What does it concern you, ape lover?' taunted a familiar voice from above.

Kami glanced up at the top of a tier, to the crouching figure of Zeel, who leaned over the edge before half-leaping to the floor. He glared at the combatants, who withdrew to nurse their wounds, then returned his attention to Kami. 'Well? As unworthy as we are to even breathe the same air as your regal self –'

'Shut up, Zeel, I don't deserve that.'

'How true.' He was clad in a fine black kilt in a tripartite pattern, with a single wide gold baldric running from his right collar-bone to his left hip, and gold armlets – a typical First Male's outfit, Kami realised – and moved with the confidence of a First, conscious of those watching him. 'You do not even deserve the pretence of respect.'

'Oh, please.' But she felt the reactions of those around her in the crowd. Things *had* changed since her departure, when Zeel had been little more than a malcontent, race-proud to the extreme but with little support. Keeping focused on Zeel, ignoring the hostility around her, she replied, 'I came to talk to you, to all of you, to find out why this is happening to us –'

'Us?' Zeel let out a harsh sound. 'There is no "us"! You're Varis's toy now!' The anger in the crowd grew almost palpable, and Zeel fed on it, drawing closer to Kami. 'He thinks nothing for us! He has a new mate now, so the rest of us can rot!'

Kami stiffened, suppressing her instinct for fight or flight, believing – hoping, really – her new special status would protect her. And she found herself in the hitherto unexpected position of defending the Firsts' actions. 'That's not true – it is his right –'

'Is that what you believe? Why you ran?' Zeel asked, his expression speaking volumes about his own opinion. He spoke more to those listening than to her. 'Perhaps we should follow Varis' lead? Get ourselves some chains and take our females by force?'

His tone was mocking, facetious, but there was enough agreement around him to make Kami think that maybe the unthinkable had been whispered here, more than once. And it frightened her; not that she would show it to the likes of them. 'Such an act would be suicidal for our people, Zeel, and you know it.'

But Zeel remained defiant. 'Perhaps you would see *us* in chains, then? Is that what your time among men taught you?'

Kami glared back, but recognised his attempt to distract her, and refused to take the bait. 'You're all in chains already; you just don't see them. As for what I learned among men, perhaps you should ask your friend Djaben that? Or hasn't he told you what I gave him? Of course he did; males gossip incessantly.' She looked to the others. 'And did it shock you? About where I put my hands? My mouth?' She laughed now. 'For all your derision of humans, they can do things that would make you writhe with bliss –'

'Filth!'

The tension in the crowd reached breaking point, and she drew out her claws.

But then the spell broke as everyone reacted to the rapidly approaching presence from the tunnel mouth. Kami turned with the others to see the crowd of males being savagely cut down the centre like a till through soft earth, and the enraged figure of Varis ploughed through towards her, teeth bared, eyes narrowed. 'Kami! Are you all right?'

She was confused, then understood his anger and confusion; if what she had seen and learned was true, she was the first female to have entered the males' grounds in a long while. 'Yes, yes, of course I am.'

'Then why are you here?' he demanded, eyes glaring from her to Zeel.

The younger male took a step back and indicated Kami. 'You should never have brought this corruptive influence back from her ape lovers, Varis!'

The First Male grunted, and his frame, already large and powerful, seemed to inflate. 'Are you challenging me, Zeel? Finally, openly?'

Kami stepped back immediately, as did the males around her; if the challenge was given, and taken, they would need space. And unlike before, with the fight Kami had witnessed, this one would not stop until one of them was dead. But she sensed that Zeel would not, at least just now, make the challenge.

And she was right; the younger male dropped his glare to the floor. 'I do not challenge.' He steeled himself visibly for the traditional response he had to make for his show of disrespect, and dropped to all fours, shoulders close to the ground, his voice taut with humiliation. 'I . . . accept your authority.'

'Of course you do.' Varis glanced with challenging eyes at the other males, then walked over, reached out and grasped Kami's forearm. 'Come.'

She followed without protest until they were alone in the tunnel. 'You can let go now.'

He did, after a moment, and practically flung her ahead of him, as if wanting to keep an eye on her. 'Stay away from the males. You're not safe.'

No one is, she thought to herself. They kept walking, Kami still ahead of him. 'Zeel could make a challenge soon. Some female will be ambitious enough to swallow their self-respect and take his seed.'

'But she will not conceive. None of us will.'

She stopped and faced him, unable to believe what she'd just heard. 'What did you say?'

Varis looked regretful of his admission, but only for a moment. 'None of us can conceive any more together.'

'How – how do you know this?'

'That I know must suffice for you. For all of you.'

She believed him. Stunned, she glanced around needlessly, as if afraid someone else might hear. 'Then ... we're doomed?'

'Perhaps. Perhaps not. Time is required.'

'Time? But we –' Then she understood. 'Seska knows of this. You assigned her to find a cure? A wise move; human medicine is far in advance of ours.'

The First Male merely grunted in reply.

Kami's features darkened with realisation. 'You knew *before* my return. And yet you continue this farce of taking me to bear your child!'

'For what it's worth, Mia took it upon herself to bring you back here. But now that you *are* here, we will not embarrass her further by refusing to follow the Behest.' He tensed.

Kami sensed this, and understood the reason: his

markings were flared, his tail twitching, and if that hadn't been enough to tell her the confrontation with Zeel had aroused him, the front of his kilt confirmed it.

It was obvious, but Kami still wanted to hear him say it. 'What do you want?'

Varis breathed heavily. 'You. In the Lair. Now.' A moment of ire overtook him. 'And this time silent about your human lover.'

Kami led the way silently, and remained silent as she took her place on all fours on the ground. There were a few males around, eating or talking, but now their attention was drawn to Kami on her hands and knees, tail risen from the folds of her dress, as she focused on some small insects scrabbling in the grass before her. She remained fully aware of the First Male kneeling behind her and opening his kilt, freeing his cock to find its way between her cheeks, as he gripped her by the hips, making Kami move to accommodate his entry.

No human foreplay, not even the Pride grooming that could be relaxing, pleasing; it would be Varis reclaiming what was his, or at least what he thought was his. It would be rough on her, if she hadn't been aroused by her handling of Zeel, so she pictured Mark once more, Mark's hands and cock and lips, his scent and voice, soothing and arousing and reassuring her in equal measures. They were back in her bedroom now, together, intimate, untroubled by anything or anyone . . .

When Varis came, he remained motionless, voiceless, prompting Kami to glance behind her and snarl, 'Get out of me.'

He did, then rose and straightened his clothes, staring down at her. 'Stay away from the males. I don't want to see you hurt.'

She curled up against a rock and glowered up at him. 'Fuck off.'

He did. After a while she rose in turn, straightened herself up and departed, having some answers and seeking others.

'Kami?'

She turned to face Tameri, the Healer she'd last seen in Kahotep's chamber. Tameri reached out a hand. 'Come.'

'Uh, now isn't –'

The hand, and offer, remained outstretched.

Kami took both.

The Arch was a large enclosure rising and narrowing to a series of rafter-like structures, seemingly further bolstered by shafts of light from one side of the roof-top, and spindles and webs of canopies and banners that fluttered from high, gentle breezes. From here one gained access to the underground pools where the Pride bred fish.

Kami noted the females standing guard at the entrance to the Arch, wary and hostile until they had identified the females – or, at least, had identified those approaching as female. When she stepped into the Arch, she saw the females assembled as the males had been, but languishing on furs and cushions, sleeping or grooming themselves, or each other; there was no aggression as there had been with the males, but there was tension, stress. She also noticed the meats sizzling on metal poles stacked over fires, and casks of water filling up from veins opened up in the walls, further proof of their extended stay here.

The females looked up on their arrival, many rising and drawing close with undisguised awe, their voices a keen caress on her ears as they surrounded Tameri and

Kami, touching her as if she were some human celebrity encircled by fans.

It baffled Kami, and unnerved her, raising her hackles, and she looked at Tameri. 'What is this about?'

The female smiled. 'It's about you.'

'So I gathered.' She swatted at some hands touching her. 'Why?'

Tameri led her to the nearest collection of furs, and prompted her to recline as others joined her, taking places around her. Tameri reached up and stroked Kami's hair. 'Just relax. You have been through so much, my sister. Let us take care of you.'

'Yes,' agreed the female at Kami's other side: Ankhesen, obviously not as loyal as Mia believed, stroked Kami's face gently then moved her hands, down to Kami's shoulders. 'And you have so much to teach us.'

'Teach you?' She felt herself relaxing, responding to the attention, their collective concern – and curiosity – an almost palpable swaddling, stimulating influence. 'I'm no teacher.'

'You can be,' Tameri assured her, her hand slipping down to caress the soft patch between Kami's breasts. 'You *can* teach.'

The voices seemed distant, and she felt both detached from and linked to her body, her breasts now aching, her nipples now growing hard. It was someone else's thighs parting, slightly, beneath her. It was someone else's body responding to the caresses.

'Ssh . . .' Tameri slipped her hand under the fabric of Kami's dress. 'Just relax. You're with those who truly care about you now.'

'Care about you,' Ankhesen echoed, 'and love you.' The younger female's long, slender fingers reached Kami's pubic thatch and began to massage her mound.

Kami parted her thighs wider instinctively, offering easier access. She felt like she was dreaming, floating in a bath, awash with sensuality, Tameri's hand stroking her breasts while other hands stroked her legs. The thought of being the centre of attention, of affection, aroused as much as relaxed her.

Heartbeats later, Ankhesen's finger probed into the sensitive, wet pocket of Kami's sex, creating a strong but pleasurable sensation as it slowly moved around inside, discovering the softness of the smooth velvet walls.

Kami yielded to the touch, her body limp as if bound, even as her mind acknowledged the unprecedented actions; Pride members, especially females, never performed such acts. Or at least, never had in the past.

She opened her eyes once when Tameri bent down and pressed her mouth against Kami's, invading it with her tongue. Then she closed her eyes again, relishing the sensations of Tameri's tongue caressing her lips in a snakelike movement. The females drew closer, Ankhesen's fingers still moving inside her, Tameri's hands at the sides of Kami's face, tenderly brushing her cheeks and toying with the softness of her hair as they gazed at each other for a few brief moments. Waves of gooseflesh rippled over Kami, the stiff tips of her nipples tingling even harder and stabbing into the material above them.

Tameri's hand returned to Kami's breasts, her fingers circling the nipples, tugging at the hard nubs. Her palms climbed the sloped curves, kneading the warm flesh. Below, Ankhesen's thumb teased Kami's clit, the finger buried in Kami's pussy twitching like a cock.

Suddenly Tameri's mouth dropped down and captured one of Kami's stiff little buds, sucking and pulling at the nipple until she moaned and jerked. Then Tameri's teeth bit lightly into the button seized by her lips. Fire flamed through the aching nipple, but the mouth abruptly retreated and then attacked the sister button of flesh. Kami groaned and shivered as her desire grew.

Then Ankhesen leaned in to the side of Kami's head, her whispered voice suffused with a curiosity that could no longer be contained. 'Do men do this? Are they like us?'

The question made Kami blink, distracted. 'What?'

Her lips still fixed on one of Kami's nipples, Tameri looked over at Ankhesen and growled in reproach. But around them, other females began asking questions, as if Ankhesen had opened the floodgates. 'You said you had one for a lover; what was he like? Did he stroke and kiss you like this?'

'What did he smell like?' asked another.

'Tell us about the food,' asked a third.

'And the clothing.'

'Do they really keep their females in chains?'

'How can you tell what they're feeling without tails?'

Tameri withdrew from Kami's breasts and rose up into a kneeling position. 'Enough!' They went silent, their beseeching hands withdrawn. Tameri smiled down at Kami and resumed stroking her breasts. 'Forgive their eagerness to know of the outside.'

Kami stopped her, the spell broken. 'They never showed much interest before.'

'We were content before.' Ankhesen leaned in closer again, stroking Kami's lower belly. 'We were blind.'

'Blind to what we could have,' Tameri followed. 'What we *should* have.'

'Should have?' But with a cold dread Kami knew what she meant.

And if she hadn't, Tameri was voicing it already. 'On her last visit, when she helped you escape, Seska showed me what our bodies can offer us, showed me the unfairness of our taboos. And in doing so, she also showed me how little our males care for us.'

'They see us as nothing,' a female just out of sight added. 'They give us nothing.'

'Even their seed is nothing,' said another. 'We near the end of our Season, and we remain barren.'

'But the way you spoke, about your man,' Tameri continued. 'He sounded wonderful.'

'He – he was.' Kami swallowed, her mind befuddled, thoughts of Mark and Seska mingling with the sensations she was receiving. '*Is.*'

'The world is full of men,' Ankhesen murmured, punctuating her words with kisses on Kami's belly. 'Men who can give us what we want.'

'You can guide us to these men,' Tameri whispered. 'Lead us.'

Lead? The word remained cold, impossible to ignore in her brain, sobering her further. She pushed Ankhensen away. 'The Firsts, the males, won't let you go.'

The other female sneered. 'Let them – let anyone – try to stop us.' The cries of agreement from the others were almost staggering.

Kami shook her head, taking in too much. 'No. It's too dangerous –'

'Better to die out there than live like this,' Ankhesen declared, inadvertently raising anxiety around her.

'No one will die,' Tameri sought to assure everyone. 'Kami will teach us what we need to know.'

'No!' Kami sat up now, and pushed everyone aside. 'You can't go out there! Most of you don't even know a portion of any human language, let alone the laws and customs. And what about our people? They'll die as a race.'

Tameri's face hardened. 'We're dying already. Do the

Firsts really think that their plan to make you Second would return us to our former places?'

Ankhesen drew closer. 'With men like yours –'

'My man ... was one man. A rare man. Before him, there had been many others, little different to our own males –'

'Then we'll be discriminating,' Tameri insisted, her confusion at Kami's reaction bubbling into impatience. 'There are many out there.'

Kami rose to her feet, drawing herself from their touch. 'No! One or two of us is one thing, but a hundred? The risk of detection is too great; all our lives would be at risk. You don't know how dangerous it can be out there!'

'That didn't stop you leaving,' Tameri snapped, her impatience burning into indignation. 'Stop being self-ish. We'll leave soon and you can lead us, help us, or let us risk it on our own.'

'Come with us,' Ankhesen urged, drawing near again. 'We need you. You can be free again, find your man!'

'Lead us,' Tameri urged, followed by the other females. 'Lead us!'

'*Lead us!*'

13

Mark had been away for the longest time. But he was OK, she had decided. As she would be. They'd keep her here for a while, scare her – some more – then let Mark and her go, unharmed. Yes, that's it, that's what would happen, she decided, as she paced the room like a caged animal, reading the posters repeatedly. At least, when they released her, she would be able to say thank you in their own language.

Seska wouldn't harm her, she was certain.

That certainty lasted almost a minute, and only because it was bolstered by self-delusion.

She sweated, starting at every little noise outside, and prayed to no particular deity – she couldn't afford to be fussy at this point. She cursed Mark and Kami for getting her into this situation, thought about her family and almost missed them, then worked on a plan to break the light bulb and trick the males outside the room.

But it would be futile, and she knew it; this was no movie, despite the presence of creatures straight out of one. Still, despite the circumstances, she couldn't help but marvel at their nature, their very existence. Marvel – and hunger for their touch.

This was so totally insane. But seeing them, and hearing more about them from Mark, had augmented her hunger. She wanted more. She wanted to touch those incredible, oh-so-sexy tails.

Janeane knew what was in store for her, really. She

was no naive child. And with that she had an idea about how to escape her fate . . .

She spun in place as the door opened and one of the males entered, staring at her. 'Pretty.'

Janeane started at the voice, dry and rough like leaves, and watched him draw near. He was the tallest, most solidly built figure she had ever seen, Pride or human: two metres in height, perhaps two hundred kilos in muscle and attitude, coal-black shoulder-length hair tied back, aquiline nose, narrow chin. Dark curly hair clumped in a diamond on his chest, fighting for attention with bruises and scars both young and old, as well as the tracks of dark spots endemic to all the Pride. He wore a simple purple loincloth that almost reached his knees, and allowed his tail freedom. He approached, and said something in an unfamiliar language.

Janeane just stood there, fighting down her fear. 'Sorry, I don't understand.'

He drew closer, and Janeane could more easily smell the musk on him. Then he repeated a word, slowly, as if dealing with an obtuse child, before reaching up and touching his chest. 'Nalo.'

'Ah.' Fear ran through her, and she couldn't help but remember how these two had strong-armed her and Mark only hours ago, and maybe killed Mark since – but she forced such thoughts aside. 'I'm Janeane.' She tapped her chest and repeated it.

He smiled at her. 'Janeane.' It sounded so fluid, when he'd repeated it. Then he nodded to the other one, obviously his brother, alike even down to their markings, who now appeared silently at the doorway. 'Brek.'

'Yeah, you Tarzan, me Jane.'

Nalo smiled back, not suddenly biting off her face, and for the first time she felt like her life wasn't in jeopardy. But she wasn't out of the woods yet. 'Guys, I'd like to stick around and chat, but I have a *dolmus* to catch –'

She had sidestepped around Nalo to leave, in an obviously futile gesture, but he reached out and snagged her black top, his English guttural. 'No go, Janeane.'

Brek drew closer to her now. 'No go, pretty Janeane.'

Janeane swallowed again, and her heart skipped a beat, but she tried to retain a casual air. 'No go? Come on, boys, give me a fucking break. I've had one hell of a day –'

Nalo said something in Pridespeak, then repeated it with a finger to his lips.

Janeane copied it for confirmation. 'Oh, right. Sorry, boys, I can be a bit of a mouth on legs at times. But don't worry. I know when to speak and when to shut up. In fact, I can be quite laconic when I want, not get a peep – hey!'

She yelped when she felt Brek's hand slap her right buttock through her trousers and leave it there, squeezing the cheek with obvious approval. He remained close behind her, sniffing her hair and neck, while Nalo drew in close to her as well, seemingly oblivious to the growing erection behind his kilt. He caught her gaze, and reached up to let his fingertips stroke her cheek and jawline, making her tilt her head back and filling her with warmth. He was purring now, and speaking again, and a part of her tried to divine the meaning, listening to his tone. But her mind seemed to have stalled. 'Guys –' She felt dizzy, and started to move sideways out from between them.

Then Brek suddenly wrapped his arms around hers, pinning them back, and when she began to struggle, he fastened his mouth on her neck, letting her feel his teeth and his growl.

She froze.

Nalo recaptured her attention, stroking her and making soothing sounds, until she relaxed a little. Brek relaxed too, but still held her tightly. Then Nalo moved in on her tightly pursed lips and drew a long, rough tongue along them. Her lips tingled, and she gasped aloud, allowing him to enter her mouth with his tongue and probe inside. Janeane's body surged within its confinement, and she moaned into Nalo's mouth. He pulled back and stared at her with undisguised attraction as his hands descended, his claws slowly, playfully, pulling off the buttons of her blouse, baring her, then he sniffed and licked around her breasts and underarms before lowering himself, his tail flicking excitedly behind him.

Maybe this was the way they killed humans.

Or maybe this was their version of the condemned's last meal.

Either way, Janeane's thighs pressed together instinctively, as if she were afraid she might wet herself, her muscles taut in defiance of the welcoming moistness within her sex. Nalo drew close to her groin and sniffed boldly through her slacks, before looking up and smiling. 'Janeane pretty smell.'

Brek made a grunting sound, his mouth on Janeane's neck but licking and sucking, his erection pressed between her cheeks. She pushed back against it and sighed. Despite herself, she was at least intrigued by the prospect of how different it would be with a Pride male – or two. And yes, she was aroused, acutely so, whether from fear for her life or their musk. Whatever the reason, she licked her lips as she watched Nalo roughly undo her trousers, slipping his thumbs and tugging them along with her knickers down to her thighs, then her knees, then her ankles, before nuzzling at her aching mound, his tongue darting out to pierce her flesh. He was trilling against her, and the vibrations sent shivers through her frame. 'Oh God – how do you guys do this, then? Never had two guys before –'

Brek removed his mouth from her neck and loosened his grip on her arms, and said something to Nalo, who looked back up at him and nodded. Then he said something to Janeane, who was wavering in place, having to fully support herself again, her head spinning, her pussy aching. Nalo said a word to her, then pointed to the floor. At her expression, he frowned, mentally searching for the English equivalent then finding it. 'Display. Display pretty Janeane.'

'Oh, right.' She repeated the word, then started to drop to the floor.

Brek reached out quickly and tugged at her shredded top and bra; she wriggled her shoulders to remove her arms from the sleeves and bra straps and, topless, her trousers and knickers still around her ankles, she dropped to all fours, feeling aroused and vulnerable in equal measure. The males talked between themselves, then Nalo dropped and touched her, pressing down on her upper back to lower her there, parting her feet a bit more and gently slapping one of her cheeks.

And so Janeane learned the Pride female's position of invitation. She felt the cool air on her skin, her labia parted, her moistness and musk seeping out. Playfully, impatiently, she wriggled her arse at them. 'OK, boys, who's first?'

Brek. He unclasped his kilt and cast it aside, his cock erect, flaring, waiting. A male of few words, he dropped to his knees behind her, grunting and slapping her arse as he guided himself into her. She dropped her head into her arms and shifted in place, quickly accommodating him. '*God*!' He filled her up, pumping furiously into her sex with short, rapid bursts. Her breasts shook beneath her with the Pride male's onslaught, and when moans escaped from her they rippled out from deep within. A spasm of pleasure coursed through her, and Brek felt it as he grunted and slapped her on the buttocks again.

Janeane lifted herself up onto her elbows, then her knees, as Brek continued to pump into her. She looked up from under her tousled blonde locks to see Nalo squatting inches away, his own kilt removed, his stiff organ pointed at her. He was murmuring something to her. But she didn't want words. She didn't want him left out. Gasping, she focused on him. 'Nalo, pretty Nalo –' She opened her mouth and offered him her tongue.

He didn't wait, eagerly drawing closer and guiding his shaft into her mouth. Her tongue licked the length of him, tasting him, his salty maleness flooding her senses. She felt Brek tighten his grip on her, and, filled at both ends, taken and taking, she squeezed his shaft and drew out his bullets of come. It was enough to throw her off Nalo's cock, and fall down onto her hands again. She gasped as Brek withdrew, and she collapsed. She heard and felt them move about around her, but she didn't care; she was happy just to lie there for a while.

Suddenly, Janeane felt her legs being spread apart, quickly followed by a tongue on her sex. She looked behind her, excited by the touch: Nalo. He lashed Janeane's dripping pussy with long, slow laps, then worked just the tip of his tongue over her needy clitoris. Janeane groaned heavily as she felt her arousal soaring to orgasm. She couldn't believe the feelings coursing through her body. She had never been this turned on; her mind completely overwhelmed with lust.

Nalo worked his tongue fiercely up and down and in

and out of her, then added his finger, and she thrust herself up to allow him easier access. 'Come on, come on, get your cock in there –'

Nalo chuckled, and after one particularly slow swipe with his tongue along her furrow, he just continued right up and teased the entrance to her rear. Close to her, Brek's cock bobbed, firm again, and as she nestled her upper half against his thigh, she reached up and stroked his shaft, with his growling approval.

Ripples of lust soared through Janeane's body, a fullness that seemed to touch every nerve ending in her, and she arched her back and groaned as an incredible orgasm swept over her. Keeping her fist wrapped tightly around Brek's cock, she panted out her climax, humping her hips back.

Gripping his cock at the base, Nalo eased its head to the opening of Janeane's sex and pushed slightly. Brek stroked her hair as he watched his brother begin to claim his prize. Nalo slowly, carefully, pushed the head into her, filling her up slowly, millimetres at a time. Janeane cried with impatience – bastard! – and tried to wriggle onto it, but Nalo wouldn't move any faster, and started making slow grinding motions.

As Nalo eased further into her, she began to lose herself in the feelings. She humped back onto Nalo's sweet cock, all the while stroking Brek, licking the underside of his shaft as she pumped him, working herself frenziedly back and forth between the two males giving her so much pleasure.

Low moans escaped the brothers' mouths as they fucked her. Nalo straddled Janeane's thighs, gripped her hips tightly and increased his pace. She placed Brek's cock head between her lips and pumped his shaft, using her mouth and throat to milk some remaining come from him.

With a groan, Nalo shot into her. As she felt the spurts of come fill her again, Janeane shuddered from her head to her toes as the most massive orgasm yet roared through her like thunder. She lifted her head from Brek's shaft and cried aloud. Nalo's cock slipped out of Janeane then, and he and his brother sat back and watched as Janeane's body was racked with spasms. It was almost too much for her to bear, and with a gasp she slumped fully onto the cell floor, exhausted.

When she finally revived, Janeane was on the mattress, her clothes still dishevelled. Slowly, wearily, she lifted her head and looked up, starting at the sight of Seska sitting at the table before her, clad in a black silk dressing gown and looking somewhat amused, if as weary as Janeane felt. 'Good morning.'

Janeane scrambled to pull her trousers and knickers back up and close her shirt as best she could. 'What's going on? Where's Mark?'

'Did you enjoy my bodyguards? They spoke highly of your performance.' She leaned back. 'Which could be fortuitous for you.'

Janeane ignored the aches and pains as she helped herself to her unsteady feet. 'I asked you what was going on, bitch –'

Seska moved with a startling swiftness, her hand shooting out and swiping at Janeane's face, never touching her, never meaning to, but making the girl shriek and fall back onto the mattress, allowing Seska to pounce on her and hiss through clenched teeth, 'Know. Your. Place.' Then, after a moment, she calmed down, as if nothing untoward had occurred. 'I *was* prepared to come in here and kill you to protect the secrets of the Pride, once our ceremony was completed.

However, your performance with Brek and Nalo has instead inspired me to ... hire you.'

Janeane's mouth was dry, and her head and body ached; her returning anxiety over her fate only made her feel worse. 'Let me guess: cats need their toys, right?'

Seska smirked. 'Irreverent – but essentially correct. I've kept the boys amused, sated, and if Kami had chosen to return, she would have helped. But now I have you. Well?'

Janeane grunted, helping herself slowly to her feet again. 'Tempting. What's the pay and benefits like?'

'Negotiable – once you've earned my trust.'

Janeane drew closer. 'Tell me, do I get to be just the boys' toy?' She reached out slowly, tentatively, touching Seska's cheek then running her hand back into Seska's hair. 'Because girls can play with me too.'

Seska looked up at her with amusement. 'Is that right?'

'Yeah. And you know it already. I want *you*. You've felt it from me, every time you visited Kami.' She shook her head in disbelief. 'Oh my God, you've said you'd kill me, I know this, and yet – and yet I still want you.' Her face seemed to boil. 'I want to give you pleasure as I gave it to your bodyguards, Seska.'

The older female regarded her, remaining insouciant. 'That's "Mistress Seska".' Seska pulled Janeane down, grinding her mouth against Janeane's, their hot tongues swirling, sliding around each other, Janeane feeling the pronounced canines in Seska's mouth, a lingering reminder of the other's dangerous potential.

Then Seska pulled back with a smack of her lips, remaining deliciously casual, if weary-looking. 'You're still afraid. You'll say anything to stay alive. But there's enough truth in what you say.' She yawned. 'It has been a long and tiring evening. We'll talk tonight, after I deal with Mr Healey.'

Mention of Mark snapped Janeane out of her distractions. 'Mark – is he OK?'

Seska chuckled. 'He's safe. I fear I was just too much for him.'

It was a sudden, sharp twist in his guts that drew Mark out of a restless slumber, making him start and half sit up, in a bed he didn't recognise. 'Wha – I –' He squinted in the strong light filling the room, his mouth tasting like it was papered with tissue. He rose weakly, only to feel strong hands gently stop him, and to hear an unfamiliar voice suggest, 'No, don't, give yourself time.'

Mark squinted; the silhouette that owned the arms focused and cleared into the image of a young Turkish man in his twenties with short, cropped black hair, piercing brown eyes and an affable smile. His English was smooth and cultured. 'Good morning, Mr Healey.'

Mark nodded and settled back again on the pillow, his hands moving subtly under the covers, confirming his nude state. He tensed, trying to study his surroundings as surreptitiously as possible. 'Who are you? And where am I?'

'My name is Haci Guten. Mistress Seska summoned me when you collapsed.'

'Janeane!'

'Pardon?'

'A woman I was with last night – American, blonde – her name is Janeane Wade.'

'I cannot confirm her name, but a woman matching that description was with Seska, at least a few hours ago.'

'Hours? How long have I been out?'

'Nearly twelve hours; it is now mid-morning.'

Mark breathed a sigh of relief, then glanced around again. 'Sorry, did you tell me where I was?'

'You're in one of the living quarters of Ardeth and Seska Fehr. They transported you upstairs after the ceremony.'

Mark blinked, and half sat up again on his elbows. 'Collapsed? What happened to me?'

Haci rose and walked to the far end of the spartan bedroom, where a silver tray sat on a painted cabinet with a matching teapot and ornate ceramic cups. 'You reacted badly to Mistress Seska's touch.' He poured black coffee into two cups, then added cream and generous portions of sugar. 'Or rather, her claws. When aroused to orgasm, female Pride members produce potent endorphins and opiate peptides. They and their males remain immune, but if they bite and scratch humans, they can produce in them feelings of intense arousal, as well as loyalty.'

Mark's hand reached up to his chest and shoulder, touching the fresh scratches. 'The "gift" from Bastet.' He thought of that, and of the other tricks she had employed: applying pressure at various traditional acupuncture points, the incense, the dim light, the drumbeats and chanting . . .

Haci set what was obviously Mark's cup on the bedside table. 'You'll find it extra sweet, but it's necessary – not just because it's Turkish, but because your blood sugar level will be down.'

'I see,' he lied. He didn't reach for it right away, but just stared ahead. It made sense, explained how Seska managed to keep those men devoted to her. 'So why did I react like that?'

Haci sat in a nearby chair and sipped at his own cup, unable to keep from grimacing. 'Still bitter. Anyway, Mistress Seska believes you "overdosed", because of lingering chemicals from Mistress Kami.'

He finally reached out for his coffee, his thoughts just as bitter and strong. Aphrodisiacs, suggestives ... were *those* the reasons behind his feelings for Kami? His devotion, chemically induced? No, he couldn't believe it. 'Are you a Sword member?'

The young man beamed proudly. 'For nearly a year. I am fortunate to have been chosen by Mistress Seska, to use my medical skills in her service. Before her, life was ... colourless. Aimless. Now I have real purpose. We both do.' Haci finished his coffee and set his cup and saucer aside, then straightened the knot in his tie. 'Come, you must dress. She wishes to speak to you.'

'Yes.' Yes, he was still alive, but he seemed little closer to finding Kami, and the Pridelands.

14

Haci led Mark to the second floor of the building – with one of the human bodyguards always near – into a large sitting room of low couches and chairs, a room whose walls and surfaces were filled with photos, pictures and ornaments. It reminded Mark of Seska's gallery office, and he was drawn to the items, unable to resist the lure of history. The wooden floorboards creaked, and somewhere nearby a clock counted the seconds, as he focused on a series of photos of Central American pyramids and stone engravings. 'Why are these in here, with all the Turkish photos?'

Haci drew closer. 'The Pride lived there until the eleventh century, when they returned across the waters to make their home in Anatolia. Utrekh, one of their most renowned First Males, a warrior and scholar, led them. And that one is a stone clock, a representation of the Pride's Seasons, their cycles of fertility. This year is one of those Seasons, in fact.'

Mark's mind took this in, adding it to all the other details he'd been collecting for his search. 'You're obviously an expert.'

Haci beamed. 'Mistress Seska requires us all to learn the history of the children of Bastet.'

Mark took a chance. 'That will include me, too.'

'Of course. And I will be happy to help you.' And the sincerity in his guileless enthusiasm, his ignorance at Mark's now-unbonded state of mind, wracked Mark with guilt.

But he still listened, keen to hear to the tales of the Pride's journeys. Haci didn't quite come out and tell him the location of the Pridelands, but Mark had worked out a general location – central Anatolia, the uneven border between the more populated and touristy western and coastal areas, and the wilder, more dangerous eastern borders with Iraq and Russia.

It would be a process of elimination after that. And he was confident he would succeed, given time.

Then the door opened, and Seska finally strode in, followed by a more welcome sight to Mark's eyes: Janeane. 'Gentlemen, good morning.'

Immediately Haci turned and dropped to all fours, head bowed. Mark quickly followed suit, his heart rate doubling, his mouth drying, his head spinning. The seconds seemed to take forever to pass until Seska spoke once more. 'Rise, gentlemen. Mr Healey, I see you've recovered. Look at me.'

Mark met her gaze; she was standing by the drinks cabinet, pouring herself what looked like a brandy, but smelled of aniseed; she was smartly dressed in a tailored Armani business suit as she had been the other day, only this was a trouser suit rather than a skirt. She was beautiful, undeniably. In the far corner, Janeane stood, silently, her eyes averted, like some Edwardian servant awaiting a summons.

Seska stared at him some more, then, without losing sight of him, motioned to Haci. 'Leave us.' She waited until she heard the door close before continuing, holding the glass up near her head. 'I know what you're doing.'

Mark's pulse trebled now. 'Sorry?'

'I know exactly what you're doing.' She sipped at her drink. 'You're an open book to me, remember that. You're trying to fight the effects of my presence in your blood.'

Mark's pulse slowed again, a little. He swallowed and folded his arms across his chest to keep from wringing his sweaty hands. He *did* feel an attraction to her, but it was coupled with a fear. 'Is it – is it that obvious?'

She smiled smugly. 'Did you know that less than ten per cent of human communication is in words? The majority is in scent, body language, pitch and tone.' She drew closer, sighing as if bored with the subject. 'So, Kami's had her claws in you already; that explains your persistence in finding her. When I'd last talked with her, she'd been all proud that she didn't need to bind you to her will. Obviously, she's reconsidered.' She regarded him more intently. 'What are your feelings for her now?'

The thought that Kami might have influenced him, that she might be as manipulative as Seska, galled and unnerved him. But he would cast it aside until he saw her again. He wanted to reply in such a way as to wipe that smug, arrogant look from Seska's face. Instead, he settled for a simple, 'Confused.'

'Understandable. You will need time to let her influence pass.' She drew even closer to him, smiling some more at his reaction to her proximity. Her voice dropped to a silken whisper. 'And be replaced with mine.'

Mark swallowed again, ignoring the growing erection in his trousers. 'Yours?'

'Yes. You possess strength, intelligence, and adaptability – useful tools for the Swords of Bastet.'

He frowned: this contradicted what she had told him last night about the Swords. He possessed no power or money or influence – and, to his knowledge, neither did Haci. What was their real purpose here? 'And what about Janeane? Is she going to be a Sword as well?'

'No.' She walked around him, her heels clicking on

the polished hardwood floor as if to match the ticking of the unseen clock, to face the woman in question. 'But she will remain here, with you, and serve in another capacity. Won't you, my dear?'

Janeane swallowed, her skin flushed, as she nodded and replied, 'Yes ... Mistress Seska.'

And then Seska leaned in for a kiss, a naked gesture of ownership rather than desire.

Mark could almost feel his friend's mortification, a feeling he shared as well. 'And we'll remain here, as your "guests", and not be allowed to leave, right?'

Seska drew away again. 'And why would you want to leave, Mr Healey? Some Sword members would give their right arms for the opportunity to live here with me.'

He could believe that. 'And Kami?'

'You may see her again, some day. If you don't do something foolish first.'

The door opened, and Ardeth Fehr, clad in a dark-blue military uniform, entered. 'Mistress, we must leave.'

'Yes.' Seska offered a final look to Mark. 'I shall return tonight, Mr Healey. We shall discuss things further, then. In the meantime, both of you learn as much as you can, as quickly as you can.'

Mark said nothing, but simply watched them depart, forcing back that longing he felt for her, then focused on Janeane. 'Hey there.'

She nodded back, then drew closer, wincing.

'What's wrong?'

'Nothing, just used some muscles last night that had cobwebs on them.' She wore a plain black figure-hugging T-shirt, and jeans that normally would have had her barred from entry through the front door. After an awkward moment, they embraced, the awkwardness

171

displaced by the undeniable relief at finding each other still alive. She pulled back. 'I heard you joined Seska's little club, got the secret handshakes and decoder rings and all that.'

He nodded. 'And you?'

'I'm Seska's . . . well, let's just say I'm Seska's.'

He stopped. 'Has she scratched you? Bitten you?'

'No. *She* hasn't, anyway. Why?'

'Apparently, Pride females possess the ability to ensnare humans with their scratches and bites at the point of climax. That's how she keeps Ardeth Fehr and the Swords under control.'

Janeane winced. 'That's what she meant about her influence?' She frowned. 'She mentioned Kami. You don't believe Kami did the same to you, do you?'

Mark left it too long before answering. 'No, of course not –'

Janeane chuckled. 'Déjà vu. Kami had similar thoughts about trusting you, a few days ago.'

'You don't understand –'

'Wanna bet? You think because she has a tail and claws and sees in the dark, that she's all that different from the rest of us? Like you said last night, she's very human.' Now she faced him. 'And I am so fucking envious that she loves you as much as she does.'

He took that in, and swallowed. 'Sorry. As Sophocles said, "Trust dies, but mistrust blossoms."'

'Yeah, well, as De Niro said in *Casino*, "When you love someone, you've gotta trust them, give them the key to everything that's yours. Otherwise, what's the point?"'

Mark smiled, and glanced around once more. 'De Niro, huh?' He returned to the bookcase. 'Who am I to argue with the classics?' He scanned the spines of the large books he found, and selected several of them.

'What's up?'

'Seska will come back tonight to finish what she started. I don't intend to stick around and give her the chance.'

'Or to start with me,' Janeane agreed. 'As fun as it'd be to stay, I know I'd be living on her whim.' When Mark nodded, only seemingly half-listening, she prompted, 'Well?'

He opened one book. 'I've been piecing together clues, from Kami, from Haci, from other things. I'm sure the Pridelands' location is right in front of us.' He frowned. 'Hopefully in some language besides Turkish.'

She drew closer, and provided what sounded like a good translation of the indicated passage, then smiled at him.

And his optimism grew.

They didn't find the answer right away; he'd have been suspicious if they had.

They *did* find it, though.

But they still had to escape the building.

Seska had slipped into a business frame of mind as she strode down the hallway. 'Remind me to see the twins before we depart. Have the checks come through? Is Healey who he says he is?'

'Yes.'

'And the arrangements? The accident reports?'

'Yes,' Fehr repeated, more curtly now.

Seska stopped and faced him, noting the smirk lifting a corner of his mouth. 'Now *that* sounded irritated. What is it?'

'Nothing,' he lied, unable to meet her stare.

She regarded him, sniffed the air around them, and then slipped her fingers under the belt of his trousers and tugged him along another hallway.

'We have that appointment –' he protested.

'We'll meet it.' They entered her bedroom, Seska slipping off her jacket and casting it to an adjacent chair. 'You have your suspicions about Healey?'

Fehr leaned against the door. 'Both of them. They appeared so conveniently –'

'Sometimes food just leaps into one's lap, Ardeth.'

He glared back, the reverence he showed her before others set aside. 'He's a threat.'

'No, Ardeth. He's just a man. Ensnared. I've seen more than my fair share – most of them made by me. Yes, we could kill him, just to be on the safe side. But he *was* Kami's man. And she was my student. Do you understand?'

'Yes,' he muttered.

Seska resisted the impulse to laugh, but instead drew closer to him, wrapping her arms around him, moving in and licking at his cheek. 'I have been neglectful of you of late.' Her hand descended to his crotch. 'Forgive me.'

Fehr's arousal was apparent, despite his attempts at maintaining decorum. 'Please, Seska, there is no need –'

'I disagree,' she purred into his ear. 'There *is* need, and obligation. No, not obligation.' She pulled back and dropped to her knees before him. 'Desire.' Eye-level with his bulge, she reached her hands up to run them along his sides, then opened his trousers and briefs to withdraw his cock, drawing in the sight of the long stem and flaring head, drawing in the familiar scent, before parting her lips and drawing him in.

He groaned above her as she ran her tongue along the rim, tasting, relishing him. With a sucking motion she manipulated the loose skin insulating his dick, drawing it up to the swollen head, and then relieving the pressure, before repeating the cycle. He moaned thickly.

Strange fates indeed, that had led her to this life, this man. Sent into the world of men, with only two males for bodyguards, and sufficient wealth to purchase whatever could not be stolen, she had tracked down and ensnared Ardeth Fehr, a man she was prepared to keep as her High Priest, but found he became so much more.

Not that she trusted him, of course: like all humans, he lacked strength, speed, and cunning. She shouldered her many personal burdens.

He began bucking into her mouth, and then she felt him shoot, a huge spurt of semen striking the back of her throat, then another. She swallowed it all, purring around his helpless column of flesh, then drew back, licking her lips. 'Feel better?'

He nodded, but his face held a multitude of emotions. None of which she was prepared to address now.

No one on the main street was looking up to see the air conditioning unit pulled from its fittings in the window. Or to see the figure peer out, then quickly lower herself into the green canvas awning stretched out over the first-floor gallery windows. Some did stop and stare as the woman eased herself over the edge, dropped and rolled onto the pavement, cursing as a man followed her from the window.

Janeane gritted her teeth. 'Fucking ouch.'

Mark dusted himself off and looked around. 'What was it you said last night? Shut up and take some action? How's this?'

She told him, after they started down the street.

The Fehrs were in the air and halfway to Istanbul when they received the news.

Seska sat in her chair, focused on staying calm, staying in control, not losing it in front of anyone. Not even Ardeth, who knew her well enough to sit beside her and wait. For what seemed like ages, there was only the buzz of the aeroplane's engines.

She barely heard it now, too busy mentally clawing at herself. Stupid, stupid bitch! She shouldn't have been so soft with either of them! 'Put out a clandestine alert. Have them picked up and detained, no outside contact, no calls. Police, border patrols –'

'I know the rest. You think they'll try to leave the country?'

She frowned at his tone. 'You think he'll still try to find the Pridelands?'

Ardeth grunted. '*I* would.'

'That's assuming he knows where to go.' She glanced out at the shifting landscape below. So many decisions, so much burden ... 'Have Brek and Nalo delivered to Birdenbulmak. They are to remain, to watch and wait, but *not* to re-enter the Pridelands. In the unlikely event of Healey and Wade appearing, I want them buried out there.'

His brow furrowed, though not from the casualness of her execution order. 'Just the males? I could arrange an Army patrol –'

'Absolutely not. Any unusual activity in the area will only attract unwanted attention, both from without and within the Pride. I can afford neither.' She stared hard out of the window. 'Especially not now.'

15

'Kami?'

She emerged from the tunnel, squinting into the afternoon light. 'Kahotep.'

He knelt as usual on his perch, never looking away from his view of the surrounding mountains. 'You're not allowed to stand out here.' He paused, patting the rock beside him. 'So you'd better sit down.'

She did, forcing the shivers from her, watching the distant wisps of slate-grey clouds race across the horizon. 'I'm in trouble. I don't know how to reconcile the males and females.'

'I didn't know that was part of your new responsibilities.'

'It isn't. But if someone doesn't do something, and soon, our life here will end, either quickly from the strife, or slowly from the Barrenness.'

'Nothing ends, little one, it merely becomes something else. The cub I once knew who got herself lost in the wilderness during one of her adventures never ended. She simply became an intelligent, admirable female.' He smiled as she leaned into him, wrapping his cloak around her as she wrapped an arm around his. 'And we will not end either. We have come too far.'

Kami closed her eyes. 'I wish I shared your optimism.'

'Give yourself a few more years, and you will.' He grunted. 'But since you're young and therefore impatient, perhaps you should start with the First?'

'Varis knows more than he tells.'

'He is a leader; he *always* knows more than he tells. But I meant Mia. Reach her, and you have a better chance of reaching him.'

'Yes,' she finally conceded, the seed of an idea taking root.

Behind them came hurried, almost frantic sounds, and both turned to watch Djaben burst onto the surface. 'Kam – Kam – Kami! You're here!'

'Well spotted, Djaben, full laurels to you.'

Kahotep chuckled. 'Just like your mother.'

'You mustn't be up here,' the younger male panted, glancing down the tunnel from which he'd emerged. 'If they find out –'

'I remember another cub,' the Gatekeeper said aloud, seemingly to himself, 'who came here and listened to forbidden tales of the human world. I made certain no one ever found out about *him*.'

Djaben paused, then nodded. 'We'd best return, so I can explain how you came up here out of concern for Kahotep. For some reason.'

'Thank you.' She leaned in and kissed Kahotep's cheek. 'And thank *you*.'

He waved off her gratitude, smirking. 'I just want my solitude back, that's all.'

Kami and Djaben were halfway down the tunnel when she stopped and frowned at him with suspicion. 'So what's the price of your discretion? Another blow-job?'

'What's a –?' Then he seemed to grasp the meaning, and flushed with embarrassment. 'Oh, *that*. No. No, as ... pleasurable as that was, I would rather you focused on helping all of us.'

'What do you mean?'

'I mean you can help make things better between the males and females.'

'What, the way things were?'

'Not if they weren't right. Do whatever it takes.'

'Me?'

'If not you, who else?'

He left her at a crossroads.

Who else indeed?

The First Female glided down the tunnel towards Kami's chambers, curious and suspicious about the invitation passed to her.

She caught the scents of jasmine and honey and cooked rabbit as she slipped between the door curtains. There was Kami, reclining at a low table, setting up the board and long cylindrical playing pieces for a game of Senet, the game first played by the human pharaohs millennia ago, and kept alive by the Pride ever since. Nearby, Tameri was at the hearth, removing a cooking stick from the flames and working the cubes of charred meat onto a plate. Both females wore simple lounging tunics, and on seeing Mia, both looked up, Tameri bowing slightly. 'Respected.'

Mia glared at Tameri. 'What is this?'

Kami smiled. 'This is what the humans would call a "Girls' Night In". We have food, we have honey wine, and we have games – and of course, each other's company.'

Mia let off a noise. 'That last is a dubious pleasure.'

Tameri carried the plate of meat and a cup over to the First. 'I know you see me as the leader of the females. But I merely voice their concerns.'

'You mean you have no courage to lead?'

'Better for a leader to have wisdom than courage –'

'Girls,' Kami interjected, glancing at both females in turn. She calmed herself down, stretched back and idly played with her tail.

Tameri offered the wine and food again. After a moment, Mia accepted both as she reclined on the pillows at the game opposite Kami. 'I cannot ignore your efforts.' Still, she glared as Tameri sat between them at one side of the table. 'Who shall roll first?'

Kami handed her the dice sticks. 'Age before beauty.'

Mia narrowed her gaze, but accepted the sticks. 'Another human expression? Does it never end?' She shook the sticks and dropped them, but none came up with the number needed for her to start. She reached for her cup and drank. 'Have they corrupted you so thoroughly?'

Kami took the sticks for her turn. 'I was trained to know and understand them. Many of us studied their languages, albeit for practical purposes.' She dropped her sticks, scored a one, and moved a scarab piece. 'But we have much more to learn.'

Mia reached for more meat, finding herself hungrier than expected. 'Are we here to speak of the apes, or of ourselves?'

'I doubt there's much difference between us,' Tameri offered.

'Heresy!' Mia snapped, shaking her head.

'Not so.' Kami moved her pieces along in the symbolic march towards the afterlife. 'We have potential unrealised, unrealised by our own ignorance.'

'What has – has this –' Mia frowned to herself, at how muddled her thoughts had grown. 'You stir up – stir up trouble –' She tried to focus on the other two females, who were watching her intently, and understood. 'What have – poisoned me –'

'No,' Tameri assured her, setting aside her untouched cup. 'A diluted version of the drug I provided for you to abduct Kami. Just enough to incapacitate you –'

With a growl Mia rose and lunged for the Healer,

knocking them both over into some pillows. Kami rose to assist Tameri, only to find it unnecessary; the attack was all Mia had in her, and she now lay like a dead-weight on top of Tameri.

'Is she all right?'

'Yes,' Tameri snapped, obviously embarrassed at being taken by surprise. Together she and Kami rolled Mia onto her back.

The First was breathing roughly, and her limbs were limp, as if having completed a gruelling marathon. But her face remained animated with rage and she hissed through bared, clenched teeth. 'Count – the last moments – of your lives – on the fingers – of one hand –'

'Perhaps,' Kami conceded, drawing closer. 'Perhaps not.'

Mia whispered again, but whatever she said was lost when the other females lifted her up and carried her over to Kami's bed, then set her down gently on the huge pillows and pulled the diaphanous curtains around them.

Tameri looked up. 'The drug won't last long.'

Kami nodded. 'Let's get in position.'

Tameri squatted at Mia's ankles and waited for Kami to get behind Mia's head. Kami cradled it in her lap and pinned the First's arms behind her.

Then Tameri regarded Mia, idly playing with the end of Mia's sash. 'You've brought this upon yourself. You're as stubborn as Varis –'

'Just – just kill me –' Mia snarled hoarsely.

'Kill?' Tameri rose and straddled Mia around the waist, pinning her lower half down. She caught Mia's murderous gaze before lowering her head, her mouth, and her teeth to Mia's bared throat . . .

. . . And began kissing and licking Mia's soft, downy

skin, feeling the blood pumping rapidly just below the surface, tasting her scent. Mia frowned, growled, 'Get get off me –' and started struggling weakly.

This stopped with Kami's claws at Mia's throat, and Kami's murmur, 'Just stay still, and silent.'

Mia obeyed as Tameri descended, drawing more of Mia's flesh into view, unravelling the front of her dress to reveal full, round breasts, the nipples dark and puckered and aching for attention.

Tameri glanced up from beneath strands of her hair to see the mortification on the First's face. 'It's wrong to be denied attention, satisfaction. Especially someone as vibrant, as beautiful as you.' Tameri descended to Mia's left breast before the older female could respond, applying gentle sucks and swirls to the nipple and the surrounding skin.

The effect on Mia was immediate and positive, the female squirming as much as her enervated state would allow, making noises that could still have been protests, but ones with weakened conviction. Tameri shifted slightly, freeing one of her hands to stroke and caress the other breast.

Still above their captive, Tameri shifted, her tail thickening and flicking behind her, and she trilled her tongue against the supple flesh of Mia's breast. The three females' collective scents of arousal filled the air. Tameri kissed and nibbled the undercurves of the breast, then moved downwards, over the downy flesh of her belly, finding and teasing her tracks until they engorged with excitement.

She shifted further down, still undressing Mia, and felt the First start at having to undergo this, despite her earlier bliss. Then she lifted the folds of Mia's dress and exposed her sex, a triangle of fine sable, wonderfully scented. She bent down and kissed it.

Above, Mia was arching her head back, baring her throat as Kami's mouth and lips kissed her where Tameri had started before. She was clearly enjoying it, but when she felt Tameri move between her legs, she shook herself out of the spell long enough to look down and croak, 'No – no, you can't –'

Tameri kept her eyes on Mia's as she reached under the First's knees to lift and part the older female's legs, exposing her sex completely. 'Yes. Yes, I can.'

And with that she bent down again to the waiting prize, an exquisite iris of delicately ruffled flesh dotted with moistness, the inner sex a deeper pink, and now Tameri could drink in the sweet and heady fragrance, could watch it pulse with desire, as her own was doing now. And as she peered closer at this wet treasure, she could see the head of Mia's clitoris, protruding from the folds of flesh, tasting the air outside. She could feel the heat radiating from within Mia's body as she drew closer, to finally bury her face into the other female.

Mia moaned and writhed within Kami's renewed grip, as Tameri sought out the tiny shaft she'd seen waiting for her, her lips wrapping around, sending waves of delight strumming through the woman. Tameri's hands reached around to clasp the fleshy buttocks below Mia's tail, holding and kneading them in turn.

Tameri's lips left Mia's clitoris, and her tongue drove a trail down to sample the sweet nectar, before entering the hot, wet, waiting channel. Mia cried aloud and thrashed about, forcing Kami to hold on tighter to keep her from breaking the spell.

Tameri returned to Mia's hard little nub and began sucking on it, no longer content with gentle exploration, having awakened the First's lust. Mia went wild, the cries from her mouth reduced to inarticulate pleas and mewling.

Suddenly Mia's muscles contracted sharply against Tameri's face, and her whole body shook with release; the Healer tried to re-enter her sex, but found a climax-induced resistance.

The three of them remained motionless save for their rapid breathing. Mia was limp, though only from the afterwaves of climax. As for Tameri, she was gazing at Kami with undisguised, unfulfilled lust, obviously just as affected by what they'd done as Kami was. 'Kam –'

'I know.' And Kami wanted nothing more than to satisfy both their needs. But that would have left Mia unattended, free to do anything.

But the First seemed to understand, and made a weak nod of assent, her eyes closed. 'Go ahead –'

Kami needed no further permission, and set Mia's head down gently onto a pillow, before practically leaping over her to fall into Tameri's arms and roll out with her under the bed curtains.

Kami's breath caught as the other female's eyes and hands roamed over her; Tameri cupped one of Kami's breasts, squeezing appreciatively, before peeling open Kami's dress, bowing down and engulfing her nipple in her mouth, sucking fiercely and niblling on it. Kami moaned, biting her lip under Tameri's ministrations.

Kami was conscious of the woman's other hand descending along her belly; she opened her legs in anticipation, and Tameri delved into her hot, puffy sex. Kami cried out, and pushed herself up to meet the other female's thrusts. Her back cambered as Tameri continued her sweet assault, sensations running through Kami like an electric current. 'Get up on me,' she begged.

Tameri quickly flipped over to land on top of Kami, her thighs on either side of Kami's head, then her tongue continued where her fingers had started. Kami opened her eyes and looked up into Tameri's sex, hot and pink and glistening, her clitoris protruding from the folds of flesh encasing it; above her parted cheeks, her tail twitched.

Kami raised her head, drinking in the female's musk, then buried her face into her, darting her tongue into Tameri's wet channel, licking, sucking, finally fastening onto her clitoris, as Tameri had just done to hers. They both squirmed and cried out into each other as their climaxes finally arrived, the circuit complete.

Afterwards, they lay clasped in each other's arms, raining strings of kisses over each other, tasting themselves and each other.

'I – I've –' Mia muttered.

The females glanced up warily. But Mia seemed to have lost her fight, even as she had regained her mobility. She rose to one elbow, her hair and clothes dishevelled, her eyes wide in disbelief. 'I've never ... never felt that way before.'

Kami sighed and disentangled herself from Tameri, then crawled slowly, carefully, towards Mia, not wishing to spook her now. 'I know. It's impossible to describe; you have to feel it.'

'Yes,' Mia agreed dumbly. 'I see now.' She shuddered and fell back, as afterwaves ran through her. She laughed helplessly. 'No wonder the others – you –'

Kami slipped under the curtains and held Mia close, stroking her hair. 'We can't go back to the way things were. We have to teach the males – and ourselves. We can give them such pleasure, too.'

Mia seemed disbelieving of that; or perhaps she was daunted by the prospect ahead of them. 'When you have borne Varis's heir, perhaps –'

'It can't happen. At least, Varis doesn't believe it.'

* * *

Mia returned to her chambers. She wanted a wash, not to clear away the scents and memories of her encounter with the females, but to touch her skin, her body, and not feel the pangs of guilt.

She stripped off and put away her clothes, foregoing preparing her own bath or visiting the communal springs, but just standing in the empty pit and pouring cold water over herself from an adjacent cask. She closed her eyes and let the water fall from the tankard she held over her head, feeling her skin prickle as rivulets snaked down her face and neck, along the curves of her shoulders and between her aching breasts. She did it again and again, feeling alive and alert, as aware of the fine hairs rising on her skin as she was of her nipples hardening and tail thickening with the memory of Kami and Tameri's actions.

Gods, but it had been mind-shattering! Even now, the throbs and thrums between her legs remained strong, insistent, like an echo that never faded. Mia poured water down her front, this time watching the liquid race down her breasts and belly towards her centre, as if drawn to the heat, and she shivered as it touched that furnace of flesh.

She lifted one leg and set her foot on the edge of the bath, pouring water over her legs, then ran her hands over her skin, as if only to sweep away the remaining water. But it was more. She wanted the touch, to be touched again. To touch herself. Kami and Tameri had talked to her some more after she had recovered. Females could touch themselves. And it wasn't dirty, wasn't wrong.

Of its own accord, her hand moved to her mound, to rest there, an innocent gesture, should anyone question – and who would anyway? Her dark thatch, now matted with various types of moisture, parted with her legs.

If she leaned over enough, she could view the pink, wrinkled folds of her sex, glistening with the dirty-milk colour of its own dew, and even glimpse the tip of her clitoris.

Her fingers moved to her nub, satiating it immediately with earnest circular motions, making her mouth gasp like her sex below. Her free hand reached up and roughly kneaded her right breast, making her moan aloud. Images and sensations danced and flirted in her mind's eye, like the twisting, turning colours in a kaleidoscope. The touch of Kami and Tameri, their lips and tongues, watching them pleasure each other ... imagining Varis doing the same to her ...

She heard and scented Varis's approach, and quickly straightened up and reached for her dressing gown, slipping into it while still wet. She cursed the females for introducing her to those forbidden sensations, once tasted, never more to be denied. She cursed herself, a female into her fourth Season, for not having had the knowledge or courage to discover these sensations herself sooner.

And she cursed Varis for interrupting her, even as his presence brought with it opportunity. 'Respected?'

He entered, immediately noticing the change in her. 'What has happened?'

'I ... dined with Kami and Tameri.'

Varis grunted. 'No doubt an enjoyable experience.'

'No doubt.' She walked up to him, sensing his discomfort, determined to overcome it. Her arousal, her need were still strong. 'Varis ... do you remember when you first took me? As your First?'

His face creased with pleasant recollection. 'Yes ... You were beautiful in your inaugural gown.'

She was beside him, her hand on his belly, snaking it around him, her breasts against his arms and chest.

'And so sweet and wet, bent over, receiving you that first time, your hands on my hips ... so masterful ...'

He smiled with the memory. 'Yes ...'

'I only wanted to serve you then.' Her hand moved lower. 'I am still sweet, and wet ...'

Varis returned to the present, pulling back from her. 'Mia, no. I cannot give you my seed now, not until the Second has conceived my child. It is the Behest.'

Frustration marred her features, and she steeled herself. 'No, it is *you*. You know something about the Barrenness, something you've kept from me, from us all. What is it?'

He looked ready to answer. Then he turned away.

Her eyes burned into the back of his head. 'It *is* Kami, isn't it? I don't blame you. She is young, pretty, smooth of face –'

'No! It is the Behest! And it is because something must be seen to be done! Better to chase an uncatchable prey than to lie down and die!'

Mia stormed away, stopping to look at him one more time. 'Maybe we're already the walking dead.'

'Mia, wait –'

She didn't.

16

Mark had been riding for almost twelve hours before he realised that they were being followed.

He wasn't even sure when they had been discovered, such was the level of his fatigue. An hour after they had broken out of the Fehrs' building, he had maxed out his credit card for cash, but not before purchasing train tickets to Istanbul, to hopefully leave a false electronic trail. Then, after buying second-hand clothes and a detailed map, they rode the *dolmus* to Hakkari, the largest town on the border with Eastern Anatolia, watching the terrain change, growing wilder around them, stark hills and vast wheat fields blending subtly with the ochre-coloured soil.

By nightfall, when the moon had drawn across the sky, they were on horses rented from a local at an exorbitant price, travelling through an environment free of traffic and people. More than once, Mark felt like an explorer of an alien world.

No, not explorer. An invader, aware of the potential dangers around him, but still striving forwards. They stopped once for a couple of hours, lit a small fire and huddled together. He and Janeane had grown silent, their unspoken questions remaining unanswered. Was he one hundred per cent certain they would find the Pridelands? No. Did he see a better alternative? No.

After a quick nap and meal, they returned to their steeds, thankful that, with the terrain around them, they had chosen horses rather than a vehicle that would almost certainly have fallen prey to the many cracks and gullies in the landscape. After a few more hours, the moon had dipped into the high, distant grey mountains, leaving the sky a soft cool slate shade, freckled with stars and lightening with the break of dawn. They had left the paths long ago, and were now surrounded by a bleak, bizarre landscape, completing the alien analogy.

Cappadocia. It cut a broad swathe through the central Anatolian plateau, bordered by the Black Sea to the north and the Taurus Mountains to the south, the Euphrates to the east and the salt lakes to the west. Aeons before, volcanoes showered vast quantities of mud, ash and lava during some of the greatest eruptions in history. Upon contact with the air, the debris transformed into soft tuff stone, creating an otherworldly landscape of white stone column chimneys and fretted valleys like a wrinkled, petrified bedspread, a landscape further sculpted by millennia of erosion, and later human habitation.

It was the latter that Mark was most familiar with: the region had been inhabited by many peoples over the centuries, from the Tabal to the Greeks, from the Byzantine Christians to the Seljuks, most carving from the soft stone thousands of churches, monasteries, fortresses, even entire communities. But only the ones on the more accessible edges of the region were visited by tourists, the rest closed off for various reasons, whether because of the danger of Kurdish separatists or criminals, or to preserve the historic areas. And when one considered that the area was just a little smaller in size than Wales, or for Janeane's reference, larger than the states of Maryland or Massachusetts, it seemed less unlikely that a few Pride could hide out here.

The sun had been making itself ready to climb over

the distant mountains when Mark felt the eyes on him, burning into him from behind. He doubted if they were officials, or they would have stopped Janeane and him by now.

'Janeane –' he finally whispered.

She kept her eyes ahead of her. 'I know. We're being watched.'

'You know?'

'Used to go hunting with my Dad in Montana. And until today I've always resented what he taught me. They're not the Turkish authorities, though, are they?'

'I'd say not.' He reined his horse to a stop, Janeane following, and reached for his water bottle on the saddle. 'They may be bandits, or smugglers, and we've ridden into their territory. Or –'

'Or Pride,' she finished, drinking from her own. 'How close are we?'

He blinked ahead, aware that they were facing east, where the sun was about to make an appearance over a wall of rock. 'See that crack in the wall?'

'That's the Pridelands? It wasn't there a moment ago, was it?'

'Optical illusion. You have to be in a certain position to see it. That's the *Birdenbulmak*: the "sudden find", as described in an Ottoman tract. Beyond it is supposed to be a Christian cave town abandoned in the late tenth century – the same time that the Pride were said to have returned from the Americas, coming up from the Mediterranean, through places like Usal. The site does not appear on any modern maps.'

'Great, we're nowhere.' She shuddered. 'They're getting closer.'

Mark tensed. 'What do we do?'

But she kept staring ahead. 'We wait ... wait ...'

He was about to ask what to wait for, when it

literally hit him: sunlight, streaming now over the tops of the mountains before him. He squinted and gritted his teeth, but followed when Janeane snarled, 'Come on!' and kicked her horse into a gallop down the slope, drawing up dirt behind them.

The pretence over now, they rode furiously towards the crack in the mountain, and slowed enough to enter it safely. It was a narrow, winding fissure path barely wide enough to accommodate them on horseback, its walls rising high above them, like hands ready to clasp shut for their trespass. Wind whipped through the channel like wails. Mark, in the rear, kept glancing behind him, but saw nothing, and began to doubt their earlier assessment, perhaps brought on by exhaustion and the events of the last few days.

Suddenly the fissure opened and spat out the riders, leaving them at the mouth of the Valley of the Pridelands.

Janeane stared ahead in awe. 'Woah ...'

Mark felt the same way. The valley, bathed in dawn's early light, was an oasis of willows and poplars, the grounds thickly carpeted with cypresses and scrub brush around a winding, inviting stream that passed through the surrounding mountains. Around the valley, the hills were steep, speckled with black recesses. It was quiet, but for the birdsong and the insects and the gurgle of the stream, and the gentle rustle of the cattle, sheep and goats moving freely about.

It was an arresting, bucolic sight – though Mark had expected to see the ruins of human habitation. All there was now was the archway, a broken but still impressive structure, with a set of weather-beaten, cracked stone lions flanking it, fittingly the only evidence remaining that humans had ever lived here.

'The source of the Pride's name,' he noted, needlessly.

Janeane glanced behind her, guiding her horse forwards. 'Come on, let's get away from here. Even if the Pride aren't here, we might be able to hide in some of the tunnels.'

A futile act, Mark thought, given their pursuers' tracking skills – and he was certain they were Pride, though he was less sure of their origin – but he said nothing as he followed her through the scrub and towards the stream. The ground was soft and silty at the edges of the water, and the horses began to move towards it for a drink; the riders descended, their shoes sinking into the wet footing.

The tall grass rustled, hiding too much.

'What now?' Janeane muttered. 'Leave the horses, climb the slopes –'

Mark cupped his hands around his mouth and called out, '*Kami!*'

Janeane's mouth dropped open. 'Mark, what the hell are you doing?'

'They have to know we're here already, so we have to also let them know we mean no harm. *Kami! It's Mark!*'

'And what about the guys following us, dickhead?'

He hadn't forgotten. But before he could answer, the horses' heads shot up from the water, and they pulled themselves out of the humans' grasps and galloped off, just before two large, powerful figures rushed out from the tall grass like charging rhinos.

Mark barely had time to recognise them as Brek and Nalo, Seska's bodyguards, clad in dark human shirts and trousers, bore down on them.

Janeane let out a yelp, scarcely having time to move a few metres before one of the males pounced on her.

Mark couldn't help her, not immediately, and knew he couldn't run away, and so he stood his ground, hoping for luck.

Luck failed him; the bodyguard, whichever one it was, struck him like a wall of water, nearly knocking the wind out of him before both of them tumbled into the grass and silt, the male ending up on top. Mark looked up at the face, framed by an unfettered sable mane, at those golden eyes, the irises black slits, tapered with the excitement of the hunt – or the imminent kill. His teeth were clenched, and air gushed through them like the exhaust on some powerful engine. His spots were thick and dark; he was enjoying this.

Mark wasn't, and showed his displeasure by throwing silt into the male's eyes, then driving his knee up into his attacker's groin. The male lost his breath and balance with a pitiable cry, and Mark couldn't help but feel sympathy for him, while still driving his fist up at the male's face, connecting badly but sending him to one side and freeing himself to go and help Janeane.

Temporarily. The male, still recovering, clasped onto Mark's left leg and pulled him down again, ready to sink his teeth and claws into it, to cripple Mark before finally killing him.

But he never had the chance. Another figure appeared, moving with astonishing speed to pounce upon the male and rake his spine, making him howl.

Mark freed himself crawled backwards, his eyes on the new arrival, his heart disbelieving.

Kami.

She was fury, unleashed and unfettered, free of any constraints of civilised behaviour, human or Pride. She was a whirlwind of limbs and claws and teeth, a storm, at the heart of which lay an indomitable drive to protect her man, at any cost. The male grappled with her, did his best, but was overwhelmed by the naked ferocity now upon him, until he made pleading noises.

She didn't stop.

Mark pulled back further, recalling the ancient stories of the feline goddesses, the wielders of justice and vengeance and wrath, whose bloodlust was so overpowering it made even the gods fear them, and understood more fully than he had ever done before.

From the corner of his eye, he watched the other male rise from Janeane's prone body, and charge towards the combatants to help his brother. Mark rose as well to intercept him – only for a third male to appear and beat him to it, this one a tall, grey-haired figure in a black kilt and tunic, driving the younger male back to the ground. The bodyguards had youth and size and strength on their side, but were kept down by the older male's disciplined fighting moves and the raw power of Kami's assault.

Mark moved over to Janeane and examined her, finding little more than cuts and the odd bruise. She looked as stunned as Mark felt, neither of them speaking as he helped her to her feet. They watched the scene before them. The grey-haired male had his opponent pinned down, and spoke to Kami, his voice soothing. But Kami didn't seem to hear, or if she did she wasn't listening.

Now Mark stepped forwards. 'Kami?'

The grey-haired male looked at him and spoke in splintered English. 'No, stay back! She won't know you!'

'Yes, she will.' But he motioned for Janeane to stay where she was as he drew closer to Kami, hands outstretched and his voice louder, but not aggressive. 'Kami? It's me, Mark. *Mark.*'

Now she looked up at him, her eyes blazing beneath her dishevelled hair and her mouth open, panting heavily. She was crouched over the bleeding but still breathing form of the male, her clothes torn in the fight and now barely more than rags.

She leaned forwards, cambered, her tail rising behind her, and she looked ready to attack Mark now.

'Human...' the grey-haired male hissed behind him, stepping closer to protect him if necessary.

But Mark ignored him, ignored his heart pounding in his chest for escape, held his arms and hands out unthreateningly and smiled, showing no fear, no aggression, no mistrust. Because he had none; doubts about his love for Kami, about its possible chemical origins, had vanished with the morning dew. 'Kami, it's me, Mark. Remember? Of course you do. I can't believe I've found you again. I just can't believe it ... Everything's going to be all right now, isn't it? Isn't it, Kami?'

He kept saying her name, kept looking into those eyes. She wouldn't hurt him. And if she did, it wouldn't matter. He'd still love her.

And he watched with the others as the fury drained from her as if from an open wound, replaced with a growing well-spring of recognition once more. Her voice was hoarse. 'M – Mark? You came for me? I heard you, heard you, but – but – you came for me?'

'Of course I did. I couldn't go another day without the woman I love.'

The battered male at her feet forgotten, she leaped over him and rushed into Mark's arms, lifting him up and crying with abject relief. Everything would be OK now, he knew it.

There was noise behind them: the other brother who had been beaten down by the grey-haired male was up and racing away.

'Uh, guys?' It was Janeane, looking battered but

relieved. 'I hate to interrupt this reunion, but maybe we should take Brek's lead and skedaddle out of here too?'

'Too late, little one.' It was the older male, sounding regretful as he approached protectively beside her, and nodded towards the grass.

At the other Pride now appearing.

They walked down the corridors, meeting Pride members who regarded the visitors – intruders, Mark corrected himself – with bald fear, or curiosity, or hostility. He ignored the latter to admire the elaborate carvings in the walls and ceilings, the murals of landscapes and animals, the formidable amount of work employed to create and maintain all this. It was a far more spacious, sophisticated living space than any of the hundreds of others made in the region, most of which were little better than holes in the tuff mountains. These people had made this place their home, and he doubted if he would find any human influences remaining.

After some argument from the other Pride that had appeared, and after the battered male, Nalo, had been taken to a Healer, the humans had been escorted to the lair of the older male, Kahotep. He provided Pride clothing: for Mark a black kilt and tunic, for Janeane a thigh-length emerald-green toga, and for Kami a white diaphanous gown. Kami stuck close to Mark and Janeane as Kahotep explained that he and Kami would go to the Court to see the Firsts.

They entered a hall with ornamental pillars and roundels carved into the walls, a large hearth, and banners hanging on the walls. Varis, Mia and Zeel were there, staring at the humans with varying levels of suspicion, but it was Zeel who pre-empted the discussion with the expected diatribe. 'How dare she walk free, after crippling one of our own? And with those *things*, still alive?'

The First Male grunted. 'Nalo raised tooth and claw against my Second; crippling him seems a fair price for such stupidity.' Varis stepped forwards, his eyes still on the new arrivals. 'And they are still alive because *I* desire it. And if that changes, it will be by my desire, too.'

Mia drew closer, too, watching the First Male as much as the newcomers. 'We want to know how and why they're here. Varis wishes to hear it from them himself.'

'Varis doesn't understand English very well,' Kami pointed out.

'There are sufficient numbers of us here who can translate.'

Kami nodded but remained close to the humans as they stepped forwards. 'Varis, our First Male, our leader.'

'Just as you explained.' Mark dropped to all fours, head bowed, copying the gesture of submission he'd learned while under Seska's authority. After a moment, Janeane followed suit.

Varis was taken aback, clearly unprepared for receiving such deference from humans. But he quickly recovered. 'This is the one? The one who was your man?'

Kami breathed in, ready to leap in and protect them. 'Yes. The woman is Janeane, my best friend.'

Varis barely acknowledged the woman. 'Tell him to rise to his knees, look up at me, and tell me why he came here, and how he found us.'

Kami translated. Mark looked up, first at Kami, then at the First Male. 'I came for Kami. We feared for her safety. I found the information while a prisoner of Seska.' He paused, as the Firsts exchanged enigmatic glances, then proceeded. 'I did not come to do harm to your people, Respected, any of them. Nor to give away any knowledge of your existence to the world. I understand the reasons for your caution about humans, having learned much about the persecution and slaughter you have faced from us. For my companion, I ask for mercy. For me, I will accept whatever fate you decide.'

Varis's gaze narrowed; though he did not understand the words, he read the sincerity behind them. And when he heard the translation, he stared at Mark with a piercing intensity. 'You ... are not what I expected.' Varis looked to Kami. 'Inform him that ... I believe him.'

As Kami translated the words, Varis moved over to Janeane, who was also prone. He squatted before her, took her chin in his hand and raised her up to her knees as well, though his expression with her was less harsh than with Mark. 'And why have *you* come, pretty?'

When it was translated, an annoyed Janeane replied by reaching up and slapping his hand away. 'Not to be handled by you, pal.'

'Jan –' Kami admonished.

Behind her, Zeel stepped forwards. 'Behave, ape!'

Varis glared up at him, his face darkening. 'The day I need the likes of you to protect me is the day I turn up my tail and die.' He looked back at the prostrate woman, chuckling. 'She has fire in her blood. Are you sure she's not one of our own kind?' As if to be certain, he pushed her head down again until she almost fell forwards, then reached down and lifted up the back of her toga, gazing at her bare, tailless rear.

'Hey! Asshole!' She worked her way back up and slapped his hand away again, this time with what she hoped was a curse in Pridespeak she'd picked up from her time with the bodyguards.

Mia stepped forwards, though it seemed more to intercede with Varis than with Janeane, as he returned his attention to Kami. 'Inform them that they will never see their world or people again. But they may live among us.'

Still behind them, Zeel gasped. 'What? They invaded our territory! Come to kill us all with their weapons, their devices!'

'What weapons?'

The others turned to the new voice at the entrance to the Court: Djaben, glaring at Zeel. 'We've searched their horses and equipment. They carried no weapons, no devices to track or record our location. And they offered no resistance, made no violent moves.'

Zeel cursed him, but Djaben remained resolute.

The First Male grunted, as if the protest hadn't occurred, and stared at Kami. 'As it has always been, no human who enters the Pridelands can leave alive. The difference now is that they will *remain* alive. But there will be two conditions: one, that they swear fealty to our laws and authority, and act accordingly. And two, that you, Kami-Merysitkheti, swear to act as my Second, willingly.'

'Kami?' Mark prompted, uncomprehending.

Kami's face tightened. Once more, a member of her people was forcing her to give up her freedom in order to save the life of her lover. It would not be easy. Mark would be close, but as Second, she wouldn't be permitted to mate with him. That could be far more intolerable than if he was still hundreds of kilometres away, and safe.

'Kami?' he repeated.

The alternative, however, for both humans, left her no choice. She knelt beside both of them, and took their hands in her own. 'You can both live, but only like us, with our laws, our way of life. And you will never see the outside world again.'

Neither human spoke for a handful of heartbeats, until Mark replied with, 'I had nothing before you. Even if I had the choice of leaving, I don't want to go back to that without you. Yes. Whatever it takes.'

Emotion welled up within her as she embraced him, before looking at Janeane. 'Jan, I'm sorry you've become involved –'

But her friend raised a hand. 'Don't. I got myself into it, and no one's gonna take away the fun I'll have kicking myself about it. Then again, what will I miss? Taxes? Politics? Crap music?' She sighed. 'Well, it could be fun being around people that have not heard all my jokes before . . .'

Kami hugged her, fighting back tears, before rising and turning to Varis. 'They'll do it. And I'll do it.'

But Zeel was determined to have the final strike, sneering at Mark. 'Wise decision, ape. You'll be near Kami again. But you'll never be able to mate.'

Mark looked at Kami. 'Is that true?'

She didn't answer.

It was late in Ankara when Ardeth received the news and delivered it to Seska. 'Brek has been picked up, badly injured. He has reported that Kami and Kahotep attacked them. Healey and Wade were still alive when he last saw them.'

She sat in the darkness. 'No word on Nalo?'

He didn't say. He didn't have to.

She rubbed the bridge of her nose between thumb and forefinger. 'We are all tumbling towards an abyss. Assemble the Swords, get them ready to leave as early as twelve hours.'

'That soon? Some might not be ready.'

'Then they will be tested soon enough.'

17

Mia waited until all had departed the Court before speaking. 'Why let them live?'

Varis moved to the hearth and examined the artefacts above the fire: banners, amulets, relics of past Firsts of note.

Would he be one? Would the actions of the next few days secure his place in history? Or condemn him to infamy? 'Maybe I'm curious. I have never met a human before. They smelled ... interesting.'

'She did, you mean.'

He grunted with some amusement. 'You described them as fireless nonentities, and the men cowards and liars. But he faced me, unafraid.'

'Both did. And that is dangerous.' When he faced her again, she continued, 'If he remains, your authority is threatened, and it is hardly at its strongest now. You'll look even weaker than you already do.'

Varis' face tightened, as much from the sting of her words as the possible truth behind them. 'Then I shall prove otherwise.'

Kami never left the humans alone after escorting them out, with a need for closeness that went beyond affection for them or excitement at their appearance here, one that recognised that, for almost all of her people, their only knowledge of humans were centuries-old stories of persecution. She led them into her chambers and lit oil lamps to allow for their more restricted vision, watching them focus on her again. She blushed. 'Sorry, not used to both of you seeing me as I am.'

'Kami,' Mark began, ignoring her evident desire not to discuss what had happened. 'What did our friend back there mean?

'He's no friend. He –' She stopped as she turned to the doorway, hearing and scenting the arrival of a male, motioning for the others to remain where they were, but relaxing a little when she recognised him.

Djaben stood at the doorway. 'Kami.'

Kami stepped forwards, not taking her eyes off the male. 'Mark, Jan, this is Djaben. He helped Mia capture me.'

'Asshole,' Janeane muttered.

Kami smiled. 'He also defended you in the Court tonight – for which he has my gratitude. And he understands English.'

Janeane's face reddened.

'Food is being prepared in the Lair,' he informed them, unconcerned about the insult. But he did appear hesitant. 'You three are ... expected. I would ... would be honoured to escort you there.'

Kami breathed out. 'Thank you. Maybe we should –'

Then she saw Mark's expression.

There was a pregnant pause among the four of them, broken when Janeane straightened herself up. 'Well, I think I'll push ahead of you two greedy gutsoes, otherwise there'll be nothing left.' She sidled up to Djaben. 'Come on, let's get a table by the window.'

He frowned. 'We have no tables in the Lair. Or windows.' Then he offered the hint of a smile. 'We have some very fine rocks, however.'

Kami and Mark watched them depart, Mark asking, 'Will she be safe?'

She didn't have to answer, both of them knowing

she wouldn't have let Janeane go alone otherwise. 'Mark, I am Varis's Second. It is his right to claim me as his exclusive mate. As his property. As pointless as it apparently is.' She took his hands in her own.

'And that's it? He just takes you? You have no recourse, no rights of your own?'

'This isn't your society, Mark. It can be harsh and unforgiving by human standards.'

Never taking his eyes off her, he indicated their entwined hands. 'Are you sure *this* is allowed?'

Her face tightened. 'Do you think I *want* this? He's not a tenth of the lover, the man, you are. I have fought him since coming here. You and Janeane would be dead by now if I didn't agree to co-operate, to become the dutiful female!' She'd feared this reaction when she'd agreed, feared his male pride would exacerbate matters.

Then his features shifted, and the tension she felt in his body dissipated. 'I'm sorry. I shouldn't have reacted like that, just thinking about myself. Of course it's been gruelling for you. I realise that more now.' He glanced down, embarrassed. 'You know, this was a lot simpler when I first set out: rescue the damsel in distress from the bad guys, be the big, strong hero.'

Her love and affection for him blossomed until she almost cried, but she reined it in and squeezed his hands. 'You still can be, Mark. I don't need you to be strong enough to fight Varis or Zeel or the others to the death. I need you to be strong enough to stand by, no matter what happens, and be there for me afterwards. I need you to be strong enough to remember that what he does means *nothing*, not compared to what we've shared.' She left his hands to hold his face. 'Can you be that strong?'

Mark didn't hesitate. 'Yes.'

Kami's heart skipped several beats. 'Good. Because I

can't do this if you can't.' She pulled him into a kiss, deep and longing and bonding, their arms around each other for dear life.

Then she whispered in his ear. 'Something else: if I've been summoned to the Lair, it's because he wants to take me, publicly.' She tightened her hold on him when he stiffened. 'He's not exactly a master of fore-play; I usually have to work myself up beforehand –'

Still in her embrace, Mark's hand moved down her left side, along her waist and hips, then under the folds of her dress.

Kami frowned. 'Mark?'

'You're beautiful,' he murmured back, breathing in the scent of her hair. 'You smell beautiful. Even more beautiful than when I first saw you.'

Her breath quickened with expectation, her sex throbbing, ignoring her anxieties. 'Mark, if he scents me on you –'

'I'll be careful. Now listen . . .' He shifted in place as his hand found her bush, her swollen mound radiating heat and desire as he pressed his palm against it. Her wetness imprinted itself on his skin as he gently squeezed. 'There's nothing I wouldn't do for you. Nothing I wouldn't be. I love you, Kami-Merysitkheti. You fill my life.'

And with that, his middle finger gently stroked the lips of her sex.

Her arousal surged eagerly at the near-contact, and she pressed her breasts against his bare chest, nipping at his ear, but remaining conscious not to leave bites or scratches on him. She clung more tightly to his frame now, her tail swishing excitedly behind her as his other hand descended and cupped her right cheek, squeezing as if determined to keep her from escaping before he was through with her.

And as he stroked her, he kept talking. 'You wonderful woman, the stuff of my dreams, being here now was so worth going through what I did. To look at you again, hear your voice, hold you so close . . .'

'Harder,' she growled. 'Faster.'

He obliged, his finger now slipping into her, the knuckle of his thumb teasing and pleasing her clit, as his words became ruder, more blatant. Her nipples rubbed against the material of her dress as she pushed herself against him, gasping and cursing and sweating, aware of his own state of arousal but unable to do anything about it.

Kami came with a startled gasp, lurching backwards until Mark lifted the hand cupping her buttock to hold her. The air was thick with her musk, and her cries echoed within the chamber.

Reluctantly she withdrew and crawled to one side, her mouth open, still reeling from the orgasm, but acutely aware of what still lay ahead for her. 'I need to go. You can stay here. Take care of yourself.'

Mark knelt there, the hand he'd used on her resting on his thigh, his body flushed, as if her orgasm had seeped into him through osmosis. He waved off her apologies. 'I'm coming.' Then he smiled. 'I mean, I'm not staying here.' He staggered to his feet, his erection still prominent.

Kami nodded gratefully.

They entered the Lair and looked around. Many males had gathered around the roasting pits, from which came the scent of freshly-killed bull, and there were even females there now, though they remained at the periphery, interested in the sight of Janeane, sitting beside Djaben.

'Go to them,' Kami whispered. 'Make sure she doesn't

panic.' She doubted if Janeane would, but she wanted Mark near Djaben, perhaps the most trustworthy Pride male present.

Varis and Mia were sitting by the rock where he liked to take Kami. The First Male puffed up his chest. 'At last, the Second has dutifully arrived. Approach – both of you.'

Kami froze. 'Both ... Respected? Why do you want Mark?'

'Because I do. Tell him to come and pay respects to his First.'

After a wary moment, Kami said in English, 'Follow, Mark, kneel before Varis the way you did in the Court.'

Guarded, Mark followed, dropping to his knees, his head bowed, shivering as though from the grass and earth beneath him now.

Varis barely looked at him. 'Second, assume your position.'

Kami walked to the rock and lay over it, opening the back of her dress to expose her rear, then looked over at Mark's bowed head, glad he couldn't see ...

Varis took a fistful of Mark's hair and lifted up his head, first to meet the man's eyes then to turn it in Kami's direction. 'Second, tell him to keep watching as you fulfil your obligations.'

Kami felt the words fight with her anger before she could speak. 'Mark, he wants you to –'

'I can guess what he wants.'

Varis released his hold and walked around to the far side of the rock. 'Mia, as Kami will willingly serve now, you may stand by her pet, to ensure his ... obedience.'

Mia started, then nodded and complied; to her credit in Kami's eyes, the First Female was visibly mortified by her mate's actions, even if she remained silent and unresisting.

Varis undid his robes and unclasped his kilt, wearing only the gold bands of his authority. When he knelt behind Kami, he loudly slapped her buttocks, watching Mark's reaction before slowly guiding himself into her.

She gasped, supremely grateful that she was still wet and receptive. She barely registered his huge hands on her hips as he thrust into her, focusing instead on Mark. Mark, who displayed no shame, no embarrassment or anger or anxiety, but only his love, his love and lust and trust, all the things she wanted and needed from him. He brought alive the memories of their hours of intimacy together, not just of sex but of talk and laughter, of both of them opening up to each other in ways they'd never done with anyone else.

And though she'd known it before, Mark's presence was living proof that no one here, not Varis or Mia or Zeel or anyone else, could really own her, or touch her, let alone hurt her. It was as empowering as a surge of adrenaline.

And both lovers remained oblivious to everything outside then, just as Varis did, grunting and slapping into Kami. Until his attention was drawn, with theirs, and everyone else's within the Lair, to the far end of the chamber. There, a gathering of females, scores of them, stood stock still, watching the scene and offering a low, continuous growl of dangerous disapproval. It was a sound that chilled the spines of all who heard it, and those bold, stupid males who had ventured close to the females now retreated without shame.

Varis stopped, withdrew from Kami and rose, clutching his kilt to his groin in an unprecedented display of vulnerability, watching and listening in disbelief, until he worked up the courage to bellow, '*Stop this!*'

Surprisingly, they did, leaving the air empty. The

First Male's eyes scanned the faces of the females, seeking and finding their unwitting leader. 'Tameri! You are a Healer. But this is not healing, this is ... evisceration! We are destroying ourselves with our divisions.'

The female's resolve visibly wavered, either out of vulnerability at being made the centre of attention, or because she was responding to his words.

But then he ruined it. 'Return to us, and it will all be as before.'

The females began to file out.

Varis turned and shot a finger at Kami, who had risen and stood beside Mark. 'Do you see her? You should follow her example!'

Tameri stopped at that, looked at Kami and replied, 'Perhaps we will.'

And left with the others.

The Firsts didn't stay long after that.

But Mia did not follow Varis to their chambers. He called after her at a crossroads. 'Where are you going?'

She stopped and glanced behind her. 'Does it matter to you any longer?'

'Of course it does!' Varis stood, uncomprehending, his heart pounding. He remembered once being told as a cub that Firstship was a burden, not a pleasure. He hadn't truly understood this, not until Seska had brought him the terrible truth about their people's present calamity. And he had carried that truth within him, revealing nothing, not even to his dearest mate, ever since.

It had seemed the proper thing to do tonight: to keep Kami and her man in their place, and demonstrate to the females the futility of their current actions. It should have been logical, even to the likes of them.

Now, he saw it for the folly that it was. 'Mia . . . I was wrong.'

'Yes, you were.' When he turned to her, she continued, her face hard. 'Proud, arrogant idiot. When the females see you taking Kami, they do not see her supporting your rule. They do not see you trying to conceive for the sake of the race. They see you taking her. And no amount of self-delusion can change that.'

'Mia –' He reached out for her as she turned away again, but she hissed at him. His face flushed with anger. 'There are things you don't understand!'

'Nor do I care to any more. You torment them, torment us all, like some cub with a captured hare.' She let out a harsh sound. 'You are pathetic.'

He snarled and swung out. She dodged the swing, extended her claws and dropped into a fighting stance, growling.

But he merely glared at her now. 'If I am so pathetic, then leave. Be sullied no longer by my company.'

Mia rose, and almost seemed to reconsider leaving. Then she slowly backed away.

Kami and Mark sat with Janeane and Djaben; little was said, or eaten. When Kami expressed a desire to be alone with her man, Djaben agreed to watch over Janeane.

It was in her chambers when Kami found her voice. 'You're angry. At me.'

Mark lay on the throws with her, his arm around her, shaking his head slightly. 'No, not you. Varis.'

'Mark, don't –'

He waved off her concerns. 'I'm not going to start trouble, promise.' He breathed in, and seemed to have to force his next words out of him. 'Kami, something else. The scratches ... I learned about them. What they can do.'

She stiffened in his embrace. 'Mark, the enthralment only works if I scratch you when I climax. I always avoided doing that when we were together. Please, believe me –'

He shushed her rising concern. 'I believe you. I *do*.'

'I'm sorry I didn't tell you before, I never would have done it to you –'

'I know, darling.' He swallowed. 'Kami, you need to know something else, too. In order to find you, in order to stay alive, I had to join the Swords.'

'Yes?'

'I – I had to ... have sex with Seska.'

'And?'

He blinked. 'I – I just want you to know that I didn't have any choice –'

'I know, darling.' She smiled, echoing his reassurances. 'You did it to find me, rescue me. You couldn't have done that if you were dead. If you'd chosen honourable fidelity over staying alive, I'd have killed you.'

He smiled back, and shifted; her scent was strong here, like her bedroom back – home? Or was this her home, and that other place a dream? – and he couldn't help but react to her body, pressed against his. His erection made its presence known beneath his kilt, but he ignored it, both of them ignored it now, as they ignored the inevitable anguish that would follow from being reminded of the restrictions. 'So, what now? You go to work, I stay home and keep the cave clean?'

She sat up, resting her chin on his chest as she stared into his eyes. 'First, we sleep. Then later, we go for a bath.' Her nose twitched. 'I love your scent, Mark, but –'

He chuckled. '*But*, I've been on the go for a while without a wash. I get it.'

Life among the Pride was different, Janeane had been assured in her talks with Djaben in the Lair. There were no clocks, no calendars, there were jobs but no wages, no work schedules or timetables or creditors. Everyone did what they did, when required. No one went without food or clothing, medicines or shelter. If someone wanted something, like a special cloak or honey wine, a story or a grooming, one needed only ask. There was time enough, each taking according to his needs, each contributing according to his gifts.

Utopia? Maybe.

It was hardly the case now. The tension here reminded her of the turmoil in her former home, with people living in separate rooms, living separate lives, uneasy silences whenever they met in common areas, the slightest argument escalating to a pitched, dirty battle. It was nasty and bitter. And dangerous for all concerned. She looked at Djaben, still beside her. 'So, what's your story?'

'Story?'

'Yeah.' She drew her knees up to her chest. 'You're helping Kami and us now, but you were one of the ones who kidnapped her.'

He frowned and shifted. 'I was ordered by the Firsts. I know Turkish, and some English –'

'Yeah, but –' She was aware of him waiting and watching her; waiting and watching was something these people seemed to do a lot, reminding her of Kami's toms back home, the way they observed everything with that inscrutability of theirs. 'Tell me, Jay, did you think what your Big Kahuna did was right?'

The male's face darkened, his spots rose and his tail

swished nervously behind him. 'No. But he is First, such is his privilege . . .' His eyes dropped. 'Truth be known, I wish I had never found her. She would be free, with her man, as you would be free. And Mia and Varis would have sought another course of action. I am responsible for all this. No wonder Tameri spurns me now. I am wretched.'

Janeane's anger wilted at his genuine remorse, and she realised she was attacking the wrong target.

Then their attention was drawn by the approach of Mia, who stared hard at Janeane. 'I would have words with you, alone.'

Janeane looked to Djaben. 'Would that be safe?'

'How dare you?' the First Female declared. 'Varis has promised your safety, so long as you obey our laws, live like us!'

Still, Janeane looked at Djaben, who nodded, clearly trying not to get any more involved. She rose and followed Mia down a narrow corridor and into an alcove, or what Janeane assumed was an alcove; it was confined, and pitch black, though perhaps not to the Pride female. Janeane didn't ask: she was determined to show no weakness before Mia. It was eerie and disorienting, however, and she felt more than a trace of fear. Mia was close to her as she hissed, 'Why did Seska send you?'

In the confined space, Janeane became acutely aware of the female's scent, her body heat, the brush of her gown against Janeane's clothes. Janeane swallowed, feeling an unexpected reaction, but focused on the equally unexpected question. 'Seska? She didn't. We had to break out ourselves. Or didn't you hear? Her boys nearly killed us –'

'You expect me to believe that? Plots and machinations are as much second nature as breathing to her.

Were you and the man sent to stir further trouble among us?' She let out a harsh laugh. 'Hardly necessary, it seems.'

Janeane swallowed, her head spinning slightly, either from the events of the past day or from proximity to this woman, who reminded her of Seska, though in different ways. Both females exuded authority, an enticing, exciting and commanding presence, but Seska's was marred with a bitterness, a coldness, that Mia seemed to lack. 'Look, lady, all Mark and I cared about was finding Kami and getting the hell out of here. If you still don't believe me, feel free to bite my ass.'

Janeane felt the female shift in front of her, and heard a change in her voice. 'Maybe you were sent to seduce Varis? Corrupt him with your human ways?'

Now Janeane laughed, and in doing so became aware of Mia's breasts brushing against hers. 'Not that I couldn't give it a try, I've had –'

Mia suddenly pushed her back, up against the smooth stone wall behind her, one hand clamped around but not squeezing Janeane's throat. Mia snarled, '*No!* It is unbearable to see him with Kami, without some ape making things worse!'

Janeane swallowed, fighting to control her pulse, and made no attempt to free herself, but instead reached up through the dark, slowly, between Mia's arms so as not to alarm her. Then she gently touched the female's face and placed her palm flat against her cheek, feeling the heat and skin and muscles beneath. Her voice betrayed some fear, and something else. 'As I was about to say, I've had men, and Pride males. Sometimes I've even enjoyed it. But I much prefer the company of women. Or Pride females. If one attracted me enough.'

Mia moved against her, and Janeane recognised

something there. There was anger, yes, but not genuine malice or intent to harm – and there was definitely a longing. She took a chance, letting the thumb of the hand touching Mia's face swivel out and brush against the female's full lips, feeling them part slightly, feeling the moistness and the breath escape from them and from the nostrils above. Janeane's sex pulsed, and she breathed in the female's scent, which seemed to have grown stronger now. 'And maybe you feel the same way, too.'

'I – I –'

Janeane pushed her thumb in slightly, barely penetrating Mia's mouth, and gasped as the tip of the female's tongue brushed against the tip of her digit; when their bodies swayed, each felt the other's nipples erect and aching against their clothing. It was insane, Janeane knew, to feel this way after all that had happened. And yet here they were, in the dark, their hungers strong and growing stronger. Maybe it was something about how easily these people acted upon their instincts.

Mia dropped her grip on Janeane's neck. Janeane pulled her in, found her mouth with her lips and kissed her, hard and hot and with an unleashed hunger. Mia responded, almost feverishly, embracing the woman as if grasping a lifeline.

But then, all too soon for Janeane's liking, she pulled back, breaking the spell, sounding as unsettled as Janeane felt. 'If you prefer the company of women, or females, I suggest you stay with ours.'

Janeane's head spun, and she breathed out, her arousal still strong. 'Thanks. And if you change your mind, call me.'

'Call you what?'

18

It took Janeane a few moments of recovery, and of following Mia's directions through the passages, before she reached the haven of the females, in the Arch. Kami and Djaben had described their attitudes and activities, and what Janeane saw now confirmed it: females keeping their own company, fending for themselves, many staring with open-mouthed fascination at Janeane.

The provisions and travelling clothes they were preparing was something new, however. 'Going on a trip?' she asked no one in particular.

A dark-skinned female turned to her, reached out and took her hand. 'Welcome, sister! Your arrival was most fortuitous!'

Janeane's breath quickened with the female's lingering touch, which was soon joined by Tameri's other hand. 'Is that right?' She guessed what was next, but asked, 'Tell me more, "sister".'

The Healer drew closer, partly focused on her pitch and partly seeming distracted by Janeane's closeness, as if fighting the urge to explore further. 'Later.'

Kami had mentioned this, too. 'I know this game.'

'Game?' Tameri's touch moved along Janeane's skin, making her shiver. 'What game do you mean?'

'This.' Janeane tried to indicate Tameri's hands, and all the other hands now touching her, stroking her, sending her temperature rising and making her pussy throb. 'All this.'

'Oh,' the Healer breathed huskily, her lips kissing

Janeane's bare arms then moving up along her shoulders. 'You mean our seducing you, to get what we want from you?'

Janeane swayed, and lost her balance; hands caught her, and gently lowered her to some furs. She was startled, though not alarmed, by how quickly she had given in to them. 'Yeah. What *do* you want from me?'

Tameri drew herself over Janeane, slipping out of her toga, her tail swishing against Janeane's legs like yet another hand. She caressed the woman's face. 'We want to bathe you, groom you. We want to find out what you taste like. We want to know how you react when you come. And we want you to learn the same from us. And then later, we'll talk.' The Healer smiled. 'Is that acceptable?'

Janeane smiled back as she was undressed. 'Let's find out.'

The enclosure was like a sauna, the steam rising from the water bubbling out of the porous walls. Mark was amazed at the intricate and sophisticated set-up, where the rock surfaces were carved into many ditches that fed down into sunken baths, the water controlled and stopped by traps and spigots made of stone, with parts that would not wear out for centuries. There were stone-carved tables and shelves for soap and towels and clothes, while above, indirect sunlight reflected down through an air chimney from a polished brass mirror; Kami took a moment to work some positioning ropes and adjust the mirror for maximum reflection for the time of day. Mark watched her, then frowned as she froze and turned, glaring past him. 'Get behind me.'

Mark did, quickly identifying the reason for her reaction: Zeel and several other males had appeared, their unacknowledged leader sneering at him as he spoke to his friends. 'Yes, this is the one, the tail-puller she rutted with.'

Kami sneered back. 'Bathe another time, Zeel. It's not as if you have to do it to please a female, as they wouldn't display for you if you had the last cock in the world.'

Zeel spoke in English now, all the better to try to intimidate Mark. 'Take care of him, Kami. Varis may have ordered their protection, but humans remain fragile. One trip in the dark –'

'– Can cost you far more than him.' And before the male had a chance to reply, she smiled and added in Pridespeak, in a tone that wouldn't alert Mark, *'You threaten him again, I'll hunt you down and kill you.'* She looked at the others. *'Every mother's cub of you.'*

The males froze; one stepped back. Nalo's condition had not improved, apparently.

'Now go,' she growled.

They retreated, Zeel being the last.

Mark breathed out. 'What did you say to them?'

'Oh, I was just telling them that they were lucky you didn't lose your temper, that in your world you were a master warrior who'd killed hundreds.'

'Uh-huh.' He removed his tunic. 'And what did you *really* threaten them with?'

'Threaten? We have a saying: "Males threaten, females act".'

'I'll have to remember that.'

She knelt at one bath and touched the water, finding it a little cool for her tastes, and worked the hot traps. 'He's an idiot. But like many idiots, he has followers. We're conservative by nature.' She lifted her toga up over her head and flung it to an adjacent bench, enjoying his reaction to her being naked in a relatively public place. 'Well, maybe not all *that* conservative.'

He chuckled, but glanced around once more before tugging at the clasps to his kilt. Her hand reached up and encircled his. She undressed him. 'And now we stand here being shy,' she joked, before glancing down, noting his thickening erection. She smiled. 'Hello again.'

He blushed, in a very sweet way.

'Come on.' She took him by the hand and led him down the steps into the bath, descending until they were waist-deep, then bobbing down to her neck, relishing the warm, comforting, all-over embrace. Mark followed, then reached for the soap and cloths. When he returned, however, he found Kami's hand on his neck, her eyes looking into his.

'Rise,' she said.

He did as she asked, feeling the cool air on his arms, shoulders and chest as she ran the cloth over him. 'That horseback ride was gruelling. Do more, please.'

Kami did just that, massaging the muscles of his neck and arms, then turning around to do his back, her touch strong but gentle and hungry for his. 'Now, me.'

They turned, and she purred as Mark's lathered hands moved over her shoulders and arms. She arched her head back and breathed in. 'Don't forget my breasts.'

'How could I?' But he hesitated. 'Is it ... is it safe?'

'Of course. We can't have intercourse, that's all. That's the only recognised sexual act here.'

'Oh.' After a moment, he complied, his hands cupping her flesh, stroking and caressing her, the pink, sweet-smelling lather foaming between their skin.

Kami bit her lip but still let out a gasp, and backed herself against him, feeling his groin at her buttocks, his cock softened a little but still prominent, and pressing against her active tail. 'Mmm, you're good.'

'You inspire me.' He sighed himself. 'I thought I'd never do this again with you.'

Kami felt herself tingle as his hands descended to her belly then moved below the waterline, and he drew in closer to her neck until she felt his breath on her skin. 'Neither did I,' she whispered.

'It was only a couple of days, but I missed you so much.'

As his hands moved down to the tops of her thighs, she turned in his embrace and faced him, her breasts against his chest, his penis twitching against her bush. 'And I, you. But we're together again . . .'

'Yes.' His eyes danced as his hands moved up her back, all pretence at washing forgotten. They kissed; he was eager enough for that, and she relished the taste of his tongue, relished the feel of their bodies pressed together, his cock growing once more. She smiled against his mouth when his hands descended to her bum, touching the base of her tail.

Then Kami caught the errant scent, glanced over Mark's shoulder, and saw Mia, half-hidden at the doorway to the baths. Watching.

Kami almost laughed aloud. Instead, she kissed Mark again, then pulled him down. Still clinging together, they lowered themselves to their throats in the water to wash off any lingering soap, before she guided him out of the bath. 'Come on, let's dry off before we catch cold.'

They stood together, towelling each other down, taking care, enjoying each other's touch and closeness once more. And during this, Kami took in Mark's scent, his body rhythms, once more – and noted Mia, remaining unseen, at least to Mark, although her changing scent betrayed the older female's growing arousal.

Kami's sex moistened, and she took his hand and

guided it towards her labia, along her wet flesh. 'Enter me, Mark. I need you there.' She reached over and grasped his penis, moving the foreskin slowly back and forth. 'Keep touching me. That's it. Oh, you gorgeous bastard...' She shuddered as he brought his head down towards her breast and began sucking on her nipple. Her hand moved faster over his cock, and he somehow managed to keep them both steady despite his own obvious aroused state. She could smell him as she worked the velvety skin up and down the length of the shaft, until his breath hissed and his eyes glazed over, the lids closing, his own efforts on her doubling.

She felt his body stiffen, tensing as bullets of come shot from him and spattered onto her thighs. He left her breast and gasped against her. 'I'm – I'm – that was – was –'

'Yeah, I know.' Kami had spasmed into climax when the hot, sticky fluid had struck her, and she remained on the cusp, moaning aloud, as she felt it drip down her legs. He'd stopped stroking her, letting her muscles push his finger out. She released her grip on his pulsing organ. 'That was good.'

Mark grunted. 'I've left you a mess.' And with that unnecessary confession, he guided her still-shaking body to an adjacent stone bench.

She glanced behind her, purposefully catching Mia's eye, then set herself down, ignoring the coolness of the polished surface, and spread her legs lewdly, watching and feeling the semen now dripping like melted candle wax towards her inner thighs.

Mark dropped to his knees in front of her, his dick still hard and hanging heavily forwards, staring at her legs, at his deposits upon them. Then he reached for a damp cloth, and gently, lovingly, cleaned her.

She dabbed her finger in one of the remaining milky grey globules, tasting it and moaning with approval. Mark smiled, drew closer, and began kissing her inner flesh. The sight of him, and the feel of his tongue on her skin, was almost too much to bear, and she growled as she took a handful of his hair. 'Now get in there, please . . .'

And he did, evidently overwhelmed with a desire to please her, his tongue eagerly lapping at her swollen sex, up to encircle the tip of her aching clit, then down again, partly of his own volition, partly at her verbal prompting. His tongue pierced her, filling her, and when he purred, she lay back fully on the bench, ignoring the cool surface and the cramp in her tail. 'That's it . . . that's it, my beautiful man . . .'

At the doorway, Mia departed; Kami smiled to herself. Yes, Mia, run off and report back to Varis.

Or better yet, be inspired.

Mark was growling into her now, lapping down, then up to the roof of her pussy, doubling his efforts, sending ripples of delight radiating from her sex to heat and charge the rest of her body. She pushed up against his face, then felt a cramp in her thigh. 'M – my legs . . .'

Without stopping, he slipped his arms under the backs of her thighs and lifted them up to set them on his broad shoulders, easily supporting her. *Good man.* She moaned and cried out again, ready to burst from within once more . . .

Mia shivered as she appeared on the surface, looking up at the cloaked figure on the perch. 'I would have words with you, Gatekeeper.'

Kahotep never moved, never even looked down behind him. 'I live apart to keep my senses sharp, and my mind uncluttered. You are not helping with that.'

'If something is not done, there will be nothing left for you to watch over.' She strode forwards, wrapping her arms around herself at the caress of a cool wind, but not attempting to climb up to him. 'The tension grows. Varis keeps his own counsel now. Humans bring their corrupting ways to us. Our world is unravelling.'

'Then seek a weaver, not a sentinel.'

'You may choose to hide out here and trade witticisms with the wind, but –'

With a sudden twist, Kahotep turned and leaped from his perch, landing from the three-metre height with a grace belying his age. Then he stood tall before her, angry and determined, his scent still potent to her senses. 'Don't speak to me of choices, "Respected". I've made them. As have you. And Varis. And all others. And we must live with their consequences, good and bad. Those who refuse to face this simple fact are the ones who hide, not me.'

He slowly paced around her, drawing in her scent, easily perceiving how aroused she was. 'Your sex mewls for relief. Humans with their "corrupting" ways would easily sate themselves. But our proud First Female, clinging to the restrictions of the Behest, hides behind denial and guilt.'

He was so close, so ready to take her … she shivered. 'Passions and instinct drive us, Kahotep. Without the Behest, we would have torn ourselves apart long ago. And perhaps taken your beloved humans along with us.'

'So you say.' He leaned in closer, until he could almost lick her ear, and his voice dropped to a whisper. 'If not believe.'

Mia pulled away, as afraid of his next move as she was of her own. 'Solitude and age have rattled your mind.'

'And yet you seek my counsel.' Kahotep smiled humourlessly, and leaned back against the nearest rock, regarding her. 'Fear not, Mia. Everything will change before you know it. The only question is how, and by whose hand.'

The Vault was long and narrow, winding downwards into the mountain like a spiral staircase. The air was torch-lit, musty and dry, affording maximum protection for the items kept here: huge clay coffers filled with Roman, Egyptian and Greek gold coins; jewel-encrusted Indian and Mayan statues; ancient swords and shields; golden cups and proud ebony cats, and even more modern canvas oils and watercolours.

The phrase 'treasure trove' could have been invented for this place.

But to Mark it was nothing compared with the historical value of the items also preserved here, as described by Kami. 'Lost plays by Aeschylus, the complete Hesiod's *Catalogue of Women*, unexpurgated copies of the Hebrew Abodazara, accounts of the Hun incursions against the Pridelands, scrolls saved when the Christians burned the Alexandria Library ... Mayan folding-bark books, manuscripts from Charlemagne's court, Pope Gregory's secret campaign against the Pride, letters by Galileo about the Academy of Lynxes, the Ottomans, the Seljuks, the Nazis, the Americans ... Information, secrets gathered and kept safe here by the various incarnations of the Swords of Bastet.'

'Good Lord,' he muttered, reaching out tentatively to a tablet of markings, almost afraid to touch it. 'The history of the ancient world; you've saved it ...'

She held a Chinese jade tiger. 'Some of it. Many of those points involved us. It was our history, too. We didn't always destroy.'

He drew closer to touch it, and saw her fingers, so close, so touchable ... he withdrew. She looked at him, ignoring his evident need to stay so close to her. 'I can teach you the languages: Pridespeak, Cuneiform, Hindi. Teach you things no other living human has ever known. Make you privy to secrets millennia old. And you'll be able to add your knowledge to ours.' She smiled. 'Think that can occupy you? Becoming one of our historians?'

He looked back at her, and the enormity of the time ahead of them – Kami serving Varis, Mark standing by, perhaps sneaking moments alone with her – struck him only then. He knew there were few people he'd miss in the outside world. Yet he'd miss the world itself, and the freedom he shared with Kami out there, despite her having to disguise her true nature among others. But he set aside his doubts, determined to make the best of the situation. 'Yes. Yes, I can.'

And Kami read the doubts on his face, the sadness, emotions mirroring her own. She too loved the outside, the travel, the music, the food and the people. They would both miss it. But they would both be determined not to show this to the other. They would be very noble.

She wanted him. Fully. Openly. And no more Varis. And Mark wanted her.

They really had no other option.

It was the most luxuriating experience Janeane had ever experienced. She lay surrounded by half a dozen female bodies, their collective heat and scent so inviting, inviting her to sink into the indulgence of it forever.

But she couldn't. Not now. She watched as Tameri licked at the undercurves of her left breast. 'Well?'

The Healer looked up from under her tousled hair and smiled. 'You taste as good as you smell.'

'Uh-huh. Now what's your pitch?'

'"Pitch"?'

'Yeah.' Janeane sat up on her elbows and looked around absently for her toga. 'You've sugared me, worn me out – and it was fucking amazing, by the way – and now you tell me what you really want from me.'

Tameri almost looked ready to protest, then thought better of it. She reached for her own clothes. 'We had turned to Kami to teach us about, and lead us to, the world of men. But she refused.'

Nearby, one of the younger females snapped, 'She was selfish.'

'Hey, watch it, kid, that's my friend!'

'Yes, Ankhesen,' Tameri agreed. 'Kami did what she thought best. Just as we're doing what *we* think is right.'

And the males are doing what they think is right, Janeane thought glumly. She rose unsteadily to her feet. 'And you believe leaving the only home you've known, and risking your lives among men, is the right thing to do?'

'Of course.' Tameri rose as well, indicating the assembled females, all preparing for their journey, or comforting each other. 'We are no longer content to be as we were, bound by the Behest, by the intransigence of the Firsts and the males' stubborn stupidity. We want our freedom, we want our needs met. Kami chose not to help us. But you, you're human, imprisoned here, treated as little better than a pet. You above all know what awaits us in your world.'

'Yeah, I do. That's what scares me.' Janeane glanced around again. She could read the expressions and body language of many who were far from happy about leaving. 'And what about those who want to stay?'

Tameri looked distinctly uncomfortable with the question, obviously an issue broached before now. 'In the end ... we agreed that we had to retain a united stand against the males.'

'Oh? You all agreed?'

'What other choice have we?'

'You can go back to the males. Try to work things out with them again. I'm not saying all of them are up for it, but I know some are, like Djaben.'

'Djaben?' Tameri regarded her with a inscrutable suspicion. Then she shook her head. 'They are idiots, unable to grasp the obvious.'

'Now who's being stubborn? Jeez, you're like those tourists I deal with who get pissed off because the locals around them have the gall not to understand English. Do you even get what the males are going through as well?'

The Healer shook her hands from Janeane's. 'You are human, you cannot understand.'

Janeane remained unfazed, folding her arms across her chest. 'So much for sisterhood.'

Then Tameri did something unexpected: she dropped to her knees before Janeane, and looked up with full, genuine need. 'If you help me, help us, I swear to become yours, always. I'll serve you. Protect you. Be anything you want. *Please.*'

Janeane was taken aback, and she was forced to admit that the idea was enticing – and not just because of the female's offer. After all, Kami had gained so much being in the outside world, hadn't she?

Before she could confront the dilemma, however,

another female approached, and said something that prompted Janeane to ask, 'What's up?'

Tameri rose. 'Kami's with her man in the Lair. They are . . . entertaining each other.'

19

The meal had been a form of spiced beef kebabs, cooked over the fire she'd made, with honey wine. The talk as they sat on the grass had been of their first meeting, their first meal together, their first lovemaking, the way each had fulfilled the other in ways they could never have realised beforehand.

And as they ate and talked and laughed, they sat close and held hands, Mark stroking her hair, Kami gasping with disbelief at how far they'd come in such a short time, and how far they could still go.

It had not been an easy decision to make, far from it; it had been difficult enough to even bring it out into the open between them. But once it had been, it was like an animal freed from a cage and let loose, unwilling to return. Then there had been the question of Janeane's safety possibly being at risk after Kami and Mark broke their oaths, but Kami was assured that her human friend would be protected by the other females.

She suddenly pulled Mark into a kiss, snaking her tongue into his mouth, exploring his inner cheeks. They embraced, his fingers in her hair, his stubbled face brushing against hers, and their kiss intensified, and multiplied.

Kami drew back, her hands working the clasps of his robe, gently easing it from his arms and shoulders, then leaving it crumpled behind him. Now he wore only his kilt. She saw his eyes, a slightly panicked expression in them as he tried to hide looking about, looking about at the growing numbers of Pride members watching them in an eerie, rapt silence.

She squeezed him gently. 'Look at me, Mark. Not them. They're not there. We're alone.' She ignored them too, only once acknowledging their presence by growling at a few who were coming too close.

Kami traced her fingers over the broad outline of Mark's jaw, then back into his hair, so thick and soft in her hands. Breathing harder, moaning softly, she ground her pelvis against his, feeling the hardness of him pressing into her as the touch of his hands aroused her further.

A cool breeze drifting their way made her shiver. His fingertips traced their way up her thighs with long, deliciously slow strokes as they kissed again. His fingers moved between her legs, carefully parting her lips and letting one finger slip inside.

Kami moaned into his mouth, and reached down to take his penis in her hand, feeling it pulse, feeling it long to be inside her. She gave him long, languid strokes. Kami could almost hear the collective, excited beatings of the hearts of those assembled, instinctively drawn to the forbidden, thankfully keeping away, but still watching – which was what she and Mark wanted anyway.

She pulled back from his mouth and murmured, 'Lie back.' She wanted to show them all the myriad wonderful ways lovers could fuck, wanted to make love to Mark for hours. But there was little time, she knew.

Mark drew back, and she could see that he was forcing himself to keep his full attention on her. She smiled, kicking aside her discarded clothes to bend over and offer her mouth to his shaft, licking the underside before plunging the length of it into her, sucking and relishing the reactions of her people almost as much as the scent and taste of him. Mark twisted beneath her, his self-conscious apprehension evidently forgotten, then slapped her bum. 'Give me a taste.'

She happily obliged, twisting and setting her lower half over his waiting, eager mouth, then squirming in delight as his tongue touched and teased her needy clitoris. Her tail flicked excitedly above her, as if to challenge those around it.

Then Kami rose, crawled over him, and offered him one final, tense moment, her parted, waiting sex radiating moist heat on his straining cock. 'Last chance to stop.'

Mark nodded – then grabbed her waist and rose upwards, spearing her from below, his breath escaping from him in a low grunt. Kami called out, her limbs flooded with the rapture of the reunion of their bodies that she had craved for so long. Both lay still, as if Mark had squandered all his energy in that first thrust, then Kami bent forwards, tasting his forehead, his lips, the salty tang of his sweat, as her inner muscles rippled along his length.

'Mark,' she murmured, a prayer on her lips.

And, as if at a command, he began to move again now, gently lifting upwards, almost fully withdrawing from her body before slipping back into her inch by delicious inch, their fit ideal, their movements natural as if having been practised over years instead of days. Her tail thickened and rose as she bent forwards again, allowing him access to her neglected breasts with his mouth and tongue. Her hands on his shoulders steadied her, her claws piercing him, no longer caring about leaving marks. In fact, she wanted him marked, for her own, marked for all to see.

His thrusting became more insistent as he grew unable to bear such an agonisingly slow pace. Parting from his mouth, she puffed, 'Wait – wait – take me – behind –'

He nodded, acknowledging the greater agenda here; she knew he must be feeling so blissful that he would agree to anything. But she clung to him, refusing to let him withdraw, instead twisting about, her superior form easily manoeuvring until she was on all fours and Mark was on his knees behind her. Her tail flicked up and stroked his face.

In that position, Mark went wild, losing control, the rude slapping of their bodies building her up to a climax. She lowered her head to the ground and pushed her body back against his, until his cock was stroking against her G-spot, sending thrumming motions through her like a plucked guitar string. Now her limbs quaked and she could barely control her movements except to push and gyrate. Around her, the crowd was silent.

Suddenly Mark's body went rigid, and he threw his head back as he called out her name. Kami responded to his surrender with her own as their bodies locked together, pumping into one another. She felt giddy with the sensation as she squeezed him, harder, harder, milking him thoroughly, savouring every bullet of come he shot deep into her.

They remained in place, feeling the ebbs drift away, until Kami sensed that they should separate, and did so. 'Turn around.'

'What?'

She twisted into a crouching position, ready to protect him; when he turned, he saw the objects of her concern drawing close, and that intense, delicious feeling of contentment evaporated sadly like water on the wall of a furnace.

'Kami –'

'Stay calm,' she whispered. 'If he was out to kill us, he would have attacked already.'

Varis and Mia parted the surrounding crowds, while Zeel brought up the rear. 'See? It is as I claimed! They have defied your authority!'

The First Male, however, looked sad rather than angry. 'Congratulations, Zeel. Feel free to lick your tail in triumph.'

Zeel's cruel glee dissipated. 'Need I remind you of their agreement?'

'Not unless you want to be gutted like a fish.' Varis ignored him and stepped forwards. He spoke, as Mia translated. 'Human, you swore an oath of fealty to my authority. It took little more than the passage of a day for you to break that oath.'

Mark managed to close the clasp to his kilt in time. 'Respected, this was my doing, not Kami's. I'm responsible.'

Kami, however, was less in a hurry to clothe herself. Or the truth. 'No, Varis. We're both responsible. This was *our* choice.'

The First grunted. 'Your choice? To die?'

Kami drew closer to her lover, her tone respectful but resolute. 'To *live*, if only for a few moments, true to ourselves. I will not submit to you again.'

'This wasn't meant as an act of defiance,' Mark continued, taking Kami's hand. 'But as a demonstration, to show the males, to show all of you, what you can have together. Mutual satisfaction, mutual fulfilment.'

Now Mia drew closer to her mate. 'Varis, I know the Behest would demand punishment for their actions –'

To her surprise and Kami's too, the First Male shook his head. 'But it would be dishonourable, given what I know. And I have caused enough dishonour already.'

Before anyone could question his enigmatic words,

the Pride within the Lair tensed as one, and turned to one particular entrance to see dozens of females swarming out, staying close together, claws bared, hackles raised, until they reached the centre. The tension within the assembled Pride doubled, as Tameri stood at the head of the pack, clad in toughened leather straps reminiscent of ancient Pride body armour as worn by males – and forbidden to females. Her hair was clasped back, her expression fierce and determined. 'Varis! You will not harm them!'

The males had reacted to the new arrivals with tension and renewed hostility, and Varis had been no exception, but Kami credited him with his effort to ignore it and maintain his composure. 'No, Healer, they will not be harmed.'

The growls among both males and females had begun to grow like an invading storm, and Kami looked around for the best direction to take with Mark if hostilities broke out, as she feared was inevitable. 'Tameri, we're in no danger –'

'Not any more,' Tameri agreed, still sounding fuelled by righteous anger. 'Varis is a fool, but not such a fool as to challenge our might. Now come with us. We're going, now!'

'You're going *nowhere*,' Varis informed her darkly, bristling, Tameri having pushed the right buttons to put him on the defensive. Around him, the males tensed further, some looking towards those females closest to them, like Kami and Mia.

The latter stepped forwards, ignoring the growing threat. 'Healer, what you taught me the other night . . . I can teach my mate.'

Behind her, Zeel too stepped forwards. 'Enough of this! We should have these insane females chained! Made to service their betters!'

'You want us, little male?' Tameri snarled, her teeth bared, as the tension escalated. 'Try to claim us!'

'Kami –' Mark started.

She gripped him, ready to lift him up and carry him to safety if he wasn't quick enough. 'Don't move a muscle.'

Suddenly the debate was halted, as all Pride ears caught something in the air at once. They began scrambling about urgently. It took Mark and Janeane a few seconds more to hear it, an animal-like cry steadily rising, like a growing wind through the Lair.

Mark asked Kami over the commotion, 'What's that?'

'The Carnyx, from Kahotep's Keep. His alarm. Invaders.'

Kahotep heard the male creep up behind him and ask, 'How many?'

'Twenty, more.' He sniffed the air again, frowning. 'With fire.'

'Fire?' Varis peered over the edge to the archway below. 'Two incursions in as many days. We're becoming quite the attraction.'

'Maybe eight centuries in the same place is time enough?' Kahotep suggested, the thought lost as he leaned forwards and sniffed again. 'Back off, you're distracting me.'

Few within the Pride could speak to Varis and expect to be obeyed without question. Kahotep was one of them. Clear again, he concentrated on the intruders, his voice low but audible enough for those waiting for information. 'Twenty, maybe more. Human, male – one Pride female – two others – unfamiliar –'

'Seska,' Varis muttered.

And he descended.

*   *   *

From the ravine below, the flickering of handheld fire torches blazed, as figures appeared, strode through the archway and stood at the mouth of the valley.

Seska led the way, flanked on her right side by Ardeth Fehr. She was clad in a regal Pride gown of creamy white, Ardeth in black robes of human design, while the men behind them were clad in Pride tunics, kilts and armbands. They carried clothes, blankets, and personal items, all approximating Pride design, but no weapons or modern paraphernalia.

Seska stepped forwards, carrying two small bundles in her arms. And as she stared into the valley, knowing she was watched and heard, she called out, 'Varis!'

For a moment, there was no reaction. Then a shape rose in the darkness and descended at its own pace to the floor of the valley. The First Male stood in their way, ready for anything. 'Your return is fortuitous, sister. And you've brought company.'

She smiled. 'More than company, brother.' With a nod from her, the men put down their torches, then dropped to one knee, heads bowed. 'Saviours.' She indicated the bundles in her arms. 'And this is Salidji, and Amahte. My son and daughter. Family.'

It was a strange and tense assembly within the Court, Varis, Mia and Zeel at one end of the table, with Seska on her own to the side, standing near Tameri as the Healer examined the infant children; Ardeth had remained outside the Pridelands. On the opposite end, Kami was watching, and poring over scrolls provided by Seska, while in the background Mark and Janeane watched, with Djaben and Kahotep translating when necessary.

Tameri wrapped up the second infant and stepped

back. 'They appear normal, healthy six-month-old Pride children.' To Seska she offered a cool, 'Felicitations.'

'You found a cure for the Barrenness,' Varis stated. 'Who is their father?'

The Priestess looked at Kami as she replied. 'Ardeth.'

That made the assembly start, Zeel reacting first. 'Human? You mean they're filthy half-breeds?'

'Your tongue will dig your grave,' Seska hissed through clenched teeth. 'Curb it.' She regained her composure once more before continuing. 'The Pride side dominates. It always has, whenever we had children with humans.'

'Impossible!'

'Kahotep,' Mia began softly, never taking her eyes from Seska. 'Take the children into your care, in case this discussion turns ... heated.'

The Gatekeeper drew close, sought and received assent from the infants' mother, and gently accepted the bundles, then returned to Djaben and the humans. Seska took that as her cue to elaborate. 'The Pride have always kept themselves isolated from the outside world, as much out of the need for survival as for the preservation of our culture. Such isolation has, at times, caused a weakness in our fertility, as it would with any secluded human community. And at those times, we need humans, male or female. It has always been the documented solution.'

'Has it?' Tameri frowned, suspicious. 'And what documents are these?'

'Those not purged long ago, by the First Male Utrekh.'

'*What?*' Zeel's hands balled into fists. 'You lie!'

Seska looked to Varis. 'Brother?'

The First Male looked at each in turn, then nodded, as Seska continued. 'Eight hundred years ago, when our people took a perilous journey across the Atlantic to finally settle here, many adults, scribes, died along the way. Utrekh used that loss as an opportunity to ... amend the Behest, and misplace aspects of our history and culture with which he personally disagreed, such as the notion that the Pride would need human help, in any capacity.' She nodded to Kami now. 'Well, Student?'

Kami glanced up, annoyed and distracted, then turned to the others. 'It appears true. In fact these records fill in certain gaps in our knowledge about our people, knowledge considered lost during the great journey.' She shook her head. 'Ironic: we've spent centuries altering human history, never realising it had been done to ourselves as well.'

'You knew,' Mia began, staring hard at Varis, as if seeing him for the first time. 'You and Seska knew of this all along, and you said nothing to me, to any of us.'

'I knew,' he admitted, unapologetic. 'Seska learned the truth, from its only remaining uncensored source: the scrolls she inherited when she became Priestess. When the Barrenness overtook us, she told me, but I didn't believe her. I didn't want to. The very idea was ... demeaning.' He spared an almost embarrassed glance at the humans present. 'I ordered her to confirm the truth, indisputably. And she did ... the results lie sleeping in Kahotep's arms.'

'They were born not long before I escaped the Pridelands,' Kami noted. 'But you kept them secret from me.'

'You were determined to go off alone into the human world, rather than remain with me.' Seska grunted. 'Had something happened to you, my children would have been compromised.'

Mia never turned from the First Male. 'That explains your sister. Why did *you* remain silent? Why did you continue to mate with Kami?'

'I kept silent to protect you from the truth. And I mated with Kami because to do otherwise would have invited more dishonour, more humiliation upon you. And it would have invited more questions.'

'You weren't ready,' Seska interjected. 'Given your attitudes towards humans, none of you were ready, not until the times had grown desperate enough to require what you would consider desperate measures. And *I* needed time. Time to prepare suitable men, which I did. The results remain guarded in the Lair. And time to prepare our females ... which Tameri did.' She looked at the Healer. 'After some instruction from me.'

Tameri flushed. 'You used me. Six months ago, when you were last here, you used me.'

'I *awakened* you.' To the rest, she explained, 'The amended Behest taught us that sex is proper in only one position, and for one purpose. But the scrolls handed down to each Priestess detail the full sexual potential to which we can aspire, and the many ways of achieving satisfaction – ways humans have always known, if not always approved of. Such skills were considered essential for the Priestesses, who kept the secrets guarded.'

'But why?' Mia asked.

'Knowledge is power,' Janeane said from the side-lines. 'Especially sexual knowledge. In my own society, women began gaining political power following sexual liberation. And I bet suppressing it was this Utrekh guy's way of keeping your women in line.'

'Very astute,' Seska affirmed. 'You're cleverer than I first assumed.'

Janeane snorted. 'And you can fuck off.'

Seska continued. 'Yes, I awakened Tameri, and encouraged her to teach other females.'

'So that they can separate themselves from the

males?' Kami deduced, clearly shaken by the revelations, but quickly recovering. 'Why provoke sedition?'

'Sedition was not my goal; I had not anticipated that they would plan to leave the Pridelands. Through Tameri I gave the females the means to prepare themselves for the men's arrival; climaxes will assist in conception. And of course to comfort themselves in the interim, because I knew I couldn't trust the males to provide it. Their feelings don't extend beyond what they hide behind their kilts.'

Kami looked around the room. She saw Varis, arrogant and imperious but genuine in his love for Mia, and stung by his sister's condemnation. She saw Djaben, wanting to heal rifts without knowing how. She saw Kahotep, strong and wise, now purring to the two infants in his arms.

Then there was Mark, caring and intelligent, brave and trustworthy . . .

And she wondered how she could ever have been as blind as her former mentor.

Seska moved to the Firsts now. 'Mia, I have personally selected those men in the Lair, not only for strength, but for their health and intelligence. And I've trained them, taught them our language, our customs and manners, and other useful skills. They have nothing in their old lives to keep them from swearing their total fealty to you, and our people. They will give our females what they want.'

'So that they will then reject Pride males?' Zeel accused.

'Not all females want the same thing from males,' Janeane noted again. 'I've talked with a few of them. Some will want to conceive. Some will want the intimacy that humans seem to provide more easily than your own males. Some will prefer merely that their

Pride mates learn, and think a little more of their needs. As the females will need to think about the males' needs.'

'And it's not something that can't be learned,' Mark finally piped up. 'You're the strongest, most tenacious people I've ever known. You've adapted and triumphed over every challenge you've ever faced, over war and persecution and disaster. This latest hurdle can't be the most formidable, and the rewards can be ... incredible.' He swallowed and stepped back. 'Sorry.'

'Don't be,' Varis assured him. 'You're one of us now.'

'And what of your heir?' Mia asked her mate. 'Can Kami provide it?'

'No,' Kami herself answered. 'Even if it was possible, I will not.'

'Nor will you have to,' the First Male confirmed. 'You are freed of your obligation as Second now. Seska's children are of my blood, and will succeed me when their time has come.'

The assembled were stunned by his announcement. Seska drew up proudly. 'I have considered this possibility. It will be an honour, brother.'

'Does Ardeth know about this?' Kami asked.

The older female frowned, as if annoyed at her assurance being questioned. 'Ardeth cares nothing for my children.'

Varis watched Kami's reaction to this, then looked at the rest of the group. 'All of you but my mate and my sister, await us in the Lair. I will be along directly.'

Those assembled departed, Zeel conspicuously keeping his distance from the rest. 'The First's brain must be addled, to speak such nonsense. We will not stand for it.'

Kami ignored the bait, instead wrapping an arm

around Mark's. 'Good words there. You knew how to scratch their backs.'

'Thanks. I've always wanted to do a Captain Kirk speech.'

'Who's Captain Kirk?'

Many had gathered in the Lair, males and females, all eyes on the men camped in the centre of the enclosure, guarded by order of Varis until further notice. If the men felt threatened or intimidated, they didn't show it, talking and even laughing among themselves.

Mark scanned their faces from a distance, nodding. 'I recognise one of them: Haci. Bright, friendly kid. Medical background.'

'Indeed.' This came from Tameri, who studied the young man, to the concern of Djaben, standing near her but obviously not near enough. Then she left to speak with the other females.

Moments later, Varis entered, conspicuously alone, and strode to the highest rock, clad in his best outfit. Silence settled on those assembled as he addressed them. 'Hear me: truths have been revealed this evening. Great, terrible truths. About us. About our past. And about our relationship with men. You will see me here again, soon, to speak further of these, though I have no doubt that these truths are already spreading among us like a scent.

'I have been told that these men before us literally carry the seed to our salvation. Over the following five days, we shall test the truth of that claim. May Bastet watch over us all.'

'Five days?' Mark echoed, once Kami had translated. 'Will that be enough time?'

Kami nodded. 'We know very quickly when we conceive; the entire gestation period itself is very short by human standards. And the females know the deadline, so they won't dawdle.'

Then she turned, as Varis appeared. 'Seska's human mate. Is he like your man?' the First Male asked.

The question took Kami by surprise, but she felt able to answer truthfully. 'Yes. Strong, in his own way, if a little too much under Seska's thumb.'

The First Male nodded, then disappeared without further explanation.

20

Much of the tension seemed to have lifted following Varis's speech, and Tameri suspected it was mostly due to the collapse of some of the wilder theories – including one that the men were really some tailless Pride who'd found their way here from some other remote part of the world.

But with this relief came a new, uneasy expectation. She had quickly spread the truth, but not everyone greeted it the same way. Zeel had returned to his tail-lickers for them to complain among themselves, while others chose to watch and wait. Many, like herself, were frankly excited. And yet all stood like cubs eager yet afraid to be first to jump in the river.

She looked over at Kami's humans, sitting at the sidelines. Perhaps if they – no, that wouldn't be fair. They were speaking with Djaben about something. Her heart ached; she had missed his company, his humour and earnest thoughts, and though she wanted children, she wanted him as a mate, to. 'Ankhesen, Ishel, our guests will be hungry. Bring food, wine.'

'Tameri?'

'We wanted to find men. Now men have found us.' She strode out, hoping she was presentable – something she hadn't thought about in a long time.

Closer now, the men's scents were stronger, similar to Kami's man. They had set aside their travellers' clothes, and wore simple tunics and kilts, chatting and looking about in wonder, clearly fascinated by being here.

Music, flute music, suddenly sounded, and Tameri turned to the man Mark had indicated. He sat cross-legged on the ground, playing a replica of one of the Pride's own wooden flute staffs. It had been a long time since music was heard here, and eyes and ears turned to him.

Tameri walked over to him as he finished his song. 'Beautiful. Does it have a name?'

The man called Haci set aside his instrument. '*And I Love Her.*'

'Did you write it?'

He smiled a very pleasing smile. 'I wish.' He was young, smooth-faced and dark-skinned, with a healthy head of black hair. His eyes, like all humans', seemed small and pale, their skin unmarked, like babies. And, of course, they were freakishly tailless. But he was far from repulsive. 'My name is Haci Guten. Please honour me with your company.'

His accent was strange, but he employed the traditional Pride invitation perfectly. She smiled and reclined on the grass opposite him. 'I am Tameri-Mnoti. I am a Healer. May I hear another song?'

He smiled. 'As many as you like.'

Varis and Kahotep marched back towards the slope after returning the infants to Ardeth, Varis offering, 'That was illuminating.'

'For both of you, I think. He is another good man; just don't start thinking all are like them. Will he do as you suggested?'

'It will be his choice.'

'Your sister could curse you for your interference.'

'It would not be the first time.' As they reached the top of the slope, Varis surveyed his starlit land. 'What a fool.'

Kahotep stopped at his perch. 'Who?'

'Utrekh. Suppressing knowledge that his people would need. Why did he do it?'

'Why did *you* do it?' The older male enjoyed the reaction on the younger one's face, then looked up at the sky. 'When I have joined him among the unwearying stars with all our other ancestors, perhaps I shall ask him.'

Varis grunted. 'Can you come back and tell me what he said?'

Kahotep grunted back. 'A long arduous lifetime here to earn my place in the afterlife, and you expect me to return and instruct you. You always were an odd cub.' He returned to his perch. 'You love Mia so much, that you will not give her up, even at the cost of not producing an heir of your own.'

Varis looked away. 'Yes. I suppose that does seem odd.'

'No. Not odd. Admirable. Worthy of any First Male I have known.' When their eyes met again, he continued. 'But maybe you shouldn't give up the notion of an heir too soon? With these humans here –'

'What? Seska only brought in men.'

'Kami's friend Jan-Neen seems to possess distinctly unmanly properties. And both you and Mia find her ... attractive.'

'Mia? I don't understand.'

Kahotep waved him away. 'Then leave me to my stars, and seek enlightenment elsewhere. Or do you expect *everything* to fall packaged and labelled into your lap?'

Varis departed, still confused, but strangely feeling more optimistic than he'd had in a long time.

* * *

After their last encounter in the tunnels, Janeane had not expected to be hearing from Mia again – to Janeane's disappointment. She'd hoped to approach her again soon, until events from the outside overtook everyone. But now, Mia had come to her, stated that Varis had summoned them both back to the Court, and said nothing further. And as they walked silently together, Janeane could almost feel the tension growing from her companion, as if they were gradually wading deeper and deeper into molasses. 'You know, a wise man once said that leadership was a harness –'

'Tell the wise man to be silent.'

Janeane bit back a retort as they entered the Court. Varis awaited them alone, freshly washed and clothed from the look and smell of him. He straightened up as they entered, a steely gaze almost hiding the trepidation that stiffened his movements. He said something in Pridespeak, Janeane definitely hearing Mia's and her own name: a greeting.

Mia remained cool as she replied, and for a moment, Janeane stood there, reading their tones, their body language. Varis remained nervous, but determined, Mia distant, suspicious. Janeane was ready to step back. It could go in any way.

And then it went in a way Janeane didn't expect.

Varis suddenly knelt before Mia, head bowed, arms crossed over his chest.

Mia let out a gasp, swallowing. 'Varis –'

He looked up at her, his face an open display of contrition, his words in Pridespeak almost choked. Janeane didn't need a translation to know he was apologising.

Mia couldn't take her eyes from her mate, and as she took Varis by the shoulders and guided him back to his feet, they embraced with such a powerful intimacy that Janeane looked away out of a sense of propriety she never thought she'd employ here.

The Firsts conversed together again, and at times Mia appeared shocked and embarrassed. A minute passed and more, and it was all Janeane could do to stop herself from just blurting out a demand for a translation.

Then it came, from Mia. 'Jan-Neen, Varis – and I – still desire an heir. I cannot provide one. You can, however.'

Now the woman understood the reactions: she felt them herself, and more. 'Me? You mean, like the way he treated Kami when she was Second?'

'No, not like that, I swear. That was the product of an ancient – and stained – Behest. We ask this of you, not demand it. And it will only happen if agreed upon by all parties. You will not be our property, but our ... lover.' She stepped forwards, reached out tentatively for her hand and took it. 'Both of us.'

Janeane felt faint with excitement as much as desire. She held onto Mia as if for support. 'You sure about this?'

The air, and the tension soaked within it, hung heavily between them, as the two women drew closer, then held each other and kissed, Janeane almost painfully aware of her nipples growing taut, erect against Mia's own. She felt her stomach do somersaults as Mia's tongue caressed her lips in a snakelike movement, deep and urgent. And Janeane reached around to clasp Mia to her, drawing her even closer until their breasts were squashed together.

Close by, Varis gasped, his own arousal evident, but made no moves to join them – just yet. Which Janeane silently appreciated. Her female friends had satisfied her, yes, but she wanted to make love to *this* female, be with her. And Varis, too, yes; he had that irresistible combination of command and humility now, and she would be delighted to take him.

But first, this female ... Janeane reached up and clasped Mia's face in her hands, holding it firmly but tenderly, feeling her react strongly, melting and galvanising, her tail swishing excitedly behind her, until Mia clutched her and pulled her close again, murmuring, 'Varis has heard that I have mated with females, as you have. He has heard that it was better than what he and I have shared –'

'Not better,' Janeane murmured back, looking over at Varis who now appeared aroused and rapt, and unsure what to do with his hands, if the way they moved over his strong, bare biceps was any indication. 'Not really. Different. And he can learn things to make it better –'

Mia purred against her neck. 'Can we show him?'

Janeane's hands drifted down over the First Female's bare back, down to a pair of full, fleshy cheeks. She squeezed them, before reaching for the base of Mia's tail, which she stroked, feeling the blood race within. Mia moaned, and Varis gasped again, clearly finding it difficult to resist the urge to join in.

Mia turned in Janeane's embrace to face Varis. 'That's what I told him. He promised not to speak or interfere until we gave him leave to join.'

Janeane looked over Mia's shoulder at the male and smiled. 'Is that right? Then let's show him something worthwhile.' And with that her hands moved up, to cup and caress Mia's breasts through her gown, feeling the nipples harden further – then, with a deft slip, she peeled the cloth from the First Female's shoulders, baring her breasts, displaying the darkened, thickened tracks. Her tail twitched eagerly against Janeane, who reached up and stroked the bared breasts, as Mia reached up and behind her to run her fingers through Janeane's blonde hair.

Varis looked ready to break his oath. But he didn't.

Mia turned once more in Janeane's embrace, letting her gown fall to her feet and baring her rear and tail to her mate, as they kissed again, then smiling as she whispered, 'You like being in charge?'

Janeane smiled back, delighted that Mia seemed to have overcome her apparent earlier embarrassment about her desires. 'Sometimes I do. Sometimes I don't.'

'Good.' And with that, Mia twisted them about, reversing their positions so that Janeane faced Varis, and Mia was behind her, her arms around the younger woman, caressing her before the male.

It seemed to have grown deathly quiet, and all that Janeane could hear was the rush of blood in her own body and the laboured breathing of the spectator of her seduction. Her eyes remained locked on Varis's, as Mia's hands reached up and tugged at the clasps of Janeane's toga. It dropped easily to her feet, and Janeane reined in her gasps, her arms trapped under Mia's superior strength, her vulnerability – and her excitement – growing more acute as Mia's hands caressed her aching breasts. Her nipples seemed to reach out to greet Mia's touch, and Mia's warm hands traced Janeane's contours to her hips.

The tingling sensations were driving Janeane mad with desire and fear and excitement. 'I – I – want to lie down – please –'

Mia kissed her neck, watching and enjoying Varis's reaction as her hands snaked down towards the woman's blonde bush, almost touching, almost ... 'As you wish.'

They lay on a set of furs, facing each other, Mia

letting her hand return to Janeane's sex, to gently stroke around Janeane's moistness, touching every part as if it were the last time she would be there, rather than the first. When she reached the uppermost fold hooding the clitoris, the electricity flashed through Janeane as she writhed and squirmed and moaned under Mia's strong yet caring touch.

As Janeane's animal noises grew louder and louder, Mia slipped a hesitant finger inside, never leaving the delighted clitoris. Janeane clutched her, wanting to touch her, to love her as she was being loved. Her voice went ragged. 'Let – Let me – Let me touch –'

'Yes – *please* –' Mia released her probing hand and turned around so that she straddled Janeane, who could now bury her face into Mia's waiting folds of pink. Janeane, anticipating this, helped her move, and when Mia had turned completely around Janeane reached up to enfold each firm buttock beneath the long, thick tail. Then she pulled herself up until she could tenderly kiss her way slowly up the inside of Mia's thighs to the sensitive, engorged parcel of lusting flesh. And when she had arrived she immersed her face in the honey-scented sex poised over her, relishing the exquisite taste.

Mia shuddered in Janeane's grasp, in the grip of passion and pleasure. They buried themselves in each other's innermost folds until their faces were coated, and their tongues glided out to probe the swollen flesh of each other's sex, exploring just how aroused and ecstatic they had become. The touch of the tongues on the most sensitive parts of their bodies made them writhe and twist in frenzied possession, and their hot tongues lasciviously continued to invade each other, bringing hot saliva to moisten and oil the swollen flesh, and leaving it tingling and hungry for more.

Meanwhile their hands did not remain idle, creeping around to each other's buttocks and slowly and sensuously stroking them, with not a contour missed, arousing them even more. Nearby, Varis moaned in frustration and delight, and they echoed him, but with immense satisfaction instead, each spurring the other onwards as they nuzzled and worshipped.

Mia found Janeane's clitoris with the tip of her tongue, gently greeting it and sending spasms through both lovers. Janeane let out a growling moan into Mia's pussy, then quickly followed her lead and let her moist tongue delicately probe until she found Mia's own as well. Mia involuntarily arched her back under the urging of Janeane's warm hands still massaging her rear, her tail swishing about furiously. Sharp cries erupted as an intense climax coursed through her.

The sound was marvellous to Janeane, marvellous and sensual beyond imagination, and arrived just before her own release. The eruption ignited in her pussy and shot like a bolt of lightning up through her exultant body, radiating intense heat as it went. Only when it reached her head did she finally disengage and erupt in groans of utter agony and delight.

Their racked bodies flailed and thrashed in convulsions, the world around them briefly forgotten and beyond all caring. Time passed unnoticed.

Until Varis cried out again, in frustration and need, pleading and demanding. Mia twisted about, moving her head up to face Janeane, kissing her once more, tasting her, before stopping and glancing from under her tousled hair at her other mate. 'Come here.'

He wasted no time, nearly ripping off his tunic and kilt before practically pouncing on both bodies, pausing for a moment, unsure of whom to touch first.

Then he moved to Mia, kissing her with a driving

lust that could not be kept leashed any longer. Still dazed, her head spinning, Janeane watched as the two Pride lovers thrashed and moaned and scratched and bit, their primal passions to the fore. It was frightening, erotic beyond measure. Varis's lips trailed along Mia's skin to her breasts, sucking hard on the nipples until she cried out and scratched him – without malice, Janeane realised. But the most arousing aspect of it all was their eyes: how they met, exchanging volumes without words. It made Janeane feel like an intruder now.

But she remained, watching in fascination as Mia, her gaze still locked with Varis's, reached out and took his hand, moulding the forefinger to straighten it out, then guide it between her legs. Janeane didn't look down; she saw it all in their eyes, their reactions, in how Varis moved his arm and how Mia moved her hips, her mouth gasping open, eyes fluttering, her hands reaching up to Varis's strong, bare shoulders. Their musk filled the air around the furs, further intoxicating the human spectator.

Mia came again, mewling, burying her head into Varis's chest. His face was a storm of emotions: fascination, fear, concern. And arousal, of course; Janeane glanced down to see his shaft, hard and throbbing, glossy at the tip. But he ignored it, holding Mia, whispering to her. She was saying something back, shaking her head – then looking at Janeane. Her voice was hoarse. 'Do you – do you –'

Driven by a greedy hunger for more, Janeane reached out and grasped his cock, capturing his attention. 'Get that thing inside me, now.'

Varis grunted, evidently understanding, then gently released Mia to lay her back on the furs, as he rose above Janeane, reaching down to grasp her hips and presumably flip her over. But Janeane stopped him, lewdly spreading her legs beneath him, smiling. 'Got no tail, you can take me like this.' Beside them, Mia whispered in Pridespeak, translating.

Varis made a growl of pleasure, then positioned himself above her, lowering his body until he pressed at her sex. Janeane pressed the opening of her flesh at the thick hardness, the wiry hair at his groin rubbing against her inflamed wetness.

He began pumping quickly, slowing only at a few words from Mia, who watched them, her skin sweat-matted and her spots thick and black.

Slowly now he thrust into her, his claws piercing her waist. She felt every ridge of him as he plunged deep into her, ripples of delight running across her skin like ants. He moaned, sounding lost to the pleasure, and, at a few more words from Mia, began withdrawing slowly until only a part of him was inside Janeane, before sliding back in again.

Her arms around him, her excitement building, she slapped his back. 'Faster! Come on! This isn't the last one we're gonna have, I promise! Mia, he can take his time later!'

Mia, smiling weakly, translated.

Varis, breathing more rapidly, quickened his thrusts to an urgent gallop.

'Yes,' she cried. 'Harder!'

He pumped into her with abandon; she felt herself on the edge of another orgasm, wanting to share it with him. He cried out, his cock swelling inside her, spurting, spurring her on, her cries mingling with his as she came, her back arching beneath him, her legs wrapping around him, clinging to him fiercely. It subsided, then rose to another peak again, quickly followed by another, like pearls on a string.

They froze in that position, lying like that for a long time, until he softened and withdrew, still holding onto her. She closed her legs, trapping his come within her, as he rolled aside, to rest between his two lovers. As Varis caressed both of them, purring against them, Janeane, lost for words, tried to keep from falling asleep, then wondered why she was bothering . . .

Haci reclined against Tameri, their bodies twisted, facing each other, embracing, kissing, Tameri surging against the man's mouth, her pussy calling out as it had never done before. His hand moved up, stroking her breast through her gown then holding her tight.

She pulled back and purred aloud, her fingers running through his hair, coarser than one of the Pride, his skin smooth, less furry. He smelled strange, tasted strange, but she liked it. And he was pleasing; he listened to her, made her smile. And wet.

Haci peeled the top of her gown away, baring her breasts, and bent down to suck on them. His lips were as soft as any woman's, and his hands moved slowly over her body, tracing the outline of her waist through her clothes, before moving up to cup the breast he was kissing.

Haci moved across to the other nipple, already erect when he took it between his teeth, gently nipping and squeezing the aching bud until she almost cried out.

He pulled back, looking concerned. 'Did I hurt you?'

'No,' she sighed, reaching up to push his mouth back onto her breast. He flicked his tongue out like a snake, tasting the warm, sweet scent of her skin, and Tameri growled when he withdrew his mouth from her.

'How did you –' She lost her words, her thoughts, leaning back until she lay fully on the grass, looking around her at the other females who'd followed her lead and ventured out to begin talking with the men, learning about them.

Some Pride males remained wary, disapproving.

It wasn't supposed to be like that.

Haci distracted her, down by her groin, brushing over it through her clothes. She could feel the wetness seeping down her crack.

She looked out, searched the faces of the males, finally calling out, 'Djaben ... come here.'

He started, as if embarrassed at being identified thus. Then he drew to her, slowly but not stopping until he knelt beside the reclining female. She smiled at him, and then pulled him into a kiss, their mouths opening, pliant and hot. Their spots darkening, they stroked each other's arms and faces, Tameri surging towards him as Haci's kisses moved along her inner thighs and upwards, drawn by her scent as much as his desire. He parted the folds of her dress and bared her pussy, a silken delta of oak-coloured hair framing heat and moistness.

Tameri gasped into Djaben's mouth as Haci teased her clit. Djaben drew back, seeking any disapproval or reprimand, but found none, and lowered himself to her breast, copying what he had seen Haci do earlier. Tameri moaned with delight, then, without disturbing Haci's work between her legs, reached under Djaben's kilt and traced a path up the inside of his leg. Wrapping her hand fully around him, she tugged gently. 'Take that off,' she whispered hoarsely.

Kneeling, swaying, Djaben fumbled with his kilt, then cast it aside and allowed all to see Tameri's hand stroking him. His face was a picture of helplessness, and Tameri smiled. 'This is my first time. You let me know if it doesn't feel right.'

He nodded, watching the man Haci, who seemed

very Pride-like now, but still different, not looking or behaving like he considered Djaben as a rival or competition, but rather a complement, a partner in the worship of this female.

Tameri released him as her body stiffened, and her legs kicked out against Haci as a climax ran through her. As the waves of delight spread through her, she saw Haci looking to Djaben and say. 'Now, come here. Take her first.'

'Take her?'

The man nodded and smiled. 'I'm not out to claim her, nor her me. She wants you. We have talked about you.'

Tameri's blood raced through her head, and she still reeled, helpless, as Djaben crawled over and started to lift her up on all fours, but Haci stopped him. 'No, try this.' He gently rolled Tameri onto her right side, guiding her leg up until her knee almost touched her belly, and her tail swished excitedly behind her. Djaben looked down with eagerness at the dark strip of fur running along her sex to her rear, then reappearing at the base of her tail.

'Go on,' Haci urged. 'She wants you in her.'

Djaben happily obliged, finding the position unusual but not impossible to achieve. Leaning in, he guided his erection into her, touching parts of her that usually went neglected.

'Yes!' Tameri cried enthusiastically, drawing him in, as the weight of him pressing down on her outer thigh.

'That's it,' Haci murmured, stroking her, watching. 'Don't lean too hard on her.'

The male listened and shifted slightly; Tameri seemed visibly relieved, and Djaben moved faster into her. Haci's stroking was now replaced by his lips and tongue along her skin, her breasts. He nipped at her, sending delicious little shards of bliss through her, conspiring to tighten the strings of her desire to produce hitherto-unheard notes. She came again, her orgasm shaking her body, sending a spasm from the back of her neck right down through her quivering thighs. It triggered Djaben's own climax, and he gasped, pumping deep into her.

She floated; both acutely and distantly she felt Djaben withdraw at Haci's quiet urgings, before they swapped places. She closed her eyes and listened as Haci undressed, knowing he would very soon be inside her. Closer, Djaben knelt before her, the scent of him, and her on him, reaching her nostrils. She licked her lips and took the opportunity to switch sides, keeping her thighs clenched shut to retain all of Djaben's seed inside her, not wanting to lose it, even if she would end up bearing Haci's child. Then Haci was behind her, and she rested her upper half on Djaben's naked lap, her arms around her waist, pushing her breasts up, his still-wet, subsiding shaft resting against her skin. Djaben held her, purring. Haci entered her, taking her back up to a crescendo at a slow, blissful pace.

Sheer delight.

21

Seska did not jump when Varis had summoned her; she was his sister, after all, and enjoyed a respected position among the Pride both for this and for her work as a Priestess. Besides, she was busy enjoying the fruits of her triumph in the Lair. Tameri had broken the ice an hour ago, and now dozens of Pride females, males and men were spread throughout, eating, drinking, talking and coupling in various combinations, a cathartic release of the tension of the past few months. Although there were a few couples, even a female pair or two, most involved a female with two males, or a male and a human. It wasn't the entire Pride – many remained stubborn, or afraid. But it was a start. A good one.

She smiled to herself with satisfaction as she finally rose and departed for the Court; with her own children now destined to be Varis's heirs, arrangements would have to be made here.

She stopped as she entered the Court, looked around. Kami and Mark were there, having left the Lair not long before Seska had been summoned. Then there was Varis, and Mia, obviously reconciled and post-coital, reclining together, Varis grooming Mia, Mia grooming ... Janeane? Their scents, and their expressions and body language, said enough, but Seska still offered an insouciant, 'I take it matters have changed somewhat here?'

'You take it correctly,' Mia replied, leaning in to

breathe in Janeane's scent again. 'Jan-Neen will bear Varis's heir.'

Seska's whole body tightened, and she knew her intense dissatisfaction at this turn of events was showing, so she took a moment to calm down before responding. 'Congratulations, Ms Wade. And here I was, worried that you wouldn't be happy here.'

Janeane smirked at the obviously false statement. 'Yeah, well, between taking care of these two, and keeping my posse of female admirers wanting more love secrets satisfied, it's gonna be hell on earth.' She yelped as Mia, running her fingers through Janeane's blonde locks, tugged playfully.

Seska looked away in disgust towards Kami and Mark, holding each other. The older female was more satisfied by the loss of control Kami showed on seeing her, and played on it. 'Ahh, the young lovers, reconciled. What is wrong, Student?'

'Ex-student. How easily you forget: you sent your lapdogs to kill Mark and Janeane.'

Seska enjoyed regaining some advantage, folding her arms across her chest. 'How easily *you* forget, little one: my responsibilities to the Pride in the outside world preclude any sentimental restrictions. Of course I sent Brek and Nalo to deal with two potential threats! And thanks to you and that aged fool Kahotep, I will need replacements.'

Kami tensed further, her tail straightening out. 'Be thankful my man and my friend were not harmed, or staff replacement would be the least of your worries now.'

Mark reached up and touched her arm. 'Kami, let it go, it's not worth it.'

She looked at him again, her features softening.

'How touching,' Seska murmured with amusement.

'Yes, it is,' Mia said behind her, holding onto Janeane. 'We should appreciate the relationships we can forge with humans.'

Seska turned to her. 'Do not preach to me of human relationships, I –' Then she glanced up at an approaching scent, a new figure entering the Court. '*Ardeth*?'

The eyes of the others followed hers to the black-robed, black-cloaked man striding closer to Seska, his face a stony mask. 'Good evening, Seska.'

'Seska'. Not 'Mistress Seska'. But she ignored the omission as the blood drained from her face, and her voice dropped to an aghast whisper. 'My children –'

He cast off his cloak. '*Our* children are safe, and on their way home.'

She relaxed, but only for a heartbeat. 'You fool! Do you know what you've done? No human who crosses into our borders can leave! Why have you trapped yourself here?' She glanced at the Firsts, waiting for a reaction from them.

But instead, Varis continued grooming Mia, never looking up, but instead saying, 'I see no human here who shouldn't be here.'

Aware now of more going on than she had anticipated, Seska drew in her reserve once again, and drew closer to Ardeth. 'Why *are* you here?'

'To speak my mind.' He turned in place, bowed towards the Firsts, then straightened up. 'Matters arose this evening amongst yourselves regarding my children. These matters were discussed without my presence, or consent. This was disrespectful to me. This will not occur again.'

Seska's mouth opened, stunned. 'Ardeth, what are you doing?'

He ignored her, and continued. 'I am aware and accept that my children are Pride, and carry within their blood a noble and worthy legacy. But they are still mine, and I wish them to acknowledge and embrace their mother's heritage – and my own.'

Varis listened to Mia's translation of Ardeth's words, then at the end looked up, disentangled himself from his lovers and rose, facing Ardeth. Seska tensed, awaiting Varis' inevitable violent reaction to the demands of a mere human . . .

Varis bowed.

Everyone else within the Court seemed to hold their breath, as the First Male straightened up again then glanced around. 'All of you, leave. Seska's mate needs time alone with her.'

As the others rose and filed out, with Varis the last, Seska grabbed the First's arm and stopped him. 'I demand to know what this is about, brother!'

He eyed her, as if she were deliberately asking the obvious. 'Perhaps you forget, sister, but the Pride could not continue to exist without the help of this man. And if his price is respect from us, and time alone with you, then he shall have both, and more.' Now he raised the arm she held, his eyes darkening. 'And Seska, I remain First Male above all, including you: *never demand anything from me again.*'

She released her hold on him, and watched him exit. Then she turned back to Ardeth. 'Listen to me, you fool –'

Now he turned to her, his dark eyes angry and determined. 'I listen, Seska. I always do. But I'm nobody's fool. Not even yours. For too long you have treated me as an inferior. You love me, yes, but you don't respect me. You have refused to recognise that you need me as much as I need you. We are partners, Seska. I am the father of our children. And you have no right to decide their future without me. I will not allow it.'

'You will not . . . *allow* it?' She reached for him.

His hand shot out with a speed worthy of a Pride male, and grasped hers first.

Her face darkened. 'Release me!'

'No.'

She moved, more swiftly than any human could anticipate.

Except, apparently, Ardeth; with a few fluid twists of his body and limbs, honed by a lifetime's training in the martial arts, he grasped and squeezed Seska near her neck; she collapsed like a house of cards, though Ardeth caught her, and lowered her limp form to the furs. She was still conscious, gasping, her eyes wide in shock and disbelief.

Now Ardeth knelt beside her, gently drew the hair from her face, and removed the cords of his robes, swiftly and expertly binding Seska's hands before her, then her ankles. She glanced up and snarled through clenched teeth, 'Stop this, Ardeth! Now!'

'I do not seek to be your master. But nor will I be your slave. Acknowledge this, and we will speak of freeing you.'

With a snarl she struggled again, ignoring the pain that came from fighting against her bound position. But Ardeth merely watched and waited and kept her down as she completely lost control, screaming incoherently until her voice was lost and the strength had bled from her.

Distantly she felt the pain end, as she slumped with exhaustion, sobbing. And Ardeth held her tightly, whispering, 'You have been strong, my dearest one. Strong for so long, in your duties as Priestess, mate, mother.

But you are not alone. *I* am strong too, Seska. Trust me to stand by you.'

She nodded finally, weakly, her voice a wisp. 'I do – I do . . . Release me, please . . .'

But he didn't. His scent filled her nostrils, engorging her spots and tail.

It had been a long time since she had captivated him. Or had needed to.

Hungers long buried awakened. She knew it. He knew it.

His cock throbbed against her thigh.

She struggled again, but had no strength left; not like his, a strength driven not by vengeance or anger or a need to dominate her, but by a love, a need, a passion.

It was as if she were seeing him for the first time.

Ardeth shifted her in place, and set her over a large wool-packed pillow. Then he fumbled with her tattered clothes, bared her rear, and worked at his own robes.

This would not be rape, not truly, she accepted – but it would be submission.

He grasped her hips, and moved her about as he pleased. Seska's claws dug into the pillow as he raised her haunches up, parting her thighs. And Seska, exhausted and weakened, could not stop him.

But rather than anxiety or dread, there was only the sudden delicious taste of surrender, surrender to a mate she never realised could be worthy of that trust.

Her man knelt behind her and entered her, finding sweet wet resistance, then surrender here, too. He pressed almost his full weight onto her buttocks, then drew out a slow, succulent rhythm, burying his length into her, then retreating.

She looked away, buried her face into the pillow and moaned, until he slapped her rear and raised her again.

'No, Seska. No hiding. I want to hear you. And I want you to see me take you.'

She turned her head, staring up at him as he took her, filled her up.

She had taken many men, many males. None had ever taken *her*, not like this. Restrained as she was, her sense of vulnerability was unexpectedly exciting beyond measure, sending pulses of desire so strong they made her whole body shudder.

But he pulled back, until he slid out of her again and made her gasp. And then he was rubbing his cock head against her crease, nestling at the opening of her sex before sliding it down to touch her clit. She tried to push back, but he held her, made her wait, made her want him all the more, until her growing lust threatened to consume her. She could feel herself contracting. She heard herself begging him with a hoarse, weakened voice – unless it was all in her mind.

But then, seemingly without any warning, Ardeth drove forwards again, down into her, parting the soft, silky walls once more, filling her and pushing her into a fire of sensation. Ardeth stroked in and out of her, carrying her sensations into a blossom of orgasm that made her tremble uncontrollably, every muscle contracting as if from an electric charge. Somewhere along the way her body melted, but was held in place by her man as he continued to drive in and out of her, slowly but powerfully, like the piston of some great engine.

Seska moaned aloud, the aftermath of her orgasm draining but not dissipating, keeping her on a high, the outward stroke of Ardeth's shaft creating a terrible void within her, the inward strokes making a wonderful connection.

And as he continued to slide into her, the sweet

slickness of her now making the penetration all but frictionless, she used the muscles of her sex to squeeze him, making him gasp with the resistance and unexpectedly bringing another wave of pleasure crashing through her.

She had never had sex like this before. It had been primal and chaotic among the Pride; had become an art and discipline when she'd first studied the scrolls to become a Priestess, and in recent times had become – a chore. Pleasurable, yes, but still a chore. Even with Ardeth.

No more. Now he pumped harder into her, his need asserting itself, and it was with a luscious delight that she realised she would come again when he ejaculated into her. Her awareness, and impatience, were undeniable.

He drew back, until she thought he might pull out of her completely again, but then he cried out and drove into her a final time, sending his come into her, then again, and again.

She thought she was prepared for it. She was wrong. The strength of his climax took her by surprise, as did the heat of his come as it struck her insides, touching her nerves like lightning strikes. She came, the final orgasm as deep and shattering as the first.

Time passed, her sweat-matted hair covering her face, her feelings those of detachment, barely registering his pulling out of her, though his withdrawal triggered a miniature tremor within her. He removed her bonds carefully, then held her close as if she might now fall apart, nuzzling into her and kissing her neck.

And as she lay beside him, her bliss ebbing away slowly like heat from a dying ember, apprehension crept in. What did this mean now for them? How would this change them? Would he wish to leave his role? Would she lose his help? Would she lose *him*?

But, as if he'd read her mind, he murmured, 'Rest now, my wife. Then we shall return home and see our children.'

She rested, trusting him.

And trust built, slowly, days after Seska and Ardeth had departed, among the Pride and the newcomers, especially after the first conceptions were confirmed. The Firsts stood upon a rock near the river in the valley, presiding over a rare display: the Pride, assembled in the open. Most of the males stood in one group, most of the females in another, but many mixed in the middle, along with the humans, all taking places on the ruins of steps and pillars and walls. It was high noon, the sun offering a harsh heat and light that made the humans squint beneath protective cloaks.

Varis was resplendent in his finest outfit, the gold portions glimmering in the light, and his face was just as bright as Mia's beside him as he spoke. 'For so long, we have looked upon humans as our enemy. We have remained apart, hidden in a world that is as much ours as theirs, remaining only legend. Sadly, the day has not yet arrived when we can step out into the open.

'But we can step closer to that day, by embracing our potential, and by welcoming those humans who have joined us.'

The assembly cheered. Mostly.

Perched higher than the others, Kami looked across and saw Zeel and his closest allies, silent. Uncharacter-istically silent. As if they had grown to accept this most radical change in their society.

Or had reason not to draw undue attention to themselves.

Clouds had invaded the sky as day became dusk, then the deepest indigo of night came, and they hid the last slivers of the moon. The valley was deserted, blanketed in shadow, the livestock at the far end, away from the entrance.

And not close enough to react to the dozen males creeping slowly, silently through the brush and towards the passage through the mountains.

They stopped only when a voice broke the darkness. 'Going somewhere, Zeel?'

From a perch nearby, Varis rose, a shadow among shadows, but visible enough for Pride senses, once he chose to conceal himself no longer. 'Arise. Show some courage, for once in your miserable life.'

Zeel did as he was told, and his friends followed sporadically, watching as other Pride emerged from the holes in the slope behind Varis, all apparently following cues from the First Male. Above them, a thunderclap shook the mountains. 'Look away, Varis. Pretend you don't see or scent us. You've exhibited such talents already days ago, when you let that human rape your own sister. I swear upon Bastet we will return when we have what we need.'

'And what is it you could get outside, that you don't already have here?'

'You know already! Human women, like the one you claimed for yourself, to bear your heir! We now accept that we can no longer conceive with the females here, and that we need humans for our survival!'

'I applaud your common sense. Then you must also accept that you cannot just walk out and abduct women for your purposes.'

'Seska did!'

'Seska brought in volunteers, concealing their fates from the human world.' Varis leaned in closer. 'I doubt if you would be as meticulous.'

Zeel snarled. 'You would see our lines end! Eliminate our right to contest your claim to Firstship!'

The First Male tensed. 'If you wish your lines to continue, then I may – *may* – speak with my sister about recruiting women for such a role. But Zeel, you can always challenge me more directly. In fact, with these actions, you've done it already. Haven't you?'

Zeel didn't reply, but the tension within him, within his band, within the Pride surrounding them, was tangible, thick and poised.

And someone – no one later would know who – set them off.

It didn't last long.

When it was over, Kahotep escorted Mark and Kami out from the tunnels and down the slope towards the floor of the valley. Mark held a fire torch, though a part of him didn't want to see what was left of Zeel and his closest followers.

Varis was there, scratched and bruised but still standing, as were most of his fellow warriors. He glanced up, his eyes reflecting the torchlight. 'And so it ends. Your assumption was correct, Kami; you have my gratitude.'

She nodded, unprepared to lose any sleep over the loss of Zeel and his cronies.

Mark, however, felt less ruthless. 'I'm sorry there couldn't have been another way.'

Above them, thunder clapped again. 'Would that I shared your regret, human, but as First Male I can ill afford it. Zeel's absence will make the changes to our way of life all the easier.' Now Varis breathed in the cool, ozone-charged night air, and didn't quite look at them. 'We are returning inside now, before the storm arrives ... If you two do not follow, I can assume that you were additional casualties of this fight. But if you *do* follow, this opportunity – this offer – will not arise again.'

Kami blinked, scarcely able to believe what she had just heard. When it did finally sink in, she could only cling onto Mark's arm and whisper, 'Thank you, Varis.'

'For what?' Only the shadow of a smile betrayed his official demeanour as he strode away with the other males.

All except for Kahotep, who handed Kami a heavy-looking satchel. 'Some more appropriate clothing for the outside, along with food and money. I will speak privately to Jan-Neen and the others, and pass on your farewells.'

She accepted the bag, then, overwhelmed by the sudden change in fortune for Mark and herself, embraced the Gatekeeper. 'I shall miss you so.'

The male squeezed back. 'And I you, little one. Look up at the stars sometimes, and think of me.' When they parted, Kahotep moved to Mark and clasped his forearm. 'Watch over each other, as Bastet does. You'll not go far wrong.'

'We will.' Mark looked at Kami, unable to believe this was happening.

She smiled and took his hand. 'Let's go.'

They stopped upon leaving the ravine and dressed, unable to walk far out there in bare feet. Six kilometres from the Pridelands, the rain began, and by the time they reached the cottage, it was in full force, soaking them.

The cottage was in a stark enclosure, with ancient

wooden rafters supporting a tin roof that now offered an endless drumbeat from the rain, boards over the windows that rattled with the wind, and a door that sat in the doorway rather than being attached to it. She knew the place immediately: she had made her way here months ago, when Seska had helped her escape the first time.

It was almost pitch black, Mark's torch long since extinguished by the rain, but Kahotep had included flints in the satchel; within minutes, Kami had started a fire in the hearth with kindling and ancient newspapers.

Then she rose and turned to Mark, who was clearing away some of the debris and making a place on the floor with their cloaks. 'Take off your clothes.'

He looked at her, seeing her silhouette in the small but growing fire behind her. Then he nodded. 'You're right, we'll catch our deaths in these wet things.'

For a moment, the sounds of their undressing joined the rain patter and the crackle of the fire. Then they embraced tightly, overcome with shivering and relief. Kami's hands moved up to his shoulder-blades, then his neck. 'M – Mark – we're – we're free –'

'I know –' Briskly he rubbed along her spine, down to her arse and tail. 'Still can't believe it –'

Neither could she. The possibilities ahead of them were so many now: settle in Turkey, go to Britain, or somewhere elsewhere. Anywhere. She started giggling, then laughing.

Mark pulled back, holding her face, then kissing it. Moving her lips to his face, then his ear, she stopped and whispered, 'The fire won't be good enough. We need to make love, Mark.'

'Makes sense.' He laughed softly. 'Even if we weren't wet.'

Kami pulled him back into an embrace, kissing and licking his neck, her hands stroking his back as her tongue entered his mouth. He shifted in her arms to accommodate his growing erection, his breathing ragged.

When she drew back, she took his hand and guided it to her bush, to her pussy lips, letting him feel the heat and moistness, even as she reached down and stroked his cock, feeling it spasm and thicken. She caught the scent of it as it rose, licked her lips and led them both to the clothes on the floor. Kami shifted to give her tail room, then reached for him again, relishing the way he responded to her touch.

He beamed at her mischievously. 'Wicked woman, I thought you wanted it inside you?'

'I do, I do,' she crooned.

'Are you sure?' His own fingers caressed her swollen, sensitive lips, carefully venturing within to collect her juices and massage them into her outer lips, then teasing her clit until she lifted her pelvis up to meet him. 'I can do this instead...'

'Inside me, Mark Healey!' she growled, smiling, her eyes wide.

'OK, OK,' he laughed, lowering himself onto her.

Kami sighed as she felt the first hot inch of his penis slide between her wet and longing lips, her hands reaching up under his arms to clasp his shoulder-blades and pull him down further, deeper. Mark bit his lip as she completely swallowed him.

Kami echoed the reaction, clutching him, savouring the union of their bodies once more. Beneath her, her tail ached, the reason she didn't like this position, but she ignored it.

But something must have shown on her, or in her,

because Mark twisted them around until he was on his back, with Kami straddling him.

Grateful to him for the change of position, she purred and moved her fingertips over his chest and arms. She squeezed his cock with her pussy until she felt she could take all of him in her body and keep him there forever, never to part again, feeling closer to this man, this wonderful man, than to anyone else.

Kami leaned back, pulling him up to a sitting position, wanting him the way she had had him in that field, the day she told him her story. Above them, the sky thundered again, but she could hear almost nothing but their breathing, and the moist rubbing of flesh around flesh. She tightened her sex again, and he pushed back in reply. He clung to her, one hand in her hair, cradling her head as they kissed, the other hand supporting her back as they rocked, acutely aware of the hardness and slickness of his cock as he moved in and out of her.

Kami's hands moved over his back and shoulders, her own pleasure intensifying towards orgasm as he began nipping at her shoulders. Her claws dug into his skin as she cried out, spurring him on, and she felt his balls draw up closer, soaking with the fluid seeping from her sex.

Mark pulled back from her as they quickened their pace, looking into each other's eyes as he grunted with each thrust, making her pussy shudder again, still on the edge of her climax, and she responded with a steady, complementary growl of indulgent pleasure. She arched backwards, her face pointing up as if daring the gods to surpass the bliss she now felt, and he moved in to kiss and nip at her breasts and nipples, settling on one and providing a sharp sucking.

It was enough to tip her over the edge, and on the crest of that wave, she felt him twitch and stiffen, and he thrust savagely up into her, making inarticulate cries drowned out by her own as another peak overwhelmed her. They sang together, both wanting the moment to be trapped and preserved forever as he flooded her with hot, sticky come.

She fell upon him, her body twitching and trembling, their sweat mingling in echo of their sexual fluids. They clung to each other, immobile, even after Mark's cock began to wilt, slipping its own way out of Kami's sex; afterwaves of Kami's orgasm conspired to push him out further.

But when Kami began to shift her whole body, Mark's mouth was at her neck, hissing, 'Don't move.' And then he added, 'Please.'

'OK.' Her voice sounded strange, as if she hadn't heard it in days, and she remembered an almost identical conversation, days ago. Mark was kissing her again, and his words indicated he remembered it too. 'We don't have to move; you can get me hard again, back inside you.'

She blinked. 'What? Are you kidding? No way.'

Then they laughed quietly, knowing better.

Visit the Black Lace website at
www.blacklace-books.co.uk

LOOK OUT FOR THE ALL-NEW BLACK LACE BOOKS – AVAILABLE NOW!

All books priced £7.99 in the UK. Please note publication dates apply to the UK only. For other territories, please contact your retailer.

PAGAN HEAT
Monica Belle
ISBN 0 352 33974 8

For Sophie Page, the job of warden at Elmcote Hall is a dream come true. The beauty of the ruined house and the overgrown grounds speaks to her love of nature. As a venue for weddings, films and exotic parties the Hall draws curious and interesting people, including the handsome Richard Fox and his friends – who are equally alluring and more puzzling still. Her aim is to be with Richard, but it quickly becomes plain that he wants rather more than she had expected to give. She suspects he may have something to do with the sexually charged and sinister events taking place by night in the woods around the Hall. Sophie wants to give in to her desires, but the consequences of doing that threaten to take her down a road she hardly dare consider.

CONFESSIONAL
Judith Roycroft
ISBN O 352 33421 5

Faren Lonsdale is an ambitious young reporter, always searching for the scoop that will rocket her to journalistic fame. In search of a story she infiltrates St Peter's, a seminary for young men who are about to sacrifice earthly pleasures for a life of devotion and abstinence. What she unveils are nocturnal shenanigans in a cloistered world that is anything but chaste. But will she reveal the secrets of St Peter's to the outside world, or will she be complicit in keeping quiet about the activities of the gentlemen priests?

GONE WILD
Maria Eppie
ISBN O 352 33670 6

Zita seems to have it all – a great job in TV, a cool flat and a fit cameraman boyfriend. But when the boyfriend heads off on a 10-week shoot in Cuba, telling Zita not to get up to any mischief, that's exactly what she does. Soon she is discovering her bisexual side with her girl pal Nadine, and partying for all she's worth. But it's when she agrees to shoot a promo for Nadine's DJ set that things get really wild; dozens of loved-up clubbers are about to descend on Nadine's country house retreat for a weekend of orgiastic hedonism that's bound to get out of hand. On top of this, Zita is growing increasingly attracted to Cy – an enigmatic buff young painter and t'ai chi naturist. When things get too hot to handle, Zita's option is to fly out to Cuba to see how her boyfriend is getting on. What she's about to discover throws their relationship – and Zita's libido – into overdrive.

Coming in November

MAKE YOU A MAN
Anna Clare
ISBN 0 352 34006 1

Claire Sawyer is a PR queen with 'the breasts of the Venus di Milo and the social conscience of Attila the Hun'. At the sharp end of the celebrity food chain, she is amoral and pragmatic in equal measure. When the opportunity arises to make a star out of James – a down-at-heel sociology student and guest on a reality TV show – Claire and her friend Santosh waste no time in giving the young man the make-over of his life. They are determined to make him magazine material, tailoring everthing from his opinion in clothes to his sexual preferences. Determined to transform him into the beau of the Lndon celebrity circuit, the girls need to educate their provincial charge in the sexual mores of modern women. What they don't bank on, is their new living doll having a mind of his own!

TONGUE IN CHEEK
Tabitha Flyte
ISBN 0 352 33484 3

Sally's in a pickle. Her conservative bosses won't let her do anything she wants at work and her long-term boyfriend Will has given her the push. Then she meets the beautiful young Marcus outside a local college. Only problem is he's a little too young. She's thirty-something and he's a teenager. But Sally's a spirited young woman and is determined to shake things up. When Mr Finnegan – her lecherous old-fashioned boss – discovers Sally's sexual peccadillo's, he's determined to get some action of his own and it isn't too long before everyone's enjoying naughty – and very bizarre – shenanigans.

Black Lace Booklist

Information is correct at time of printing. To avoid disappointment
check availability before ordering. Go to www.blacklace-books.co.uk.
All books are priced £6.99 unless another price is given.

BLACK LACE BOOKS WITH A CONTEMPORARY SETTING

BLACK LACE BOOKS WITH AN HISTORICAL SETTING

☐ THE LION LOVER Mercedes Kelly   ISBN 0 352 33162 3
☐ THE AMULET Lisette Allen   ISBN 0 352 33019 8
☐ WHITE ROSE ENSNARED Juliet Hastings   ISBN 0 352 33052 X
☐ UNHALLOWED RITES Martine Marquand   ISBN 0 352 33222 0
☐ LA BASQUAISE Angel Strand   ISBN 0 352 32988 2
☐ THE HAND OF AMUN Juliet Hastings   ISBN 0 352 33144 5
☐ THE SENSES BEJEWELLED Cleo Cordell   ISBN 0 352 32904 1
☐ UNDRESSING THE DEVIL Angel Strand   ISBN 0 352 33938 1   £7.99
☐ THE BARBARIAN GEISHA Charlotte Royal   ISBN 0 352 33267 0   £7.99
☐ FRENCH MANNERS Olivia Christie   ISBN 0 352 33214 X   £7.99
☐ LORD WRAXALL'S FANCY Anna Lieff Saxby   ISBN 0 352 33080 5   £7.99
☐ NICOLE'S REVENGE Lisette Allen   ISBN 0 352 32984 X   £7.99

BLACK LACE ANTHOLOGIES

☐ WICKED WORDS Various   ISBN 0 352 33363 4
☐ MORE WICKED WORDS Various   ISBN 0 352 33487 8
☐ WICKED WORDS 3 Various   ISBN 0 352 33522 X
☐ WICKED WORDS 4 Various   ISBN 0 352 33603 X
☐ WICKED WORDS 5 Various   ISBN 0 352 33642 0
☐ WICKED WORDS 6 Various   ISBN 0 352 33690 0
☐ WICKED WORDS 7 Various   ISBN 0 352 33743 5
☐ WICKED WORDS 8 Various   ISBN 0 352 33787 7
☐ WICKED WORDS 9 Various   ISBN 0 352 33860 1
☐ WICKED WORDS 10 Various   ISBN 0 352 33893 8
☐ THE BEST OF BLACK LACE 2 Various   ISBN 0 352 33718 4
☐ WICKED WORDS: SEX IN THE OFFICE Various   ISBN 0 352 33944 6   £7.99
☐ WICKED WORDS: SEX ON HOLIDAY Various   ISBN 0 352 33961 6   £7.99

BLACK LACE NON-FICTION

☐ THE BLACK LACE BOOK OF WOMEN'S SEXUAL   ISBN 0 352 33793 1
      FANTASIES Ed. Kerri Sharp
☐ THE BLACK LACE SEXY QUIZ BOOK Maddie Saxon   ISBN 0 352 33884 9

To find out the latest information about Black Lace titles, check out the website: www.blacklace-books.co.uk or send for a booklist with complete synopses by writing to:

Black Lace Booklist, Virgin Books Ltd
Thames Wharf Studios
Rainville Road
London W6 9HA

Please include an SAE of decent size. Please note only British stamps are valid.

Our privacy policy
We will not disclose information you supply us to any other parties.
We will not disclose any information which identifies you personally to any person without your express consent.

From time to time we may send out information about Black Lace books and special offers. Please tick here if you do <u>not</u> wish to receive Black Lace information. ☐

Please send me the books I have ticked above.

Name ....

Address ....

....

....

....

Post Code ....

Send to: Virgin Books Cash Sales, Thames Wharf Studios, Rainville Road, London W6 9HA.

US customers: for prices and details of how to order books for delivery by mail, call 1-800-343-4499.

Please enclose a cheque or postal order, made payable to Virgin Books Ltd, to the value of the books you have ordered plus postage and packing costs as follows:

UK and BFPO – £1.00 for the first book, 50p for each subsequent book.

Overseas (including Republic of Ireland) – £2.00 for the first book, £1.00 for each subsequent book.

If you would prefer to pay by VISA, ACCESS/MASTERCARD, DINERS CLUB, AMEX or SWITCH, please write your card number and expiry date here:

....

Signature ....

Please allow up to 28 days for delivery.